A
CERTAIN
SUMMER

ALSO BY PATRICIA BEARD

*Blue Blood & Mutiny: The Fight for
the Soul of Morgan Stanley*

*After the Ball: Gilded Age Secrets, Boardroom Betrayals, and
the Party That Ignited the Great Wall Street Scandal of 1905*

Good Daughters: Loving Our Mothers as They Age

*Growing Up Republican: Christie Whitman
and the Politics of Character*

A
CERTAIN
SUMMER

A Novel

PATRICIA BEARD

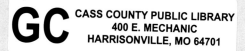

GALLERY BOOKS

New York   London   Toronto   Sydney   New Delhi

G

Gallery Books
A Division of Simon & Schuster, Inc.
1230 Avenue of the Americas
New York, NY 10020

Copyright © 2013 by Patricia Beard

First Gallery Books trade paperback edition May 2013

GALLERY BOOKS and colophon are registered trademarks of Simon & Schuster, Inc.

For information about special discounts for bulk purchases, please contact Simon & Schuster Special Sales at 1-866-506-1949 or business@simonandschuster.com.

The Simon & Schuster Speakers Bureau can bring authors to your live event. For more information or to book an event contact the Simon & Schuster Speakers Bureau at 1-866-248-3049 or visit our website at www.simonspeakers.com.

Designed by Kyoko Watanabe

Manufactured in the United States of America

10 9 8 7 6 5 4 3 2 1

Library of Congress Cataloging-in-Publication Data

Beard, Patricia.
A CERTAIN SUMMER : A Novel / Patricia Beard. — First Gallery Books trade paperback edition.
pages cm
1. Conduct of life—Fiction. 2. Seclusion—Fiction. 3. Security—Fiction. 4. Summer—Fiction. 5. Wauregan (Conn.)—Fiction. I. Title.
PS3602.E2523C47 2013
813'.6—dc23
2012041002

ISBN 978-1-4767-1026-6
ISBN 978-1-4767-1027-3 (ebook)

For David Braga

PROLOGUE

NOTHING ever changed at Wauregan. That was the island's purpose, its life force—and its myth. If there were questions, there were answers, either in the Rule Book devised by its founders and unaltered in half a century, or in the collective memory of its summer people.

The colony's traditions had survived two world wars and the Great Depression, yet in the summer of 1948, undercurrents and disruptions caused by the recent conflict swirled and sucked.

Helen Wadsworth was not alone in needing the island's serenity to soothe her, although her situation was singular. The other women in the colony were either reunited with their husbands, if sometimes tenuously, or were war widows. Helen was officially neither.

Four years earlier, her husband, Arthur, had been reported "missing, presumed dead" on an OSS mission in France. Since then, the War Office had not elaborated on the original statement. There was one person who might be able to tell her more, but like so many men who had returned from combat, particularly those who had served in the secret service, he had been practically mute on the subject. Frank Hartman, Arthur's OSS partner and godfather to Helen and Arthur's son, Jack, said he believed that Arthur had been picked up by the Gestapo the night they were to escape together over the Pyrenees. He had provided the barest details about why he had slid out of the noose, while Arthur had been captured. It seemed to Helen—but so much of what Frank and Arthur had done in France was classified, so what did she know?—that Frank might have been able to find out from their friends in the Resistance if the Gestapo had killed Arthur or sent him to a prison camp. Yet once Frank left France, she supposed he was out of touch. All she was sure of was that both men were involved in "operations," and that Arthur had been the short-wave radio operator.

And so it was that Arthur was still "missing." If he were alive, she was certain he would be home, yet Frank assured her that she should not entirely give up hope. Now Frank had taken a job at the successor to the OSS, the Central Intelligence Agency, where he could access the files, and said he could dig deeper.

Yet even as Helen grieved and doubted, on this brilliant early summer day, the promise of Wauregan was so seductive that when she boarded the first ferry of the season, she felt her spirits lift.

The ferry edged out of its slip toward the open water, and Helen smelled the salt breeze and felt the pull of the island, with its dense fogs, shining days, peaceful early-to-bed nights, and memories of better times when she and Arthur had been together, watching Jack playing at the edge of the sea. "It's like seeing myself as a child, only through my parents' eyes," Arthur had once fondly remarked.

Aboard their private boat, Waureganites were already in their own world. The island was surrounded by the moat-like Great Bay on one side and the ocean on the other, protected from anyone with malevolent intent, not just thieves or kidnappers—although among families as rich as those who inhabited this special community, there were always concerns—but also from people who meant no harm, but chewed gum with their mouths open and talked in unmodulated voices.

Members of the colony were so secure in the circle of safety they had drawn around their summer world that even three-year-olds could ride their tricycles along the paths near their houses without a parent or nursemaid striding behind. When Jack was four years old, Helen had sent him a few houses down to borrow some curry from Fong, the Chinese chef who worked for a neighboring family. Fong, who often gave Jack cookies, poured a spoonful of curry into a twist of waxed paper and handed it to him. Jack, thinking it was a new kind of treat, opened the twist, stuck out his tongue, and licked it up. Despite the coughing and choking and tears, Helen thought if that was the worst thing that happened to her little boy when he was out on his own, they were lucky.

Only a few years earlier, the Lindbergh baby had been kidnapped from his crib in New Jersey, and partners at the House of Morgan, of whom there were a number in the colony, were assigned bodyguards for themselves and their families. It was only at Wauregan that they were not followed by men with guns. There, they could believe, as four generations of Waure-ganites had, that they would always be able to summer safely, guarded by an elderly night watchman on a bicycle, who was armed with no more than a flashlight.

Changes had followed the war, but most members of the colony tried to behave, at least in public, as though nothing had interrupted the way things always had been. In the larger world, it could be hard to adapt to the newly sharper edges of business, and small "s" society. At Wauregan, they could live the way their parents and grandparents had, without feeling they were out of step with a brash style that was taking hold "off-island."

Waureganites attempted to ensure that the only people who knew about their island were others like themselves. If a visitor blabbed to a gossip columnist, he or she would never be invited back. The season before the war, Arthur invited their friends, the Count and Countess de Voubray, to visit. The count, mar-ried to a midwestern heiress who had been a schoolmate of Helen's, believed that all Americans liked to talk business, and asked one of the stuffier members of the community what he did for a living. The businessman—a bank president, as it hap-pened—later told Arthur he didn't care how closely related his friend was to the French once-royals, Wauregan was not the place for him.

The banker shook his head gravely, and reminded Arthur, "In certain summer places, we try to leave all that behind and just be good neighbors." Few at Wauregan would disagree.

Like most watering holes that harbored the rich, Wauregan was an object of curiosity, but hardly a temptation to robbers. Not a single door on the island was locked. There was very little to steal. The cottages were comfortably furnished, then left alone until the curtains rotted from the damp and sun, and sweating glasses left interlocking stains on the tables. As for jewelry, the women wore their wedding and engagement rings (preferably handed down in the family) even on the beach. Otherwise their finery consisted of a strand of pearls for the Saturday night dances, and costume jewelry clip-on earrings. Some women even forgot to pack those.

A distinguishing quirk was the tradition of going barefoot, a legacy of the Jazz Age. Not wearing shoes, except for church and tennis, was the passkey that opened the door to summer. Waureganites spent July and August toughening their soles, picking boardwalk splinters from their toes, and scrubbing off beach tar that floated in from ocean-bound tankers. Whether the rain pelted down or the sand scorched, the absence of shoes was a badge of belonging. Even at the formal dances held in the simple red barn known as "the casino," a building even more ramshackle than the sprawling shingled edifice of "the club," while the men wore dinner jackets and the women long dresses, their feet were bare. At the end of each seaside season, when the wives groped on their closet floors for their city shoes, they were apt to find them fuzzed with green mold, and too tight for feet that had spread.

When the ferry made open water, Helen stood up, sidled along the bench past Jack and his nanny, Kathleen Corrigan, and went to the tiny, dark head. She closed and locked the door, removed her prescription sunglasses, and squinted near-sightedly to check that the floor was dry. Then she took off her spectator pumps, unsnapped the stockings from her garter belt, rolled up belt and hose, and stuffed them into her handbag.

With her shoes slung in one hand, she returned to her seat by the window, stretched out her long legs, and wiggled her toes. Looking down at her bare feet, she had the sense that she had found something she had lost and had been missing: a carefree summer, the past, and childlike joy in small things.

Kathleen, tidily tucked between Helen and Jack on the aisle, reached down, collected the pumps, and packed them into her satchel. She had worked for the Wadsworths ever since she was hired to care for Arthur in St. Paul, Minnesota, when he was a small boy. Thirty years later, she still disapproved of the barefoot custom. In Ireland, she had been one of seventeen children. Going shoeless was an indication of poverty, not privilege.

The ferry was crowded and noisy that first weekend, as summer friends stopped to greet each other. On his way down the aisle between the two rows of benches, a former Army officer leaned across Jack and Kathleen, put a hand on Helen's shoulder, and asked, "Any news?" One of his eyebrows was permanently raised, the result of an emergency operation in a field hospital. His tone of concern was offset by the eyebrow, which gave the misleading impression that he was a man of irony. Helen sometimes did think she heard a hint of disingenuous interest when people asked about her husband. "Missing in action" meant mystery, and mysteries have long lives.

"Nothing yet," Helen said politely. Feeling smothered by the well-meaning but thoughtless question—if Arthur's fate had been discovered, every Waureganite would know by now—she firmly removed the man's hand.

Jack watched him maneuvering along the aisle between dogs and small children, toward his wife, seated by a window in the forward row, apparently wanting to be among the first to spot the island. "Snoop," Jack said, with a fourteen-year-old's crack in his voice. "Why can't they leave it alone?" For him, "missing" did not feel like a titillating puzzle; it felt like abandonment. Long after others would forget the ambiguity of Arthur's disappearance, Jack would be left with the plain fact that, dead or alive, he was gone. Jack was as patriotic as any boy who had grown up during the war, but sometimes it made him furious that his father, who was *too old*, he told himself, had volunteered to become a spy and risk his life, when he had a child who needed him.

He stood up, lurched as the ferry hit a wake, and turned his back on his mother and the nursemaid who would soon be denied the opportunity of making him pick up his clothes and mind his manners, for he would be going to boarding school in the fall. Helen and Kathleen watched him slouch down the aisle, head bent, and push open the door to the outside deck, where a group of boys was clustered, laughing into the wind.

Kathleen made a little clucking sound, and Helen lightly touched the soft, thin old skin on the top of her hand. "Never mind," she said. "We're almost there."

Looking out over the glittering water, watching for the island, Helen thought that if ever there was a place that knew its place, it was this quiet New England summer community. Even its name was said to mean "pleasant" in the Mohegan language. Not "glamorous"; not even "exclusive"; although it was certainly that. Just pleasant.

Its initial board of governors—late Victorian financiers and professional men from the older strata of New York Society, with a smattering of midwesterners—had believed that the cities were unhealthy in the summer. The heat-reek of steaming horse manure and decomposing garbage was too disagreeable for their families to endure. A man of standing could hardly expect his wife and children to spend the hot season in town. Yet they were determined to avoid the glitter of Newport, the social competition of lush green Southampton, and the inconvenience of the Great Camps carved into the Adirondack wilderness. Instead they would establish an antidote to the Gilded Age, a resort where its residents could escape the heat and the grandeur. Thus Wauregan was born.

The original plan worked, as one Gilded Age followed another, was knocked down, and eventually re-created in a different style. By the mid-twentieth century, Wauregan was known among those familiar with East Coast summer watering holes as the proud relic of an age that had been extinguished nearly everywhere else.

Before the first structure was built, the founders established strict bylaws and wrote a Rule Book, with the stipulation that it was never to be updated. The Wauregan Association would be run by a board of directors, with committees responsible for each aspect of island life: the club, the catchall red barn casino, the church, sports, and whatever else came up. Only married couples with children could build, buy, or rent a house. The tennis courts were closed until church was over on Sundays, to encourage attendance at services. When automobiles became common conveyances, they were forbidden on the island. Waureganites walked, rode bicycles, or pulled small children and groceries along in little red wagons. To mollify the nineteenth-century Temperance faction, it had always been against the rules to sell liquor. The compromise, still observed a hard-drinking half-century later, was for cottagers to buy their whiskey elsewhere, and store the bottles, tagged with their names, behind the club bar.

Even the style of the houses was determined by covenant. Built on stilts so the water could rush under them when the tides ran high, every house was clad in unpainted shingles, with green or white trim. Some, like the Wadsworths', were imposingly large, multi-gabled and porch-wrapped, with a warren of rooms on the third floor for the staff, and paling fences to hide the drying yards where laundry was hung in the fresh air. Soon the buildings weathered enough that they resembled members of a family who looked alike, but would never be taken for twins. Yet despite the attempt to blend in, they loomed above the flat, sandy landscape, with its clumps of spiky beach grass, thickets of bayberry bushes, and the low, wind-twisted trees known as "volunteers." Hardly anyone attempted a garden. The wild roses that lined the cement bikeways and boardwalks were enough. There were no lawns to be mowed, no gardens to be weeded. One older woman, who took great pride in her herbaceous borders on the mainland, admitted to Helen that gardening could be a viciously competitive "sport." She said she was always relieved to let the outside staff at home take care of her showplace, so she could stay out of the game for two months.

While the founders were as conservative about their refuge as they were in their business and family lives, they were reckless, even arrogant, in their choice of an unstable barrier island for a retreat meant to last for the ages. The fragile spit of land caught between the Great Bay and the unpredictable ocean could be submerged at any time. Wauregan was so narrow that even in the houses at its center, cottagers could hear the waves thudding and hissing on the sand, and inhale the ozone sea air that makes dogs yawn and sends even adults to bed early. When dense fogs dropped over the island, other sounds became part of its atmosphere: the rhythmic clang of the wave-struck bell buoys, the long warnings of foghorns, and the adenoidal horn announcing the ferry's arrival, as it emerged through the mists. Helen loved the fog, when the air was so rich with moisture she could feel it. Usually, air was just there, but fog had life.

Jack was the fourth generation of Wadsworths to inhabit the family's big old shingled firetrap on the beach. There he clung to the hope that if every summer were the same, one Friday night his father might come back on the boat with the other men. When he used Arthur's sports equipment, he was precise about replacing it where it belonged. He screwed his father's old tennis racket into its wooden press the way Arthur had shown him, turning the top right and bottom left screws first, repeating the process on the other side, so the racket wouldn't warp. After he came back from fishing, he hung Arthur's rod carefully on its hook, sorted out the tackle box, and placed it on its shelf in the shed next to the outdoor shower. He slept in his father's childhood bedroom, amid trophies from the 1920s that propped up children's books whose pages were marked with brown spots like the freckles on old hands.

For Jack, the house was filled with his father. Sometimes he lay on his stomach in the living room and squinted through the cracks between the floorboards, where he could just see the sand, five or six feet below. His father had lain there side-by-side with him one stormy day when the sea sloshed under the house and slapped at the pilings. "Look," he had said. "See how close to nature we are." Jack was just six then. He thought his father had whispered, "And how temporary everything is." When Jack felt particularly sad, he went back to the same place and lay facedown, where no one could see that his eyes were filled with tears. He stayed there until the sand below was blurred and the floor had damp marks on the wood.

It was true for Helen, too, that Arthur's absence seemed less absolute on the island than in the vast stone house in St. Paul where he had grown up next door to her, and where they lived after his parents died. There, her husband was always home at the end of the day, except in the summers when they used the family apartment in Manhattan, close to his grain company's New York office. Despite Wauregan's reputation as a family place, during the week the colony was the nearly exclusive domain of women and children. Any man who wasn't retired was in the city from Monday morning until dinnertime on Friday.

Before Arthur went to war, he had spent summer weekdays in New York. Helen had slept alone on the island more often than she had slept there with her husband.

Yet wherever she was, sorrow was her companion. At times she felt as raw as a peeled shrimp, certain that her husband was dead, that he had been starved and tortured in a prison camp, or was wandering around Europe, unable to remember who he was or where he belonged—a "displaced person," as those without homes to return to were called. She cherished the times when she dreamed that he was with her, and she could see him clearly and hear his voice. She would awaken and imagine that she could go downstairs in the morning and find him at the breakfast table.

Jack optimistically reminded her that a person who is declared missing in action is not considered dead for seven years from the time he was last seen or heard from, but she did not encourage him to hope. Each year she dreaded turning the calendar page to August, the month she had learned that her husband was missing, because it brought her closer to the time when his life would be formally over. In 1948, there were three more years to go.

On that sunny day at the end of June, when the ferry landed, and Helen, Jack, and Kathleen stepped onto the warm wood of the Wauregan dock, they each hoped that this place would soften the pain of loss. Even if Arthur never came back, he had left something indelible of himself here, in the house his grandfather had built.

Yet even orderly Wauregan could not always keep its promises. That summer, the Wadsworth household would notably lack what Helen remembered that the poet Baudelaire called *luxe, calme, et volupté*. Jack would be shocked into beginning to grow up and Helen would become determined to find answers to the questions about Arthur's absence that haunted her.

It would also be the summer she fell in love again.

CHAPTER ONE

"WHAT do you mean, you're worried about Helen?" Sally asked. It wasn't even July Fourth and the gossip had already started. It was funny, she thought, that when many of the men were away at war, there had been so much less barbed chatter.

Sally Carter and Betty Spencer, who had been known as "Betty Boo-hoo" when she was a little girl, were sitting under Betty's umbrella on the beach, watching the sandpipers pick and prance in the foam at the edge of the sea. "Of course, it's awful not knowing if your husband is dead or alive, but that's been true for years. Why now?"

"She must know he's dead," Betty said, with something in her voice. "That's not what I'm worried about. It's the men."

"What men?" Sally asked.

"Our men."

"You can't be serious. Helen would never go after anyone's husband."

"But they might go after her," Betty said defensively. "My Malcolm, for example." She lowered her voice. "He was practically a sex fiend before the war. Now, and don't you dare repeat this"—she paused and, unable to say the words, held out her pointer finger, and bent it, so it looked limp. "He's lost interest in me. We barely talk, except about the children. And sex? Never."

"What does that have to do with Helen?"

"She's beautiful. She's alone. And maybe she'd welcome a little attention."

"That's a lot of C-R-A-P," Sally snapped. "She's still waiting for Arthur. You know they grew up together in St. Paul. They were inseparable from the time they were tiny. Arthur's grandfather was 'the Grain King' and Helen's was 'the Empire Builder.' One of them built the railroad, and the other used it to ship his wheat. And with Helen's mother so sick, I think she spent more time at the Wadsworths' than she did at home."

"That's the thing: she didn't really have a mother, did she?"

"No. It was pretty awful. Mrs. Gladsome was in and out of institutions. Helen never knew when she'd be at home, and when she'd suddenly be gone. She told me about it when we were in boarding school. She and Arthur were always happiest in each other's company. When we had a dance with St. Mark's, he filled in every dance on her card with his name. We all knew those two were meant for each other. They were like brother and sister and best friends and lovers—but not till they were married, of course. Nothing could come between them.

"As for Malcolm and his limp finger, haven't you noticed how the men who were in combat seem different, muffled or amplified, or something else I can't quite explain? They try to hide it, whatever 'it' is, but these houses are so close to each other, sometimes you can hear the man next door wake up screaming in the night. Who knows what they relive in their dreams?"

"I don't want to imagine," Betty said firmly.

"I do," Sally said. "I want to know what Dan went through while he was away. As for Helen, she isn't a husband stealer. If anyone made a pass at her, she'd make sure he didn't do it again."

"There's another thing about Helen," Betty said. "She didn't grow up here."

"Neither did you," Sally said.

"Yes, but I had a strict mother and I always knew right from wrong. I remember hearing that the first sign of Helen's mother's illness was when she started sleeping with the gardener, and the chauffeur, and anyone's husband she could get. That was before she was certifiable. And in the summers, Helen's father took her to Europe, instead of coming to a place like this. Who's to say she really cares about the rules?"

"I say so. You're right that Helen had a horrible childhood," Sally said. "It makes her want even more to have a stable family life. The last thing she'd do is get involved with a married man.

"As for not growing up here, if I remember right, your mother was a hat model when your father met her and introduced her to the Colony Club and Wauregan. And wasn't your grandfather an Irish cop? This is *America*, Betty. You belong here, and so does Helen. She loves the island. Helen would never do anything to make trouble. She calls this her 'safe place.' If she could hear you, she might not be so sure."

Sally caught her breath and stopped. Defending Helen had brought out the anger that surfaced when she was confronted with unfairness, and made her feel light-headed and reckless. "I'm warning you," she said. "If you even hint that Helen is husband bait, I will tell everyone in this place about the night you screwed the captain of the Australian tennis team under a tree at the Merion Cricket Club, and the next morning admitted you never found out his name. So much for 'knowing right from wrong.'"

"You wouldn't!"

"Don't test me," Sally said. "I'm sorry you're having problems with Malcolm, but that doesn't have anything to do with Helen. It's that damn war the men won't talk about, as though being back at Wauregan can just erase the past few years."

When the men were mired in muddy trenches, on bombing runs, and in deadly battles, their dreams of the colony were as vivid as Technicolor movies with big-screen happy endings. It might be unrealistic to hope that a small insular summer place could restore what the war had stolen, but battlefront life and death were so surreal it was hard to recall even an ordinary peacetime day. The warriors' anticipation of the perfect families waiting for them in an ideal community were like the fantasies people at home shared during rationing. For years, they would discuss the delicacies they would enjoy when they could buy anything they wanted, only to find, after a few postwar feasts, that for the most part, even good food was just food.

Sally stood up and brushed the sand off her legs, while her rickety beach chair folded in on itself. "Dratted things," she said. "You'd think now the war's over the club could buy some new ones. I've got to go. I'm on my way to Helen's, as a matter of fact. In case you're wondering, I won't tell her what you said. This place is too small to start feuds."

"I didn't mean . . ." Betty began, but Sally was out of earshot by the time she could figure out what to say next. She reminded herself of all the times she had thought how wonderful it was that the granddaughter of a Boston policeman could end up listed in the *Social Register*, with her children in the best schools, and thought that Sally was quite right: "This is America." Still, Helen was the daughter of a crazy nymphomaniac mother. Didn't those things run in families?

Sally and Helen settled on the sea-facing side of Helen's porch, where a breeze gently combed through their hair, lifting it off their necks in the morning heat. Sally would never have considered discussing her problems with "Betty-boo," but Helen was her closest friend, and she, too, was having trouble at home. In a voice choked with humiliation, she confided that her husband, Dan, the president of the Wauregan Association, had made an offhand comment about what had happened when Paris was liberated and he went there on leave from the Navy. "'The Parisians went wild,' he said. 'It looked like every woman in the city was ready to lift her skirts for an American soldier.'"

"Uch," Helen said. "That's a little vulgar."

"So then he said he saw this prostitute who had hair exactly the same red as mine. He told me it was the hair that made him do it."

Helen snorted. "I hate to laugh, but what a lame excuse! Why did he have to tell you? He didn't come back with a disease?"

"No, thank goodness," Sally said. "He came back shut down

and angry, and he won't tell me what happened when he was away. Occasionally, he'll burp up a little tidbit, but mainly it's just the bare facts. I know his ship was attacked and sunk, and most of the sailors were lost, but when he told me about it, he said. 'You haven't seen anything until you've seen the sea on fire.' He was talking about a kind of hell, but his voice was soft, as though he were describing a Turner sunset. He has horrible nightmares, then claims he can't remember them. He won't say what it was like to be there—and then he tells me *that*!" she said. "About some woman."

Helen gave Sally a sympathetic blue-green look from behind her tortoiseshell glasses. There was so much she, too, wanted to know about the war.

Sally went on to tell her that Dan had followed his confession of casual infidelity by remarking that her hair was like the red light in a brothel window. He said he was sure that while he was away, it had attracted plenty of attention from the soldiers and sailors and airmen she "fed" at the canteen in Times Square, "making those condescending little quotation marks in the air," Sally said angrily. "He was never like this before." Her voice dropped, until it was almost a whisper. "What could have happened?"

Helen was not entirely surprised. During the war, she and Jack and Kathleen had moved to New York for the duration. The house in St. Paul was meant for a big family and a complete staff, and with only the three of them in residence it felt hollow and cold. She had always wanted to live in Manhattan, and she used the Wadsworth family apartment, enrolled Jack in the best boys' school, and volunteered for the Red Cross. After an intensive nursing course, she signed on for night duty, so she would only be gone when Jack was in bed and Kathleen was in the apartment.

She was assigned to the docks where wounded soldiers were unloaded from the hospital ships. The scene had a disturbingly surreal quality. It took place in the blacked-out city, with hooded flashlights illuminating the men who had been laid out in rows of stretchers. The disembarkation began at ten-thirty. The official story was that the soldiers were off-loaded at night to avoid traffic, so they could be transported to the appropriate facilities as quickly as possible, but that was a cover-up. The government didn't want civilians to see the extent of the damage, for the same reason that at the start of the conflict, newspapers and newsreels were forbidden to show pictures of dead soldiers. The Red Cross nurses were required to sign a confidentiality agreement, swearing that they would not discuss what they were doing.

Each night, when the ships disgorged their human cargo, doctors walked along the lines, assessing each man's injuries and deciding where he should be sent for treatment. Helen was responsible for making certain that the men in her area were taken to the right ambulances, and recording who went where. Some of the soldiers were so badly injured she found it hard to look at them. The blackened burn victims were the worst. After them, the cases she found most disturbing were the men who had to be strapped into their stretchers because they could suddenly turn violent, or who stared, unblinking and silent, and didn't answer when she bent over to welcome them and ask their names.

She remembered when her mother had stopped talking and lay in her bed in the sanitarium, never turning her eyes away from the glamorous portrait of her younger self. Helen's father had brought the picture to be hung opposite her bed, as though to remind her of who she was, or once had been. When that didn't work, he switched it for a painting of the family and Helen's mother's much-loved dog. Helen was so young when the painting was made that she could almost understand that her mother would not recognize her as the child in the white dress, sitting on the floor of their library, holding a little Papillon on her lap. But surely, she thought, she might have had some response to the image of "Blizzard," with her perked ears and the white butterfly stripe bisecting her forehead. She had brought that dog to her marriage, along with her ladies' maid. Helen had thought that the maid, always known as "Mam'selle," had been more important to her mistress than the little girl sitting close to her mother's satin ball slippers. Even if it was unthinkable to include a servant in a family portrait, Mam'selle was there, a ghostly pentimento, with a protective, possessive hand on her mistress's shoulder.

After the war, with Arthur still gone, Helen stayed in Manhattan. Jack was happy at his school, and for Helen, as a woman on her own, life was more stimulating than in St. Paul. She continued to work for the Red Cross at a veterans' hospital that attempted to rehabilitate men who suffered from what had openly been called "shell shock" in the last war, but now was only acknowledged in the most extreme cases. No matter how terrified and confused the veterans she worked with were, they evidently believed it was unmanly to talk about their experiences. Whether they feared that unleashing their emotions would throw them further off balance, or were simply behaving the way they had been brought up to act, in a society where "boys don't cry," the results were the same: silence and bravado, until finally, in the soldiers who were most likely to be cured, there came a loss of control, the lightning, and thunder, and hailstones that broke the unbearable heat of memory.

"Listen," Helen told Sally. "The men we're trying to help? They're so traumatized, they're in a hospital, but it's hard to get even them to say more than 'I only did what anyone would do.' When you find out what they've been through—and you have to, or they'll never get better—you can hardly believe it. I try to be like the doctors, who don't let it upset them, but I can't be that detached. Once they start talking, sometimes I want to put my fingers in my ears, and say, 'Stop! Don't tell me.'"

"How about the heroes?" Sally added. "With medals for bravery? You'd think someone would say, 'Bart Littlefield won the Distinguished Service Cross for—what is it? 'gallantly risking his life under the most dangerous circumstances'?—and then tell us what the 'circumstances' were. But they act like it would be barroom bragging. The only higher award than the Distinguished Service Cross is the Medal of Honor, usually awarded to the family by the president, because for the most part, you have to die to get it. Remember what Bart said when someone congratulated him? 'I was just lucky.'"

"I don't think it's so much that they're shutting us out, as afraid that speaking about the unspeakable will bring home everything they want to leave behind," Helen said.

"Still, some of them are really nuts," Sally said. "Did you know that since the war, John Williams can't eat anything with bones in it? Marjorie says he won't tell her why. But bones? What could that be about?"

"Don't even think about it. Does he eat things that *used* to have bones, like hamburgers?"

"I don't know, but Marjorie says even fish bones are taboo. Poor John. Can you imagine what he must have seen?"

"No," Helen said. "It must have been horrible. How awful to think of Marjorie cooking rice and spaghetti and boning chicken breasts, all the time wondering what made her husband suffer so badly."

"It's odd how the war took people differently. Look at Ted and Libby; do you ever remember another man commuting during the week? An hour and a half each way? He's here almost every night," Sally said.

"I know. I love watching them. Libby told me that all during the war Ted believed if he could get back to her and the kids, and Wauregan was still the same, he'd know he had been fighting for the right reasons. Not just to stop evil, but to preserve good."

Sally nodded. "I saw them one afternoon when I was walking along the beach. They were in the surf and he was holding her like a baby and swinging her in the waves. They looked about eighteen years old."

Helen smiled. Ted was shaped like a fireplug and Libby was tiny and so light that she ran like a deer.

"It's not an accident that Dan's the head of the Wauregan Association," Sally said. "I think he wanted the job because he thought this place had a magic that would cure him."

"It does," Helen said. "It just takes longer for some people than others."

She wondered, as she often had, whether, if Arthur came home, he would be so wounded that he would shut her out when she asked what it had been like in France. She was certain he would not have turned mean like Dan.

Despite their private struggles, Wauregan couples remained coupled, and tried to keep up appearances. Stories seeped out about men who seemed like troubled strangers to their wives and stumbled as they tried to reestablish relationships with their children, but most of the husbands and wives cared enough about each other that they were determined to regain their footing. Others thrashed along, some because they believed divorce was a disgrace; others because the men couldn't afford to support two households. And there were the Wauregan Rules. If a family split up, and their house was sold, neither parent would be allowed to rent a place there. Losing the island summers would be another kind of divorce. A man or a woman might find another spouse, but nothing could replace Wauregan.

Whatever went on behind closed doors, in the ways that showed, the colony's treasured sense of continuity prevailed. The children, especially, went about their summer lives as they always had.

For those who were old enough, the most engrossing activity was sailing on the gusty bay. The community had its own fleet of fat-bellied Beetle Cats, the same boats their fathers and mothers had sailed when the vessels were brought onto the island in 1921, the year they were first made. They were small and sturdy and rarely tipped over, although, as one member of the Yacht Club Committee remarked, "I don't know why we don't lose at least one child every year." Often enough, a boy or girl forgot to duck when the boat went about, and got whacked on the head; or tumbled overboard if the vessel heeled in a strong wind.

That summer, on the day they arrived, Jack told Helen he wanted to get his father's old boat, *Red Wing,* into the water again. Helen and Kathleen were in the kitchen when he announced his intentions, then wheeled around and left. They heard the stairs squeak as he loped back up to his room, as though he had gotten something off his chest.

"Do you think he wants the boat to be ready to sail when Arthur returns, or he's given up, and he's fixing it for himself?" Helen asked Kathleen. "Arthur told him it would be his when he turned fourteen."

"Ah, Mrs. W, who knows what the boy is thinking? I'll start worrying when he doesn't eat everything on his plate and ask for seconds."

"Mmm-hmm," Helen said. "Sometimes not knowing makes me want to act like Jack. Just *mad.* When a woman whose husband came back from the war complains that she feels like she's married to a stranger, I'm tempted to say, 'I'm sorry, but I don't even know if I have a husband.'"

Kathleen pursed her lips, trying to keep the words in, then her habitual self-containment cracked. "Don't you think I want to know what happened to Mr. Arthur?" she said. "Didn't I bring that boy up? I know him. If he was alive, he would have done anything—killed and stolen if he had to—to get back to you and Jack. Mr. Arthur is gone for good. It's time for you to stop fooling yourself, and letting Jack believe his father will step off that ferry one fine day."

"No," Helen said. "Arthur was working with a Resistance

group. Even if Frank doesn't know what happened, someone must."

"What if they do? It seems like no one's telling. Maybe you should find a new man," Kathleen said.

"I don't want another man. I want Arthur," Helen said crankily. Then she strode out of the kitchen and let the door swing shut behind her. She was sick of being soaked with sorrow, and ashamed of being angry at her absent husband, who almost certainly had no control over what had happened, or had been done to him.

CHAPTER TWO

TWO single men arrived with the crowd of husbands on the Friday evening ferry of the July Fourth weekend. One was Peter Gavin, the twenty-eight-year-old grandson of the redoubtable Judge Michael Gavin, whose house was across the path from the Wadsworths'. Peter, who was coming to spend the summer with his grandfather, was accompanied by a German shepherd that, as the islanders would soon learn, had been in the K-9 Corps with his Marine platoon in the Pacific. The other was Frank Hartman, Arthur Wadsworth's roommate at Yale and his teammate on the OSS mission from which Arthur had not returned. Frank was there to spend a few days with Helen and his godson, a visit he anticipated with what he feared was an improbable hopefulness.

The fog was so thick that the mothers and children and grandparents couldn't see the ferry until it was nearly close enough to touch, although they heard the grinding of the motor above the screeching of seagulls, and smelled diesel fuel from the engine room, and at last heard the deep horn that announced the boat was pulling into the dock.

The young wives looked much as they had in college when they prepared for a date. In the afternoon, they had rinsed their hair in beer, an excellent setting lotion—the smell evaporated when it dried—stuffed a sanitary napkin under the ends to mold their pageboys, and tied on a net to hold the bulge in place, with the strings of the net in a bow on top of their heads. While they waited for their hair to dry, they sat on their porches and gave each other manicures and pedicures. By the time they met their husbands at the ferry, if they had daughters, some of them would be wearing matching sundresses; the boys would have been changed into fresh shorts and tucked-in shirts; and the littlest children would be dressed for bed in pajamas and terrycloth bathrobes with the sashes neatly tied around their waists. The first thing the men would do after kissing their wives and hoisting the children into the air and bouncing them until they giggled would be to remove their shoes and socks, revealing feet that were whiter than those of the women who had been barefoot all week. Then they would put their footwear and their briefcases into the little red wagons the children had brought. The workweek was over, and they were where they should be.

Often Waureganites went down to watch the Friday night ferry come in, even if they didn't have anyone to greet, just to see who was arriving, but Helen had avoided that ritual in recent years, except when she had a guest coming. She was afraid that Jack would be scanning the deck for Arthur—just in case. She, too, might watch the men who stepped across the gap between the boat and the dock, and fantasize that her husband would miraculously appear, looking the way he did in the pictures in the albums she and Jack sometimes took out to remind themselves of the man who went to war six years earlier, when Jack was eight.

That night, Helen caught a glimpse of a big golden dog with black markings that emerged from the fog. She was looking for Frank, and he did not notice the man with the animal, but he saw her when she flipped back the hood of her yellow slicker and he thought she looked as though someone had turned a flashlight on her, making the beads of water in her tawny hair sparkle.

The crowd moved back a bit as Peter Gavin and his big dog made their way over to Peter's grandfather, Judge Gavin. When Peter passed Helen, he heard her greet another man and say, "How glad I am . . ." and saw her son balancing the man's suitcase in the red wagon, draping a tarpaulin over it as carefully as though he were tucking in a child for the night. He recognized the woman from before the war, and he was sure he had heard her husband was missing in action. Perhaps that news was old, Arthur was dead, and this man was Helen's suitor, or even her new husband. Peter scowled. Helen? he thought. Wasn't that her name? How old was she? Thirty-four? Thirty-six? She looked—he couldn't put an age on it—young.

Peter threw an arm around his grandfather and gave him a one-armed hug. Judge Gavin leaned down to inspect the dog. "Max," Peter said proudly. "Love of my life." The Judge, as he was called, smiled and pushed his upper dentures back in place with his tongue. It would be nice if a young lady were next, he thought. Be good if the boy would give me some great-grandchildren. Then they were off, two bicycles, a red wagon with a duffel bag in it, and a large dog trotting alongside.

• • •

When Helen came down for breakfast on Saturday morning, Frank and Jack were still asleep, but Kathleen, who had already had a chat with a neighboring maid, had a thorough if not necessarily accurate report.

"That Peter, across the way? Judge Gavin's grandson? The Lawrences' Mary down the row heard the Nips did something really bad to him when he was in the Pacific. She says he's going to graduate school in the fall to learn to be an architect. Same place as Mr. Arthur went to college. That Yale. Mary saw him walking his dog. She says he's as tall as his grandfather. Ask me, those men are the descendants of the great Irish chieftains. Big and handsome."

"How do you know Peter Gavin is handsome?"

"I told you. Mary saw him. She says he looks like he was drawn through a keyhole, though."

"You mean skinny?"

"Maybe, but Mary said it was something in the eyes."

"I remember him from before the war," Helen said. "Mary is right. He was very good looking."

Peter had spent every summer with his grandparents at Wauregan since Helen had first been there, but as he was eight years younger than she was, twenty-eight to her thirty-six in 1948, she hadn't paid much attention to him. The only time they had really met was just before he left for his first year at Yale, and Arthur invited the Judge and his grandson over for a drink, a gesture of solidarity. One Yale man to another—two others, counting the Judge.

Arthur made them laugh, talking about the band he and

Frank Hartman had put together when they were undergraduates. "We called it 'The DeLyrics,' as in 'delightful and lyrical.' Our sole purpose was to have an excuse to go to the girls' schools and play at parties. The qualification to join was that the guys had to look good. They didn't have to be great musicians, as long as they could fake it. None of us had perfect pitch, and we were always getting out of synch. The girls thought we were meant to be funny, and when we figured out they liked it, we got even worse. We should have been called 'The Delirious.' We had a great time. Even made a record. I hope you'll enjoy it there, too," Arthur said to Peter.

When Helen thought about the DeLyrics, it still irritated her that they focused their attention on the social finishing schools, and never made the trip to her own college, Bryn Mawr. The implication was that Yale men believed brains didn't go with beauty, or that smart girls were too challenging. Based on the women many of them married, that appeared to be true.

But that evening ten years earlier, she had also observed that Peter Gavin, who had unusual ease for an eighteen-year-old, would not need to start a band to be noticed.

At the market, Helen ran into Sally Carter, who was loading groceries into her bicycle basket.

"I hear you have a new neighbor," Sally said.

"Judge Gavin's grandson? Not exactly new, since he's been here practically all his life, but yes, he just came in last night."

"Everyone is talking about him. The story is that he was invalided out of the Marine Corps after he'd been tortured by the Japanese, and spent a year in a hospital recovering. And not just physically," Sally said. "Whatever happened messed up his head. Have you seen him?"

"Not yet."

"Or the dog?"

"*Mmm.* At the ferry. Beautiful animal."

"Served in the K-9 Corps. Trained to kill, according to my husband. Dan has already gotten calls: 'Why bring a dog like that here, with all these children around?'"

Helen liked dogs, and would have one herself if she weren't living in New York. "I don't see the Marines releasing a killer dog into civilian life," she said. Hundreds, or perhaps it was thousands, she wasn't sure, of civilians, including children, had donated their pet dogs to work with the military for the duration. She had read that at one center alone, the handlers had retrained more than five hundred dogs and returned all but four of them to their owners, and some to their handlers.

"You'll see Peter soon enough since he's living across the path from you. I know how Jack loves dogs. Just be sure this one's safe before you let him get near it."

"Come on, Sally," Helen said. "Don't let Dan get too heated up. If Peter Gavin spent a year getting his head straight, maybe he needs the dog for comfort. Leave it alone."

Saturday was turning into a steambath. After a long breakfast on the screen porch that kept most of the sand and flies away from food, Helen and Frank biked down the boardwalk and settled under the Wadsworths' umbrella in the club's uncomfortable canvas beach chairs. They chatted with Sally and Dan

Carter, and Frank told them about the newly established CIA.

"What happened to the American idea that gentlemen don't spy on each other?" Dan asked.

"We caught up to the rest of the world," Frank said. "Learned a lot from the Brits. Arthur and I were trained in a very hush-hush British spy center loaned to their secret service by an English lord who had other houses to live in. I never saw such paintings in my life, outside of a museum.

"As for spies, remember Queen Elizabeth's Francis Walsingham?" Helen remarked, glad that she remembered something from her Elizabethan history course at college. "He set the bar."

When the beach got too hot, Helen enticed Jack out of the water, where he was bodysurfing with some boys and one brave girl, and the three of them bicycled slowly back to the house and changed for lunch, served under a squeaking ceiling fan in the dining room.

"That fan needs to be oiled," Frank said, looking up. "Want me to get up on a ladder and do it when we finish lunch?"

Helen smiled. "Thanks, but you'd be surprised what a woman can learn to do when there isn't a man around. I can fix it myself, but we've only been here for a week and this is the first day it's been hot enough to turn it on. I'll take care of it later."

With lunch over, Helen suggested that instead of going back to the beach, they sit on the porch, which would be cooler, and watch the scene from the shade.

"Heat," Frank said. "It's gotten so I can't get enough of it. Even summer in Washington doesn't bother me. That winter we were in France, we had to sleep on the ground a lot, and even in the south, the inside of your bones holds the cold."

"Well, if you'd like to walk back over that blistering sand . . ." Helen began.

"No. I'd like to be alone with you here," Frank said. They moved under the overhang of the wraparound porch, where the worn wicker on the once-white chairs had little protruding twigs that scratched the legs of any sitter who didn't put a towel down first. Frank knew those chairs and seated himself carefully. He was wearing white linen shorts and a pink polo shirt. Even in the heat, there was no sign of sweat on his face, or under the arms of his shirt. Helen, who was wiping perspiration off her forehead, thought how cool and contained he was.

Frank pulled up a stool, stretched his legs out, and crossed them at the ankles, then put his glass of iced tea on the deck. He plucked the mint out of the glass and chewed it, something Arthur always used to do. The gesture resonated through Helen's body, and she remembered what Kathleen had said that morning, before Frank came down for breakfast. "Mr. Frank doesn't look like Mr. Arthur. Not with that blond hair and those blue eyes. But he dresses like him, and walks like him, and he talks the same. It gives me a funny feeling."

Helen said, "I thought you liked him."

"He's always extra polite to me," Kathleen said. "Not to criticize, but how come he's so perfect? That's what I want to know."

"Frank was a scholarship boy at Yale," Helen said. "I imagine there was a lot he had to learn. If Arthur trusted him so much he asked him to be Jack's godfather, that's good enough for me."

The view of the children on the beach brought Helen back to the porch. Watching Frank, she realized that Kathleen was right. Frank was reclining in Arthur's chair, and he had adopted many of Arthur's mannerisms. Like Arthur, he had a subtle way of changing the subject to defuse conversation that might turn unpleasant, or to deflect personal questions. While they were talking quietly about Frank's new job at the CIA, Helen wondered why he hadn't returned to the lucrative practice of law, and what about him was attracted to the role of spy.

Their conversation was abruptly entwined with the sound of a trumpet. Judge Gavin, who traditionally played "The Star Spangled Banner" on Independence Day, after the fireworks at the club, was practicing. The trumpet was a relic from the last war, when he played reveille, taps, and the signal to advance or retreat.

Helen turned toward the Gavins' house and saw Peter trotting down the front steps. He gave a signal to his dog, mounted his bike, and rode off with the dog by his side. She saw a tall young man with short curly brown hair, already streaked with lighter tones. Perhaps the sanitarium where he had been was in a warm climate, she thought. It was too early in the season for sun-streaks. His movements were strong and sure, and he did not appear as though he had been drawn through a keyhole.

"Who's that?" Frank asked.

"The boy next door," Helen said, "in a manner of speaking."

"I thought Arthur was the boy next door," Frank said. His voice sounded taut, as though he didn't trust this new neighbor, who, as anyone could see, was fit and handsome.

Helen smiled, thinking of Arthur, and their childhood together. "Yes, he was," she said. "That young man is Peter Gavin.

He went to Yale, too, before he was a Marine in the Pacific. He's summering here with his grandfather."

Kathleen came out and remarked, "Too bad the Judge doesn't play reveille every day. Might get Jack out of bed a little faster in the mornings."

"Growing is exhausting," Helen said. "Fourteen-year-olds *sleep*."

"Growing didn't tire out the boys when I was a girl in Ireland," Kathleen said. As it often did when she was remembering her youth, her brogue got stronger. "That age, they were already working. Up before dawn, at it till sunset. Didn't do them no harm, neither."

"I don't suppose it did them a lot of good that they had to quit school to go to work," Helen said sympathetically.

"Sure, and isn't that why my brothers and myself came here, Mrs. W?" Kathleen retorted.

"How do you think Jack's doing?" Frank asked Helen and Kathleen.

"Medium," Helen said. "I'm glad you're here. Since Arthur's been gone, it seems like Jack misses him most the weekend of the Wauregathon."

"What's the Wauregathon? I don't think I've ever been around for one of those."

"An all-island competition, held every year on the Sunday of July Fourth weekend—tomorrow. Arthur ran it the last summer he was here. It had a dramatic end."

"What happened?"

"I'll try to describe it to you," Helen said, "but give me a minute." She turned her chair, so she was no longer looking at Frank.

He adjusted his legs and pulled one knee up, put his arms around it, and prepared to listen. But she was silent, as the undertow of her thoughts dragged her back to a weekend six years earlier.

As Frank saw Helen's face change, he released his knee, turned toward the beach, and waited for her to be ready to talk, just as he had done when he interrogated Germans they had taken prisoner when he worked with the Resistance. He was not eager to hear about her happy times with his roommate and war partner.

Many of Helen's memories of Arthur had been handled so often they were smudged and hazy, the way the world looked when she took off the tortoiseshell glasses she insisted on wearing. She wasn't vain, but she had been told often enough that she was beautiful, and although she didn't understand men very well when she was younger, she suspected that the glasses made her appear more approachable, if a bit too much like a "bluestocking," that mysterious expression that described a woman who was too intellectual for her own good. She had noticed that some of the prettiest girls at college often didn't have dates on Saturday nights, because the boys were afraid they were dated up for months in advance.

She hadn't spent much time thinking about that particular Wauregathon, and she took a deep breath and tried to bring it back.

CHAPTER THREE

THAT Friday night in the early summer of 1942, Helen and Arthur were sitting in the living room on a cushy sofa as deep as a bed. They leaned back, facing each other, with their legs up and their feet touching, talking about the war in Europe.

"When this is over I want to reopen the French office," Arthur said. Wadsworth Grain had served an international clientele from Paris since the late nineteenth century.

"What if France ends up being part of Germany?" Helen asked.

"The French will still be French, and Europe will still need grain. If the Germans win, we'll have to deal with them anyway. Maybe we can do some good," Arthur said. "What would you think of living in Paris for a while?"

"Whither thou goest," Helen said, and smiled. "My mother would have loved the idea of my living in France. Remember that she dumped me with those mother and daughter war widows when I was only nine, so I could learn the language, then went tootling off by herself in her car? I've always wondered where she went."

Arthur snorted. "You probably don't want to know."

"If we go to Paris when this mess is over, I'd like to assign a couple of our men to work with the farmers who are being wiped out again by this war. What do you think?"

Helen thought it was a good idea, and typical of Arthur, who had been preoccupied with the fight against fascism.

"Christ only knows why Roosevelt hung back for so long. It's been clear for years that we had to get into this before the Germans took England, too," he said.

"Mmm-hmm," Helen said. She stroked his leg with her foot. "What is it about an idealistic grain merchant that makes me want to entice him up to our bedroom and take off my clothes, one piece at a time, like a stripper?"

"That won't take long, darling. Shorts, shirt, bra, panties. You're practically there already. I've been looking at you for the last half hour, wanting to unbutton your shirt and feel your breasts in my hands." Arthur swung his legs over the side of the couch and stood up. "Come here, sweetheart," he said.

Helen's face felt flushed, sitting on the porch with Frank and remembering how she had gone upstairs to make love with Arthur. She thought about what it might be like if she and Frank were to sneak into her room when everyone was asleep, and slide under the sheets, skin on skin. She wondered how many women he had slept with.

"Sorry," she said. "My mind was wandering. You wanted to know about the Wauregathon. I'd forgotten that you never came to visit over July Fourth. It's a series of contests for the children. The year I remember best is when Jack was in the eight-and-unders. They catch crabs for a race, then take them to the beach. One of the fathers draws a circle in the sand. The children put the crabs in the center of the circle and watch to see which one gets to the edge first. I took Jack down to the dock to catch his crabs, and he was petrified, dangling his little legs over the side and holding a string with a chunk of bacon on it. He was sure the crabs would jump out of the water and grab his toes.

"Did you ever know Howland Munson? He was in charge of the crab race. His widow, Alice, and I were just talking about how oblivious we were that some of the games were so wasteful. Before rationing, there used to be an egg toss and a toilet paper race, but with the shortages, they were replaced by sack races and a scavenger hunt. Now we can hardly imagine throwing eggs at each other, and letting them break and scatter in the sand. Even toilet paper: in the summer of 1942, when we were unrolling those streamers, people in Europe were already using scraps of old newspaper in the john.

"Poor Alice. Howland was such a sweet guy. Killed on the beach at Normandy. Alice has to rent her house every August, and she's working as a saleswoman at the dress shop on Madison Avenue we all go to, so she can keep Josie in private school."

Frank frowned and shook his head. "Pretty tough when a fellow's just started his career, and hasn't put aside any money yet. He probably had life insurance, but that wouldn't cover much."

"Certainly not private school, an apartment in New York,

and a summer house," Helen said. "Even with just one child. She's not the only one. Hardly anyone ever sells at Wauregan. Most families pass the houses down from generation to generation, but there are a couple of houses on the market now. Widows."

"That's a shame," Frank said, sounding sincere. "Tell me more about the Wauregathon. Did Arthur swim in the parent-child race?"

Helen made a "ha" sound. "If you were on the Yale swim team, even if your partner is your eight-year-old son, you would still have too much of an advantage. He was the referee."

Helen thought of Arthur standing in his bathing suit at the end of the "tank," the area in the bay that was roped off for swimming lessons and races. Even though she had been married to him for nine years that summer, she still noticed the muscles below his collarbone and across the top of his chest, and his strong, taut thighs. When they were engaged, they had done so much kissing that she had thought of him mostly as a face: strong-jawed, brown-eyed, with lovely straight hair that fell over his forehead—and a pair of hands that touched her gently, then urgently, until they sat back, panting, smiled at each other, and stopped.

Even after their years of married intimacy, when she watched him at the swim race, she had the same feeling of pleasure she had when she saw him doing other masculine things. She never tired of seeing the way, when he came home from work, he opened the top button of his shirt and yanked his tie down; or in the mornings, while she sat up in bed in her quilted satin bed jacket and they talked about the day to come, he knotted his tie, slinging one end over the other, adjusting the knot before he pulled it tight, then ran a finger under the back of his collar, to make sure it was straight.

She imagined Frank doing the same things and glanced at him: shiny blond hair, clear blue eyes, and regular features. Everything about him was in proportion. She looked at his neat hands with their long fingers and square-cut nails, and his narrow, elegant feet, and was reminded that he was a magnet to women. Arthur had once remarked that it was not just that Frank was handsome, but he had the ability to understand what a woman wanted. "Frank's intuitive, as well as smart," Arthur said. "Which accounts for his remarkable transformation from scholarship boy to clubman at Yale, and his success as a litigator when Bill Donovan hired him at his law firm before he started the OSS."

Frank could be the man who inspired her, if he was available. It was rare that he didn't have a woman in his life, although he never brought a date to Wauregan. If he ever did, that would mean he was serious. Helen realized she had goose bumps, and the fair hair on her arms was standing up, as though in alarm.

Frank, noticing, said, "Are you okay? You look like you're getting chilled out here. In this heat."

"I'm fine," she said. "I was just thinking about the last Wauregathon when Arthur was here," and she let herself remember again.

That day in 1942 had unfolded the way days often did at Wauregan: foggy in the morning, then suddenly clear and sunny, as the colony worked into a frenzy of competition. After lunch, while the judges collected team members' scores, doing a preliminary count, the participants in the final event assembled. The Wauregathon always ended with a tug-of-war, limited to adults and children over ten.

Helen had been salvaging unused hot dog rolls that hadn't gotten sandy and Arthur was conferring with the judges, when Jack inserted himself between two older children along the rope. If Kathleen had been there, he would never have gotten away with it, but Kathleen didn't go to the beach. She couldn't see the point. She didn't know how to swim and she didn't own a bathing suit. Her fine Irish skin burned easily, and she had no interest in sitting under an umbrella, listening to the conversations between Helen and the other mothers. Kathleen had things to do, especially on washing days. She had told Helen that hanging the laundry outside to dry was her favorite job. During her childhood, with the exception of church, doing the washing was one of the rare times she could get some peace in a household teeming with children. She had learned to plunge her hand into a laundry tub when even her mother screeched that the water was scalding. The reward was her time in the drying yard, where it was quiet and she could be alone.

Returning her attention to Frank, Helen said, "At the end of the Wauregathon, while Arthur and I weren't watching, Jack squeezed into the tug-of-war. He must have held on with all his might; he was so small, he was probably dragged off his feet. When the other team lost, they stumbled over the line, and the players on both sides crashed on top of each other. Jack got squashed in the pile. Arthur saw him first and ran over, calling me. When I got there, he was kneeling in the sand, asking Jack if he was okay. He must have been knocked out for a couple of minutes, because I remember his eyes fluttering open, and Arthur saying, 'Hello, piglet. Are you all in one piece?'

"Jack tried to get up, but when he leaned on his elbow, he fell back, crying. His arm was hanging, and it looked like his shoulder was dislocated. I felt nauseated, as though it was my own arm. We yelled for the doctor—there is something odd about seeing a doctor in a bathing suit, carrying his kit bag—and Dr. Bunbury came over. I kissed Jack on the forehead and tried to brush his hair back, and he said, 'Stop, Mummy! I'm fine. My team won!' Dr. Bunbury diagnosed a dislocation—it was pretty obvious—put a foot in Jack's armpit, extended the arm, and manipulated the joint into the socket. Jack's arm popped back in, he let out a cry, and he passed out. I was so upset my knees were trembling. Arthur picked him up and carried him back to the house. That was the excitement of the day."

Helen did not describe that evening, when she and Arthur stayed home from the Independence Day celebration and sat on their porch to watch the club fireworks, shooting out over the sea. Jack, who had recently announced he was too old for lap-sitting, had made an exception to his new rule, and was curled up on Arthur's lap, with one arm around his neck. The other arm was in a sling, and Jack was still pale and in pain, despite Kathleen's administrations of steaming hot cloths and half an aspirin. The night sky was a deep, dark blue, the stars were sharp, and glittered as though they were blinking. The fireworks display had a peculiar undertone. Helen had seen enough newsreels of battlefield scenes that as she watched, she wondered at the similarity between the fireworks and the tracers from machine guns shooting fire through the night.

When the last burst of lights dripped down into the sea, the Wadsworths could hear singing from the club deck, as the entire colony stood, hands over their hearts, and sang "The Star Spangled Banner," with Judge Gavin leading them on his trumpet. Helen and Arthur stood, too, while Jack still clung to his father, and they joined the singing quietly enough to hear the voices from the club, and feel part of the outpouring of love of country. When the anthem was finished, Jack nestled his head under Arthur's chin, and declared, "This is the best summer of my life."

"Mine, too, piglet," Arthur said.

Late that night, after they had made love, and Arthur was beginning to doze off, Helen said quietly, "If we get into this war, I'm so glad you're too old to fight."

She sighed and returned to the summer of 1948, and to Frank.

"Now that Jack's outgrown the crab race, what's he going to do today?" Frank asked.

"He's a junior counselor in the sports group. They get to help at the different events. It's a big deal," Helen said.

With thoughts of making love still clear in her mind, she avoided Frank's eye when he asked, "You've been remembering, haven't you?"

"Of course. Although the memories get fainter every year he's gone."

"Are you ready to consider that he isn't coming back?"

"Yes," she said. "And no."

"I remember the summer of '42," Frank said. "When I came to visit in August, Arthur was beginning to show Jack how to

sail *Red Wing*. Do you remember all those questions he asked—
'How come you call a boat "she"?' and 'Why's it called a Beetle
Cat? It doesn't look like a bug—or a cat.'"

Helen smiled. "Arthur was so patient. He told Jack he wasn't
sure why boats were female, but he thought it was because
fishermen and sailors who were away for a long time named
their boats after the people they loved most, and were leaving
behind—their wives and daughters. And Jack said, 'And their
mothers. Don't forget their mothers.'" She was still smiling, but
her eyes were full of tears.

"Why *are* they called Beetle Cats?" Frank asked.

"Not because of the way they look. The family who makes
them is named Beetle. I don't know about the 'cat' part, but
someone told me that because of their flat bottoms, they move
as fast and gracefully as a cat, with the same kind of balance.
Nothing to do with catamarans. I don't know where that name
comes from."

"Jack was out on the boat with us when I talked to Arthur
about joining the OSS. It had just been established in June.
Before that, remember, the president gave Donovan the title of
'Co-ordinator of Information.' He had assembled a team, and I
was on it. Until then, we didn't even have an intelligence service.
Roosevelt had to fight to get that to happen. It took a year, from
July '41, before the OSS was officially formed."

"Maybe one of the reasons Arthur was so eager to join was
that he said he sometimes felt as though his whole life had been
preplanned, without anyone consulting him," Helen said. "He
always wanted to be a little different. To be part of the world
he was born into, but not trapped in it. In a way it's surprising
that he married me. I was such an obvious choice.

"I once asked him if he chose me because it was so easy. I was always there and he didn't have to get to know me.

"He was incredulous. We were in the car, coming home from a dinner party. Dead of winter and the road was icy. 'You've got to be kidding,' he said. 'I've loved you all my life.'

"We were always a team. Once when we were little, my mother was having one of her really crazy spells. A friend of ours was giving a costume party, and Kathleen made costumes for both of us. I was Wendy and Arthur was Captain Hook, because he always wanted to be a pirate when we dressed up. My mother said I couldn't go because I was wearing a nightgown—flannel, with a high neck, cut down from an old one of Mrs. Wadsworth's. Mama said people would think she was a bad mother, and I was going to grow up to be a loose woman. And I was what? Nine?"

"So, did Arthur go alone?"

"No. Daddy intervened, the way he always did. It was just before Mama decided I was the spawn of Satan. That was dangerous. I stayed with the Wadsworths until Daddy found the right place to send her." Helen sighed deeply.

"It was always clear that you were Arthur's girl," Frank said. "I have to admit I was jealous. And while he and I were together in France, he had you, and I had no one. The war made all of us long for a safe haven. Wife. Children. A place like this. I'd buy a house here in an instant if bachelors weren't taboo. I wish I had a ready-made family, so I wouldn't have to wait—" he said, and stopped abruptly.

When Kathleen came out with a fresh pitcher of minty iced tea, and poured some into Helen's and Frank's empty glasses, Frank thought her timing was good. It was too soon to say anything more.

He thanked Kathleen for the iced tea, then impulsively said, "I wish you wouldn't call me Mr. Frank. You've known me long enough. Why not just call me Frank?"

Kathleen stepped back and held the pitcher in front of her like a shield. "When a person lives in the same house with the people she works for, it's good to keep a little distance. It's the only way to have some privacy your own self. I call my employers Mr. Arthur and Mrs. W, and you Mr. Frank, because it's respectful, but it gives me some breathing room, too. I bet you never thought of this: I've been in Mr. Arthur and Mrs. W's room just about every day. You know how often they been in my room? Almost never. One more thing. If it wasn't for you, Mr. Arthur would never have gone off to that war. I don't blame you that he didn't come back, but I don't like it. Now let's not have any more of this 'Call me Frank' business. Have a little respect for a person's job."

"Wow! I remember when you used to give Arthur and me the dickens when we were in college and stayed out all night at those deb parties he took me to. You sure haven't lost your touch."

"I hope not," Kathleen said. She brought one hand up to cover her mouth as she smiled, hiding her teeth. Dentistry had not been an option in a poor Irish family.

"How *did* you get Arthur to go off with you?" Helen asked Frank.

"He wanted to do something, and he was frustrated that he was too old to enlist. I told him about the OSS, and he said he'd think about it. Did he talk it over with you?"

"Yes. Before dinner that night. He'd already made up his mind."

"I always wondered what Jack heard and understood when he was out on *Red Wing* with us."

"Enough. He was so excited, he told me before Arthur did. He came home, and said, 'Wow! Daddy's going to be a spy with Uncle Frank!'"

"And what did Arthur tell you?"

"He said, 'We're in this thing, and it's our duty to do whatever we can.' That was the night the bluefish ran."

"I remember the church bell chiming when we were getting dressed for the dance," Frank said, "and wondering if there was some kind of emergency."

"Urgency is more like it. We have a special chime that announces a run of bluefish," Helen said. "If it goes off, the men drop everything and grab their gear and cast into the surf. Arthur was wearing his tuxedo shirt, trousers, and suspenders, and he'd just fastened his cummerbund. He stripped off his socks, dropped them into a big shell on his bureau, turned back his sleeves, and raced down to the shed to get his rod and tackle. I sat on the banquette that wraps around the binnacle in front of the picture window in the room we call 'the captain's room,' and watched Arthur and the other men casting at the edge of the surf, with their tuxedo pants rolled up. Arthur had just told me he was going to sign with your organization. I remember thinking we weren't even in the war, and my husband was ready to join some new spy service to save the world for democracy. Do you ever wish you hadn't talked him into it?"

"All the time," Frank said.

If only he truly meant it, he thought, but if Arthur were here, he would not be alone with Helen. Arthur had discreetly implied he and Helen had a deeply sexual relationship, and if that was her nature, he might be able to make the same kind of connection with her. He only had to wait three more years for Arthur to be officially declared dead. He would never have to reveal what had really happened in France, and he believed the only other person who knew had been killed. He had learned to be patient during the war, and unless something, or someone, unexpected turned up, he would stay the course. He loved Helen and Jack in the way he could love, and he would be there when she was ready to move on. Between her railroad money and Arthur's grain fortune, he could afford to stay at the CIA. He had discovered that espionage work suited him better than the more profitable practice of the law.

CHAPTER FOUR

"DID you ever see anyone sleep as hard as Jack?" Helen asked Kathleen, a couple of weeks after Frank left. July Fourth was on a Monday that year, and while Frank was staying with them, Jack had gotten up for breakfast with the adults. Now that he had to wake up in time to get to his job at the sports group, raising him was like getting an alligator out of hibernation in the mud when the water turns cool in the southern swamps.

"Not that Peter," Kathleen said. "I hear he hardly sleeps at all."

"He sleeps in the afternoons," Helen said. "I've seen him."

Helen had heard enough about Peter Gavin to arouse her interest. As the days went by, she watched him bicycling to and from his grandfather's house and repairing damaged railings that hadn't been fixed during the war when materials were in short supply. In the late afternoons, she stretched out with a book on a chaise in the sitting room that faced the Gavins' and she could see him sleeping on the faded floral cretonne-covered sofa on their screened porch. As the setting sun moved across his face she noticed that even when he was asleep, the sharp lines between his nose and the side of his mouth didn't relax, as though his teeth were clenched. She hardly knew him, yet she found that she wanted to stroke his face until it was smooth and unworried. She asked herself if she was feeling maternal, or if her desire came from another place.

Sometimes she gazed at him until her cheeks were pink and the pulse in her throat was beating fast enough that she could feel it. One afternoon, as though he sensed her attention, Peter's dog, Max, who was lying on the floor next to him, with his black muzzle between his paws and his big velvety ears cocked, lifted his head, and stared across at her. She looked back and smiled, although she had read somewhere that, in the dog world, showing teeth was a warning, not a sign of friendship. They looked at each other until Max evidently decided that no danger was coming from her direction, then dropped his head on his paws again.

Occasionally, she and Kathleen heard the Judge playing jazz tunes on the trumpet, and the sound brought up an image of a different Peter from the one with premature lines on his face. She imagined that the Judge was trying to cheer him up, and visualized the two tall men boogieing around their living room, dancing in and out among the gloomy green cotton-covered furniture and the rickety lamps with bulbs that were many watts too dull. The Gavin house had never had much style, even by Wauregan standards, but it had lapsed into a nearly terminal fatigue since the Judge's wife had died. The place reflected the sadness of a lonely old man and his sleepless grandson. Perhaps the jazz riffs were a sign that life was returning on the other side of the path.

Around the time that Helen was thinking about Peter, he had begun to wonder about her. One morning when Kathleen had just done the washing and had hung the clothes on the line, Peter noticed a full set of men's summer clothes bouncing and fluttering in the wind. When he came downstairs, he asked his grandfather, "Did I miss something? Arthur Wadsworth didn't come home, did he?"

Judge Gavin shook his head and closed his mouth in a tight line.

"Is he expected?"

"No," the Judge said shortly.

"So whose clothes are those? Surely they're too big for the little Wadsworth boy."

"That 'little boy' is fourteen. He's going to boarding school in the fall. He's pretty weedy, but he hasn't gotten his full growth yet. Those are Arthur's clothes."

"You're kidding! What's the point?"

"Every year Helen has Kathleen take out Arthur's summer wardrobe, and wash and iron everything. I think she wants to be sure if he returns, he can just slip back into the person who wore those clothes before he left."

"Doesn't she realize he isn't going to be wearing them again?"

"I don't know. There's something not quite right about the story. It's a little suspicious that his partner made it back and he didn't. The only credible hint I got from one of my friends in Washington who knows we go to the same summer place as the Wadsworths, is that Arthur may be working undercover for that new organization, the CIA. He thinks he could still be in France, infiltrating a Communist group. I suspect my friend was fishing, to see if I knew anything."

"You think it's possible?"

"Highly unlikely. Arthur was a real family man. Plus, he and Helen grew up together. I'd guess they have a bond that's stronger than most married couples. You know her mother was crazy; Helen had a real up-and-down childhood. Her father ran the family railroad and traveled a lot, and Helen was always over at the Wadsworths'. Kathleen was almost as much her nurse as Arthur's. Helen must have been a lonely little girl. Arthur was her refuge, and he took care of her, even before they knew what grown-up love meant. How's a man like that going to walk away from his family to work for the government? No matter how patriotic he is."

"You were in the last one. You know how war can change people."

"Uh-huh, but I still feel a little sick every summer when I see those clothes out on the washing line, nothing inside them except the breezes."

While Peter and the Judge were speculating about Arthur's fate, the adults in the community were talking about Max. A small but persistent group believed a dog trained to kill could revert and become vicious at any time, and was pressuring the Wauregan Association to force Peter to remove Max from the island. When one of the more sympathetic women asked the Judge about Max, he answered her so sharply that she warned the others off. Peter and Max remained a mystery, until the children on the island discovered them.

In the mornings, before sports group, before the lifeguards came on duty, while the mothers and nursemaids were making beds and cleaning up after breakfast, the Wauregan children rode up and down the narrow paths, clanking on their bikes like loose change, free to go anywhere except the beach, which was strictly forbidden to anyone under twelve not accompanied by an adult.

Soon after Peter had settled into his grandfather's house that July Fourth weekend, a few children riding past the stile nearest the club on their way to sports group heard the unusual sound of an internal combustion engine on the other side of the dunes. In a place without cars, any motorized vehicle was a novelty. They left their bikes leaning against the rack at the bottom of the stairs, climbed to the top of the bleached-wood stile, and saw a tractor with balloon-pumped tires. Hitched behind it was a bar with rubber broom strips that swayed along in the sand like a hula skirt on a fat lady taking a stroll. Peter was in the driver's seat, steering steadily down the beach, as the brushes smoothed the sand. The big dog that some of the children had been warned to stay away from trotted alongside, keeping pace with the machine, tail up, ears perked, looking left and right, as though to be sure the perimeters were safe.

Jack, who was also heading for the athletic field, went up to investigate and move the campers along, so they wouldn't be late. When they saw him, one of the boys asked, "Could you go down and see what it is?" At fourteen, Jack was old enough to be on the beach on his own. "You stay up here," he warned. "I'll come back and tell you." He vaulted down the steps, taking them two at a time, then cautiously approached.

Peter saw him coming and turned off the engine.

"Hi!" Jack said. The children watching him made him feel less shy than he might have felt with a grown-up he didn't know. "What's that?"

"Sand sweeper," Peter said. "The club bought it to clean up the beach. It gets rid of footprints and the junk people leave around." He saw Jack looking at his dog, and said, "This is Max. Want to meet him?"

Jack, who was not one of the children whose mother had instructed, "Under no circumstances are you to go near that animal," nodded eagerly.

Peter gave Max the "sit" command, and he settled on his haunches and looked up at Peter, who nodded. Then Max leaned his nose forward, gave Jack's hand a lick, and straightened up, sitting at attention. Jack looked at his bright brown eyes and the blond eyebrows, set so Max looked as though he were asking, "Who are you?" or "What would you like me to do?" His muzzle was black, as though he had been digging in the dirt, and much of his body was a reddish blond, except for a black saddle around his middle and a white patch on his chest. He swished his bushy tail and, at Peter's instruction, gave Jack a large, furry paw to shake. Jack, who had wished for a dog of his own when he blew out the candles on his birthday cake every year, instantly fell in love.

The dog's performance on the beach was too much for the children at the top of the stile. The boldest boys decided that with a grown man and a teenager as "protection," and no one watching, they could claim to be adequately chaperoned, and dashed down the steps, then walked cautiously toward the scene on the sand.

It only took a couple of days before the early mornings found as many as five children at a time sitting on the bar at the back of the sand sweeper, riding along, chattering and cheeping like birds on a wire. With the extra weight, the brushes were making shallow grooves in the sand. It was fortunate that no mother was looking down the beach as she shook out a rug on her porch. None of them knew that their children were starting their days by having an adventure with a pair of controversial veterans.

The task of driving the new piece of equipment had initially been assigned to a college boy, but he had been fired for swearing at the club cook. Peter took it on temporarily, after his grandfather suggested he might be willing to substitute until a replacement could be found. The Judge thought Peter might as well have something to do in the early mornings, because he would surely be awake. He, too, was aware that the only time his grandson slept soundly was for the couple of hours in the late afternoon when he stretched out on the old couch on the screened porch. At night, he prowled the house. Every board made its own noise, and Michael Gavin, who had grown up in that house, could follow his grandson's patrols by the treads on the boards and the clicking of Max's toenails on the wood. When the Judge gently asked about the long, wakeful nights, Peter apologetically explained, "Sorry, Gramps. I don't like to close my eyes when it's dark."

After Jack met Max, he asked Helen about the dog, and she assured him that the Marines would not have allowed a dangerous animal to come to a place where there were children.

"I read they had a program to retrain the war dogs to get used to civilian life again," she said.

"What if it doesn't work?"

"Maybe they keep them in a sort of camp," she said, although she knew that some of the dogs had been too badly traumatized or had turned mean, and had to be euthanized.

Kathleen had her own view about Max. She told Helen that some of the men who had seen action were worse than that nice animal. "Once you've killed," she said ominously, "it gets easier every time." That might also apply to a dog, but nobody really understood what Max had done in the Pacific. When anyone asked, Peter explained that he had been a "scout dog," that each dog worked with a handler, and that they slept and ate together. "They develop a bond that's hard to describe," he would say. "Sometimes all that saves a man from going crazy is the love of that animal. A lot of the dogs were pets before the war and I guess most of them never lose the ability to love and be gentle." But whomever he was talking to would look at Max, imagine him growling with his fangs bared, and lose the thread of the story.

After members of the Association Board received enough complaints, a few of the men asked Peter to bring his dog over to Bill Sorter's house for an informal interview. As Max lay quietly at his feet, front paws crossed, ears pricked, Peter told them, "Scouts like Max go out on recons to look for the enemy and warn us, or lead us to them. They only attack under extreme circumstances. *Patrol* dogs are trained to assault, but even they aren't naturally aggressive, and they only attack on command. A lot of dogs have been retrained, and are back home. I got a letter the other day from one of the handlers who wanted to know how Max was doing. He told me that something like three thousand war dogs have been returned to civilian life."

"I don't know," Bill Sorter said doubtfully. He had a scar on his hand from a time when, as a small boy, he had yanked hard on a dachshund's tail and wouldn't let go until the dog turned and bit him. He had been afraid of dogs ever since. "You got to admit, Max looks more like a wolf than a domesticated animal."

"These big shepherds look fierce, but except for a few that are naturally vicious—like people, there are always a couple who are just plain bad—you have to teach a dog to be belligerent. A lot of the time, when a dog gets hostile, it's out of devotion to a human," Peter said.

"I was on Guam with one of our handlers who had a Doberman named Skipper. The dog slept with him, and ate his rations out of his helmet. The handler was promoted to second lieutenant, which meant he couldn't work with his dog anymore—that wasn't a job for an officer. After a couple of weeks, he said, 'You can have your stripes, I want my old rank back so I can have my dog.' The commanding officer laughed and demoted him. This guy was wounded in a skirmish on one of the islands, and when he fell, Skipper stood guard over him. As soon as the medic knelt down and touched him, Skipper growled and took the medic's hand in his mouth and held it. He didn't bite, just held it. Luckily the handler was conscious, and he instructed Skipper to let go. The medic proceded, but when the soldier groaned, the dog grabbed the medic's arm and even the handler couldn't get him to open his mouth and sit back. It was some sight! Every time the soldier winced, the medic was sure Skipper was going to sink in his teeth and pull him off, but he never did.

"These animals have a special kind of loyalty and intelligence. Some of the men believed they were sent to be our guardian angels," Peter said, and exhaled. He had been so intent, he had hardly taken a breath. "Sorry. I didn't mean to make a speech."

"How come you got Max? Weren't you an officer?" Bill Sorter asked, pulling out the front of his shirt, which was sticking to him. Max's proximity was making him nervous, and he was sweating.

"That's right. But I knew his handler, and he'd shown me how he worked him. His father was a dog trainer, and my dad used to shoot over his field dogs at a club he belonged to. When the son enlisted, the boy was assigned to the K-9 unit at Fort Bragg, and he asked his father to send his dog down. It wasn't one of the kennel dogs. Shepherds aren't used for hunting. Max was his pet. The boy was killed in the mop-up on Guam and that's when I took him over. After the war was over, I was sent to Japan first, but then I was invalided out. Some of the men heard that I was in a kind of hospital, and they thought it would be good for me to have a companion. When I asked the doctors, they agreed. The place was a big converted country house, built by one of the Wall Street tycoons at the turn of the century. Actually," Peter said, and grinned at one of the senior bankers who sat on the board, "I think it used to be your grandfather's place."

"North Shore of Long Island?"

Peter nodded. "Overlooking Oyster Bay."

"That's it. The fortune came from the National City Bank of New York. First bank to exceed one billion dollars in assets. Largest commercial bank in the world in 1902. Hated going to Sunday lunch there. Footmen! Maids for the lapdogs! Father got rid of it and moved here as soon as Grandfather died. So now it's a convalescent home?"

"Something like that," Peter said. "Anyway, the rules weren't so strict, and Max was shipped to me. When he arrived, I hadn't been able to talk for months. I could hear words in my head, but I couldn't get myself to open my mouth and say them. But Max needed to hear a confident voice, and I found mine again. I'd guess some of you who saw the worst of it know what you carry around when it's over. Thanks to Max, I feel like the scar's healing, even if the wound is mostly in my mind.

"After I got out of the hospital, I took Max to see the boy's father and told him how his son died, and that his dog stood by him and whimpered and howled, and wouldn't leave until we took the body away. I told him both man and dog had served their country bravely, and I'd be honored if he'd let me keep Max. The old man said yes. That's the kind of visit every officer dreads, but the handler was in my platoon and I knew the family."

The men sitting on the porch overlooking the bay didn't say much after that. They had heard that Peter had suffered a breakdown when he came back from the Pacific, but they hadn't expected him to talk about it. If he had taken responsibility for a dog that had lost its master, and the dog had helped him regain his voice, so be it. It occurred to more than one of the men at Bill Sorter's that it would have helped if he, too, had had a place of refuge and a few months to absorb the shocks of the war before he came home. In a way, Peter was lucky. He didn't have a wife and children who expected that he would reappear and be just the same as he was before he learned to kill.

Jack had been working up his courage to talk to Peter about Max after their encounter at the beach. With the Gavins living so close by, he had considerable opportunity to watch the dog, and he was eager to get to know him. One evening before dinner, Jack knocked on the Gavins' screen door. Peter and Max came to the door and invited him in. "Any interest in a Coke?" Peter asked.

"Sure," Jack said. He wasn't allowed to drink Coca-Cola at home.

"I was wondering," Jack said, after he had put his nose in the glass to feel the bubbles bursting. "Would you say Max is a one-man dog or could he make friends with other people? Kids, maybe?"

"Like you?"

Jack smiled sheepishly. "Particularly me," he said.

"Why not? In the Pacific Max lived with a whole platoon, and he was everyone's buddy. When we dug foxholes to sleep in, people used to try to get near him and his handler, because they knew if the enemy was approaching, Max would alert, and they'd be ready for an attack."

"Weren't you his handler?"

"No. Officers aren't part of the K-9 Corps. His handler

couldn't take him when the war was over, so I did," Peter said shortly.

The "buddy" part sounded promising, Jack thought. He hoped Max would like him enough so he could learn how to take care of a dog, if he ever got one.

CHAPTER FIVE

THE Wauregan women ran the Children's Athletics Program during the war, but when their husbands returned, the men took over again. Before the summer of 1948, Sally's husband, Dan Carter, led the search for a new sports group director, and the committee hired a veteran like themselves.

Gunner Sergeant Red Stanley, known as "Sarge," was a career soldier in his early forties. He had been honorably discharged after he was wounded at Anzio, and had not found a new job. He thought that with his experience in training soldiers, he might be good at running an athletic program for a school. To get some experience for his résumé, he had applied for the position at Wauregan. Sarge had a steel plate in his scalp, and when the barometer was changing, he was attacked by excruciating headaches. He did not mention that he was also prone to sudden seizures. His hair had not grown back over the flap of skin that covered the steel plate, but he wore a hat, and only took it off briefly to run his hand over the smooth, taut skin on the top of his head, or scratch the place where it itched, so there was nothing about his appearance to frighten the children.

When the members of the committee interviewed a presumptive war hero who needed a job—the description "war hero" was almost automatically applied to anyone who had been severely wounded—they hired him.

Dan Carter said, "If this guy could turn raw recruits into soldiers, he's got the right kind of experience to toughen up our children. The boys spent too much time with their mothers while we were away, and it's made them soft. We need a real masculine role model. As my father used to say, 'A wishbone is fine, but it's the backbone that matters.' Sergeant Stanley won't give any quarter to sissies, cheaters, or layabouts. Those kids had better try hard and obey the rules, or they'll suffer the consequences."

That was greeted by a muttering of "That's the ticket" from the other men on the committee. No one asked if Sarge had had any experience with children.

Sarge had been in the U.S. Army his entire adult life. He was single, with no family of his own; he had no permanent home, and few options for the future. If the men who hired him wanted him to be tough, he would not disappoint them. What he had not expected was that at Wauregan he would find himself in the unique and lonely position of an outsider, once the apparent camaraderie of the interview was over.

In the Army, there had been officers' clubs and enlisted men's clubs. Here there was only one club, and he wasn't allowed to use it. As for the equivalent of other enlisted men, there was the watchman, who was in his seventies and rode his bicycle around with a flashlight all night and slept during the day. Sarge was assigned staff housing in a dormitory where he lived with the bartender and the college boys who waited tables and worked in the kitchen. Even the chef had better quarters, and the island manager and his family kept to themselves.

He had to remind himself that this job was his ticket to the next one, that his bosses were on the boards of the kinds of private schools where he imagined himself working, housed, fed, and taken care of the way he had been in the armed forces. If he pleased them, he stood a chance that one of them would recommend him for a position in the athletic department of a school where, as he imagined correctly, Waureganites and their sort ruled. He would only have to endure the Wauregan "boot camp" for two months, but his solitary status made him angry, and that made him rougher on the children than the committee had anticipated, or intended.

Jack had been going to the morning sports group since he was five, but this was the first year he was a junior counselor. The "Sports Sirs," as the gym teachers in his all-boys' school were called, were strict, but he had never encountered anyone as hard as Sarge, who acted out his rage at being treated like an outcast by taunting the weaker kids, and taking the wind out of anyone who was too successful. Jack watched, did what he was told, and tried not to attract attention.

He was a reasonably good athlete, tall for his age and wiry. His glasses steamed up, or slipped down his nose when he sweated, which could make it hard to see, but he had a strong, accurate throwing arm. At softball games, Sarge usually placed him behind the outfielder, so if a child didn't have the power to throw a ball to the pitcher or a baseman, Jack could pluck the ball out of the air, or off the ground, toss it to the waiting child, and let the boy or girl make the throw. Coed softball, which the women instituted when their husbands were away, was now firmly established, despite some of the men's objections that the girls would take the edge off the game.

One muggy mid-July morning, Jack was deep in the outfield, hoping that the little girl resolutely standing some yards in front of him, crouched over, with her elbows on her knees, could do a bit better this time. Someone hit a long fast grounder and she scrambled for the ball, but it went through her legs and out of bounds. Jack jogged off to retrieve it, just as Peter and Max were walking by the athletics field.

Peter gestured to Max to pick up the ball and bring it to Jack. Max took it in his mouth, but when Sarge saw them, he came barreling toward the outfield, his stomach jiggling under his T-shirt, yelling, "Stop! Get that dog away from these kids!"

Max had dropped the ball at Jack's feet, and he had picked it up and was standing with it in his mitt as Sarge raced toward him. Jack heard Peter command Max to sit and stay, but Jack was watching Sarge, with his red, splotchy face and his gut poking out ahead of him, as he puffed and gasped, sputtering and shouting, "I seen them vicious dogs on sentry duty. 'Detect, detain, and *destroy*'! What do you want a destroyer dog around kids for? They should have put every one of 'em down when the war was over. I seen 'em knock a man over and sink in them fangs, and rip up flesh until it was hamburger. You got a dangerous weapon there. You keep that animal away from these children. Or else. Hear me?" Then as the habit of a lifelong professional soldier kicked in, he remembered that Peter had been an officer, and automatically added, "Sir," then was furious at himself for treating the younger man as though he were his superior.

"Thousands of these dogs were prepared for civilian life," Peter said calmly, as he had already told many of the doubters. "If someone saved your life, would you have him destroyed when the fighting was over?"

"Did Max really save your life?" Jack asked.

"Keep out of this, kid. None of your business," Sarge snapped.

He squinted at Peter, and said venomously, "What're you doing hanging around here anyway, doin' nothin' all summer, while some of us have to work? You Marines think you're something special. Believe you me, us army guys were just as tough. You call yourselves and those beasts 'devil dogs.' That's a lot of you-know-what. You better have that animal put down before he does some real damage—"

"No!" Jack interrupted. "Max is a good dog," and suddenly out spurted the words, "And you're a big fat jerk."

Sarge looked down at Jack. His eyes were hidden behind dark sunglasses, and Jack couldn't see his expression, but he was scared. "Get out of here, kid," Sarge spat. "I don't want to see you and your four eyes until I'm good and ready. As of right now, you are on probation, so git going."

Helen and Kathleen were listening to the radio while Kathleen swept the sand out of the living room and Helen plumped cushions, and they were singing along at top volume. The song, a hit from a couple of years earlier, was "Zip-a-Dee-Doo-Dah." As Jack walked in, he heard his mother laugh and tell Kathleen, "Listen to that propaganda. The war's over. 'My, oh, my, it's a wonderful day!' Sixty or seventy million dead, ten million thrown into concentration camps, most of them dead, too, but look forward, not back."

"Good idea," Kathleen said. Then she noticed Jack, standing in the doorway, punching his baseball mitt, his lower lip stuck out, the expression of a boy who was trying not to cry. "Home early, are you?" she said. "Did you get hungry from taking care of them little kids?"

Helen shook her head, warningly. "What happened?" she asked.

"Sarge put me on probation."

"What for?"

Jack looked down at his softball mitt, and thumped it with his fist.

"Come on," Helen said.

"I called him a bad word."

"Which was?"

"It wasn't one of the ones I'm not allowed to say."

"Jack . . ." Helen warned.

"I called him a jerk."

Helen tried not to laugh. "Because?"

"He told Peter he should have Max put down."

Helen set down the cushion she was plumping and put her hands on her hips. Her ears had started to buzz.

"Jack?"

He looked up warily.

"Let Peter handle Sarge. You'd better ride back to the sports field right now and apologize before that man boils over. We have a whole summer ahead of us. I don't see you spending the mornings cleaning house with me and Kathleen."

"But I'm not sorry."

"That doesn't matter. Sarge doesn't have any authority over Peter or his dog, and sometimes you have to apologize to keep the peace."

Jack saw that his mother wasn't going to give in. "Would you come with me?" he asked.

"I could come along, but I'm not going to say anything," Helen said. "This is up to you." She wanted to see how her son handled himself, but she promised herself to stay out of it.

They got on their bikes and started toward the sports field, with Jack in the lead, riding fast, head down, his usual style. They were nearly there when he skidded to a stop, turned, and rode back to Helen. "Grandpa used to tell me I should fight my own battles," he said.

"Which you're going to do."

Grandpa said, Helen thought sadly. If only my son could say, *Dad says . . .*

Her father, who had given her the yellow bike she was riding as a thirtieth birthday present a few years back, had been a good surrogate, but he had died of a stroke just that winter. The house where Helen had grown up in Minnesota was empty now, and without any brothers or sisters to move in, she was thinking of putting it on the market. Yet it had been built by one of the greatest railroad men who ever lived, and she was also considering turning it into a small museum that showed the history of the territory the line traversed, and how her grandfather's railroad had settled the empty plains and given farmers the chance to turn them into rich farmland from which they could ship their crops to market.

Helen pedaled along, knowing she should not be there, but she couldn't resist the urge to protect her son on his last summer before he went away to school and had to protect himself. She had transferred her anger from Sarge to Arthur; she felt as though he had abandoned her, even if he hadn't had a choice. Dealing with a bully was a man's job. Frank could have handled Sarge, too, she thought, and realized she had begun to count on him more than she had realized. She wasn't the only mother who didn't like the sergeant's swagger, or the way he looked at some of them. If the committee were still run by women, Sarge would not have been a candidate to head the Wauregan Association children's athletics program.

She clenched her teeth and leaned over her handlebars to keep up with Jack, not slowing for corners or cracks in the concrete path, until she hit a broken piece of cement and fell off her bike. She sat on the ground and brushed grit out of the scrapes on her palms. The yellow bike was resting on a handlebar and its wheel casing was scratched, as though someone had gouged the paint with the sharp end of a screwdriver. She had loved it when her father bought her a new bike and she took good care of it. The gift reminded her of the time when she was little and he taught her to ride a two-wheeler, and when, before the war, Arthur ran along behind Jack with one hand on the back of the seat, as Jack learned to balance on his own.

Jack dismounted and leaned his bike against the trunk of one of the self-seeded pines that grew all over Wauregan. Then he sat on the sandy, scrubby side of the path next to Helen and examined her scrapes. He touched a finger to a cut that was welling with blood, and put it in his mouth and grinned. "The vampire of the Wauregan Association."

"Grandpa's bike is scratched," Helen said.

"That's good," Jack said. "Shiny new bikes are for little kids."

Helen smiled. "Okay," she said. "Let's go."

The sports field was busy with children playing volleyball or baseball, and a few girls sitting at a picnic table making lanyards, among the less useful, if satisfying, children's activities. Sarge was shouting instructions through a bullhorn. He had taken off his hat to wipe away the sweat with a large plaid handkerchief and Helen saw the shiny patch of skin over the steel plate before he jammed the cap back on his head and straightened the bill. Jack parked his bike in the rack at the side of the field and tentatively walked toward him, while Helen stood back and watched.

Sarge noticed Helen first. He looked at her in a way that made her skin crawl, as though he had been waiting for her, and had used her son's punishment to draw her to him. She grabbed her hair, which was hanging loose, and pulled it back, holding it in a hank at the back of her neck. Then she realized that keeping her arm up made her breasts jut forward, so she let her hair fall and crossed her arms over her chest.

Sarge handed the bullhorn to one of the junior counselors and stood with his legs apart, like a giant in a fairy tale. He was twisting a length of rope looped through his belt like a lasso. Helen wondered what that was for, then remembered tug-of-war, which the older boys and girls sometimes played. She couldn't hear Jack; he had his back to her, but she saw him straighten up, so his shoulder blades stuck out like little wings, as he gathered his dignity to apologize. He was getting tall, but he still had elements of the body of a little boy. She had always loved those "wings," and his vulnerable back.

Jack said something, Sarge answered, and Jack turned around to look at his mother and shook his head. It appeared that the apology had not gone well.

Helen's temples started to throb, and she walked out onto the field. "What's going on here?" she said. "I understand Jack was rude to you, which was wrong, but I also believe you insulted a friend of his. Why don't you make up and get back to the business of giving these children a good summer?"

"If you came to ask me to let him back in, the answer's no. He's a disturbance."

"That's ridiculous. He's extremely responsible."

Jack interrupted, "Max isn't dangerous. He's a hero."

"That's just an excuse," Sarge said. "Listen to yourself. The way you're going, your whole life is gonna be one big excuse."

"If my dad was here . . ." Jack began, bristling.

Sarge stared at him. "Yeah," he said, "but your dad isn't here. The war's been over three years. 'MIA' is just another way of saying he's dead, but they can't find the body. Wake up, big shot; he ain't coming back. You and your 'mummy' are on your own."

Jack hauled off and punched Sarge in the belly. It looked soft, but Jack was surprised at how much it hurt to hit him.

Sarge's face turned an ugly red. He lifted his hand as though to strike the boy, looked at Helen, dropped his arm, spat on the ground, and marched away.

Evidently, Helen thought, being brought up by his mother and his nurse hadn't turned Jack into a sissy. Damn it, she told herself. I'm going to have to punish him. But she and Arthur had taught Jack to fight unfairness and cruelty, and Jack had not forgotten the lesson. In the end, she decided that being kicked out of sports group was enough punishment and that she would wait to see what Jack found to fill his days.

CHAPTER SIX

THE next morning, when the younger children had climbed off the sand sweeper, Jack walked over to the beach, and climbed to the top of the stile, to see if Peter and Max were there. He saw Peter lying on his back, with his torso under the machine, and his legs sticking out the other side, trying to fix something.

Jack grabbed the rails of the stile with both hands, leapt over the stairs, and approached.

"What're you doing?" he asked.

"Hi," Peter said. "Aren't you late for sports?"

"I'm not going. I'm out."

"Because you called Sarge a bad name?"

"Worse. I went to apologize, and he said something that upset my mother, and I punched him in the stomach. His gut looks like jelly, but it's lined with cement."

Peter poked his head back under the vehicle before Jack could see him grin. Then he slid backward on the sand and stood up. "Something got stuck in the works on this baby. I'm trying to find it," he said. "Want to see if you can figure out what the trouble is? I'm a little too big to fit under there and I can't move around to see very well."

Jack got down on his hands and knees, turned onto his back, and maneuvered himself beneath the machine. "Hey!" he said. "Got it!" A broken shell had been stuck in the works beneath the sand sweeper. He back-crawled out, and held it up proudly.

"Good job," Peter said. "Now that you're out of sports, what are you going to do the rest of the summer? This is—what?— July 15? You've got six, seven weeks until Labor Day."

"Mom says the wood trim on the porch could use a paint job, now that we can get paint again."

"Everybody's porch around here could use some paint. How about for fun?"

"Ha-ha," Jack said.

"Max and I are going fishing off the dock when I put the sweeper back. Got a fishing rod?"

Jack smiled broadly. "It's my dad's, but I'm using it until he gets back. Could you come over to my house and ask my mother if it's okay?"

The morning chores were finished and Helen was setting the lid on the trash can in the drying yard when Peter and Jack rode up on their bikes. Max was trotting alongside Peter. The dog was on a leash, Peter's concession to the worriers, although if Max had been free, he would not have left his side.

Helen had been watching Peter from a little distance, but this was the first time the two of them had been face to face.

He had an effect on her. Not like Arthur, who had always been there, or Frank, who was—she wasn't sure exactly what role he played in her life. Peter felt like a stranger whom she somehow knew, not the boy she had met years before, but a new man.

"Mother?" Jack remembered to say. "This is Peter. From across the path? And Max. Can we go fishing when I finish cleaning my room?"

"Peter and I met before the war. Remember when you came over before you left for college?" Helen said, and held out her hand. "Nice to see you after all this time," she added—too formally, she thought.

"It's laundry day again," she reminded Jack, tilting her head toward the sheets billowing and snapping on the line. "Kathleen changed the beds and cleaned your room for you. You're free to go fishing. Just be back by lunchtime. If you catch anything, I'll cook it and maybe Peter would like to stay and share the feast. Take some of the mackerel out of the freezer for bait."

"You're an optimist," Peter said, and smiled slightly. "We'll do our best. Lunch sounds great. My grandfather's off the island for a couple of days, so I'm on my own."

"If the fish don't bite, we'll feed you anyway," Helen said.

When Jack went to get his father's rod and tackle box from the shed under the porch, Helen and Peter stood and looked at each other until she thought of something to say. "I'd like to be properly introduced to Max. I've heard a lot about him."

"You mean that he's a ravening beast and will attack without provocation."

"That, and some other things. I gather you two had quite a time in the war."

"We made it back."

"I'm sorry. I should know better. None of you men want to talk about the war. It doesn't affect me as much, since my husband's still missing, but the other wives can feel left out. I gather you don't have a wife yet?"

Peter looked at her gravely. "I have a way to go before anyone could live with me," he said. "So, no."

When Peter, Jack, and Max had left, Helen went into the kitchen and considered the options. "I'll cook," she told Kathleen. "We're having a guest for lunch."

"Mmm. That Peter," Kathleen said. "Why don't you make some of Mrs. Wadsworth's coleslaw with bacon," she suggested. "Men always like that."

"Good idea," Helen said. "We've got the cabbage and the bacon, and plenty of mayonnaise. If you'll bicycle down to the market and get some plums while I'm making it, I can bake a plum tart."

"What if they don't have any plums? That market is puny."

"Then get peaches or apples, okay?"

While Kathleen was gone, Helen finished the coleslaw, and made some of her mother-in-law's special iced tea, steeped with fresh mint and sugar and mixed with orange juice. Using the recipes made her miss Mrs. Wadsworth, who had so often stood in for her own mother when her mother was "away," as her stays in mental hospitals and sanitariums were described. But then she thought it was selfish to wish Arthur's mother were still there, in the house where she'd spent summers with her boy. She could imagine how bereft she would feel if she heard that Jack was missing, and there was only the slimmest chance he would return. Or no chance at all.

. . .

As Jack and Peter walked back to the house with a couple of striped bass for lunch, Peter asked what Wauregan was like during the war years while he was away in the service.

The war had arrived on the island in July 1942, Jack told him.

"You were about eight then, right?"

"Yup. That was the last summer my dad was here, although most of the time he was in the city. Dad's in the grain business and the army needed a lot of food. The first thing was everyone in the sailing program, or who would even be going out on a rowboat, had to go to the Coast Guard station down the beach to be fingerprinted. They even gave us identification cards so no one would mistake us for the enemy, if we were out on the water. I remember when I showed my mother and Kathleen my inky fingers and my card. I wanted to know if that meant I had enlisted.

"My mother told me it meant that I was cooperating with the war effort, but she was glad I wouldn't be going into combat. That was funny 'cause I wasn't much bigger than Max when he stands on his hind legs. What does he weigh?"

"Usually eighty, ninety pounds. More like sixty-five now. A lot of parasites in those jungles. Do a job on your stomach, man or dog."

"So I was about the same size, only not much muscle and no fangs."

"What makes these dogs so useful on scout missions isn't so much that they're strong, as that they can smell and hear a lot better than people, so they could detect any small change long before we'd get close enough to get in trouble. What happened after you got fingerprinted?"

"One day, an army troop landed on our dock. We didn't even know they were coming until we saw a green pickup truck driving across the island with soldiers in the back. They had guns and everything. They set up camp near the Coast Guard station, but I don't think the guardsmen liked that very much. They thought it was their job to defend us.

"Next thing, a soldier came around to the houses and handed out flyers with the new rules. They pinned up posters all over the place. They sure weren't interested in the Wauregan Rules. The posters said 'CAUTION: Army and Navy Regulations for Wauregan, 1942.'

"No one was allowed on the beach after dusk," Jack continued. "Not that anyone would, but you couldn't blink your lights at night in case you were sending signals to an enemy landing force. It was 'specially hard for us because our house overlooks the ocean and if we wanted to go out at night, we couldn't use a flashlight, and we couldn't ride our bikes on the boardwalk nearest the beach until we got inland. Before the war we used to go out on boat picnics for supper, but no one could even take a boat off its mooring after sunset.

"My job," Jack said, "was to pull down the blackout shades on the beach side of the house every night. Oh boy! I never realized how many windows we had. I had to make sure the shades went all the way to the sill and didn't flap, so there wouldn't be even a crack of light to help some Germans in a submarine or U-boat find us. I didn't really believe the Huns would come in so close, 'cause what would they want with a little summer place like this? But I did it anyway. I figured there must be some reason we had all those soldiers camped next to us.

"Then one day I was riding my bike home, looking out to sea. I did that a lot, because our house is sort of like the outpost in a fort, since we can see the ocean so well. I didn't really expect to see an enemy vessel, but there it was! A sub had just surfaced way out on the horizon. I jumped off my bike and raced down to a Coast Guard man who was patrolling the beach. By the time I got to him I was so out of breath I just pointed. The Coast Guard guy didn't even look. He just said, 'Thanks, son, but there's nothing out there.'

"I told him I saw a sub. And I did!" Jack said. Remembering, he became agitated. "I was thinking maybe they were going to try to take over the island, like the Americans who fought the Japanese for islands in the Pacific. But the Coast Guard man just stood there and asked me what my name was.

"I said I was Jack Wadsworth, and my father always told me to be careful that what I said was true.

"So he said to me, 'Well then, Jack Wadsworth, this is important, so pay attention. You. Did. Not. See. Anything. Do you understand?'"

Peter smiled. "I guess that told you," he said.

"You bet! I thought, gosh, but then I got it, so I said, 'Maybe it was a fishing boat?'

"'That's the right idea,' he said, and then he told me to go home, and not to go around telling people I saw something that wasn't there.

"I said, 'Yes, sir,' but you know what? When I was walking back to my bike, I heard engines, and when I looked up, I saw groups of planes flying in threes, heading out to sea."

"Good work," Peter said. "Did you keep your promise and not tell anyone?"

"Sort of," Jack said. "Remember, I was only eight years old. I told my mother and Kathleen, and that weekend, I told my father when he came back from work. That was just before he went away to do secret stuff himself. Mummy said she was proud of me, and we would keep the story to ourselves, so other people didn't panic."

"That was right," Peter said. "Still, it was important that you were keeping watch. Did you know that when the Germans surrounded Leningrad, the Russians had lost so many soldiers, even boys not much older than you were helped defend the city?"

"With guns?"

"Uh-huh. They were starving. A million and a half people died. Every hand counted."

Jack didn't think he had done much, but after the episode with the submarine, he had become even more vigilant. It made him feel as though he had a bond with his father, that they were both prepared to fight the enemy.

"How about when the war ended?" Peter asked. "I was in a hospital, but I tried to imagine what the celebration was like here. All I could think of was that for sure my grandfather was playing 'The Star Spangled Banner' on his trumpet."

"It was grand! I thought my dad would be home any day when I heard the church bells ringing the afternoon Japan surrendered," Jack said. "Probably someone heard the news on the radio and ran to the church to ring the bell. It tolled and tolled, and everyone stopped what they were doing, and headed toward the church. The minister came along, and your grandfather turned up with his trumpet, and Mrs. Beach, who used to play the organ, came up with her hands flapping, as though she couldn't wait to get to the keys, and we had a service of thanksgiving. I felt sorry for the kids whose fathers had been killed, but they prayed and sang along with us, too."

That afternoon at the end of the summer of 1945, it had been almost exactly one year since the OSS notified Helen that her husband was "missing, presumed dead," although the officer wrote that nothing was certain in the turmoil of Europe, and she should not give up all hope.

Helen cooked the bass Peter and Jack had caught, and served the coleslaw and then the tart. Suffused with good food and the peace of a clear, hot afternoon, the three of them settled on the sea side of the porch and watched the waves roll in and out, dragging the sand back and forth. Jack was innocent of the thoughts preoccupying his mother and Peter. Helen was considering asking Peter what he was planning to do when the summer was over, but decided that if he wasn't ready to get back into the "real" world, it could be awkward and unkind. Peter was thinking of asking Helen if she was going to return to St. Paul, or stay in New York, and what she did while she was in the city in the winter. But those questions came too close to asking what he really wanted to know: whether she thought there was a chance that Arthur was alive, and if not, how she imagined her life would be without him. Even if he could have brought himself to be so direct, he had had a glimpse of the answer when he saw Arthur's clothes drying in the laundry yard.

Jack broke the silence by asking Peter, "Could you tell me more about Max?" After their morning together, he had almost forgotten that at first he had been a little afraid of Max, but now he dropped his hand on the dog's neck and scratched him.

"I'll start by telling you about the first German shepherd I knew," Peter said. "He belonged to a house master at the boarding school you're going to in the fall, and for all I know, he may still be there. His name was Wotan, pronounced with a 'V' but spelled with a 'W.' Wotan was the king of the gods in old Scandinavian mythology. Shepherds are herding dogs, and when the bell rang for us boys to go to our rooms at night, the dorm master would give Wotan the command to herd, and he would dash down the corridor. If any boy was still out there he'd nip him lightly on the rear end or the leg, and we would race for our beds."

"Funny that they're bred to herd," Helen said. "I once read that shepherds are only ten percent different from wolves. You'd think they'd eat the sheep instead of protecting them."

"I guess that ten percent makes the difference. If you ask me, dogs are closer to humans than to wolves."

"Closer than monkeys?" Jack asked.

"I don't know about that," Peter said. "I've heard monkeys are cute when they're young, but can get mean when they reach adulthood. But make friends with a monkey and let me know."

"I don't know about monkeys, either," Helen said, "but I had a friend at home whose father adopted a pair of baby raccoon orphans. They lived in the house for a year and then one night, the family went out for dinner and closed them into the downstairs powder room."

Jack had heard the story before and he was already starting to laugh.

"When they came home, the front hall floor was covered in water streaming out from under the bathroom door. The raccoons have those little hands and they love to play with things, especially if there's water involved. They'd disconnected the pressure pipe to the toilet and the water was gushing out. Then they got under the sink and unscrewed the bolts between the pipes, so that water was pouring out, too. And when they finished with that they unrolled the toilet paper, so the whole room was filled with soggy wads of paper."

"What did they do with the raccoons after that?" Peter said, laughing.

Ha! Helen thought. We made him smile. Maybe he'll come around more often.

"They built them a fancy cage outside. Sort of a guest house."

"Did you have a pet growing up?" Peter asked her.

"My mother had a little dog when she married Daddy, but it was really her dog. When Mummy got sick, the dog was heartbroken, and the poor little thing died soon after. We never got another one."

Uh-oh, Peter was thinking, remembering that the Judge had told him about Helen's mother. That wasn't a good subject.

Jack stood up and stretched. "Gotta go," he said. "Time to buy some more paint for the porch trim."

"I'd better be off, too," Peter said, although he didn't have anything particular to do. He had already finished his painting job.

• • •

After they left, Helen stood at the sink and considered the lunch dishes. There was some iced tea left in one of the glasses, Peter's maybe, and she drank it.

"Fine young fellow," Kathleen said as she dried the dishes. "Looks like a movie star. You two looked good together, Mrs. W."

"Kathleen, Peter Gavin is too young for me. He'll be back at Yale in a couple of months. Plus, whatever put him in the hospital, he may look good, but I doubt he's fully healed. Don't try to fix me up."

"I believe I heard that he's going to *graduate* school to learn to be an architect. If you're not interested, how come you know so much about him?"

"Everyone knows everything in this place. Anyway, I'm a married woman."

CHAPTER SEVEN

THE porch was nearly painted and it was late July when Jack again asked Helen if he could take *Red Wing* off her blocks, and start working on her.

"She's probably not seaworthy. All those years out of the water," Helen said. She was thinking of how long it had been since she had been on the bay with Arthur. "Even when your father was keeping her in good trim, *Red Wing* was leaky. The wood shrinks in the winter cold, and swells again in the summer. The boards won't be tight anymore, so she isn't safe. Plus she needs to be scraped and painted. The sail's probably mildewed, too," she said, but when she saw Jack's expression, she quickly added, "Let's take a look. If you're willing to get her in shape, and she needs a new sail, I'll treat you. Only I don't think you can fix her by yourself. Do you have any friends who could help?"

"Mostly they're junior counselors, or they're sailing in the weekend regattas, and they practice all week. Charlie Moore could do it, but he's working on his tennis so he can make the varsity at school this year. Do you think Peter would help? I don't think he has much to do."

"Umm," Helen said. Jack and Peter had been fishing and sailing together on the Judge's boat a few times. Helen had invited Peter and his grandfather to dinner, and she saw Peter most days in the early morning. Before breakfast, she usually pulled on her bathing suit, grabbed a towel, and ran down her steps and across the sand to plunge into the sea. She swam sleekly back and forth until she overcame the shock of the cold water. When she was warmer, she floated on her back and gazed at the lighter blue sky, enveloped in pleasure.

She discovered that Peter had the same routine one foggy morning when she could just see the water from her house, and thought she might not go in. Then she decided it wouldn't be much different from swimming in the rain. As the fog lifted, she spotted Peter, smoothly doing the Australian crawl parallel to the beach. The air was still dank when they emerged and she asked him back to her cottage for a cup of coffee. After that, without discussing it, they swam at the same time, emerged from the water, and rubbed themselves dry with their towels, and Peter followed Helen up her back stairs to the porch for a cup of the coffee Kathleen had percolating on the stove.

Max always swam with them, and Helen loved watching him follow Peter into the shallows. Max's fur floated up like a little ruffle, and when he lunged out of the water, he would shake himself off, then roll in the sand until he was fully dusted and scratched. Max seemed to understand that he was not welcome on Helen's porch in that condition, and Peter would give him a good soaking in her outdoor shower and a rubdown before he could come up.

"He is such a *good* dog," Helen said to Peter one morning as Max explored her hand with his long muzzle and gave her a lick with his rough pink tongue. "Good for Jack, too. He's at a tough age. Too old to let his mother hug him, and too young for girls, but there's nothing babyish or threatening about snuggling with a big dog."

"I remember that age," Peter said. "It's a lonely time, even if you have a gang of friends. Everyone needs to be touched, but when you're fourteen, it's too embarrassing. That's probably one of the reasons boys roughhouse. At least they get some physical contact."

Many of those mornings on the porch as they watched the day come to life, they barely spoke, but while the sun scoured the shadows off the bleached wood, they sat companionably, alive to the place and the undemanding presence of another person.

Helen liked the way Peter looked when his hair shone as it dried, and the deep lines on either side of his mouth gave him a wry appearance when he smiled. When they were together, he seemed to be diverted from what she assumed were his darker thoughts, and she counted it a success if she could make him laugh. Yet even then, there was tension around his eyes and sometimes he squinted, as though he were narrowing his gaze to find the enemy.

But when he and Max were sitting close together, and he was stroking Max's fur, Peter's face softened, and his eyes were bright and clear. She would look at his arm, only a hairsbreadth away, and imagine stroking it, the way he was petting Max. The thought was so sensuous that she squirmed in her chair to stop the throbbing she felt in the crotch of her bathing suit.

First Frank, now Peter, she thought. I've got to stop this.

Peter would have liked to talk to Helen more on those shared mornings, although he, too, liked the peacefulness of their new friendship. He felt he might be able to tell her things, but below her apparent naturalness, she seemed impenetrable. Her beauty had a restrained overtone, as though she would have preferred to have it boxed up and put away in storage until Arthur came back. Perhaps when she was officially declared a widow, and Peter had few doubts that if the OSS had had no news of him for four years, he was dead—probably thrown into a mass grave somewhere, poor bastard—Helen might let down her guard. He wondered what she would be like, and decided that was a dangerous road to follow. He put the thought away until, as it did more and more often, his imagination took over and he would shake his head and try to resettle Helen into the woman sitting next to him, hidden behind her dark glasses.

When Helen found herself thinking about touching Peter, or swimming with him at night when no one could see them, she dragged her thoughts back to Arthur, and the fate she could not bear to think about. Then she was revolted at herself, starting one glorious day after another with a handsome young man for whom she felt the stirrings of desire.

Her fears about Arthur's fate aroused a sense of guilt that forced her to seek any distracting task. There were nights when Kathleen and Jack were asleep and she got out of bed to arrange the kitchen spices in alphabetical order, or line shelves and bureau drawers with fresh paper. She became compulsive about cleanliness and bought a dustpan and broom for each bedroom, and insisted that Kathleen use them to sweep stray grains of sand out of the sheets when she made the beds. If the day had been wet or foggy, she sprinkled baby powder in Jack's bed to absorb the dampness, ignoring his protests that he was not a baby.

Kathleen could not decide if Helen was still deeply "be-grieved," as she thought of it, or if, as Peter became part of their daily lives, she was falling in love. She could see that Peter was opening up with the help of Max, the Judge, and the Wadsworth household, and she silently cheered him on.

And then there was Mr. Frank, who had been calling Helen nearly every week all year, and who was coming back for a visit soon "to see how Jack was doing," he said. It was obvious that he was interested in Mrs. W, even if she hadn't figured that out for herself, and he was certainly more suitable, practically a member of the family. He also had a job, mysterious as it seemed to Kathleen, and whatever happened to him in the war appeared to have made him stronger. Maybe Kathleen liked that about him and maybe she didn't quite believe it. She couldn't decide which man she was rooting for. Or sort of rooting: she didn't think Mr. Arthur was coming home, but just in case, she didn't want to get off track.

As for the other veterans on the island, one afternoon when she brought Helen her tea, she remarked, "You know that Mr. Jackson? The one who had his arm amputated up to the elbow?"

"Of course. Has something happened to him?"

"Not that I know of. Only I was thinking he was one of the lucky ones. You can see he's been hurt. It shows on the outside. It's those other men, where it doesn't show. Except at home. And then their wives start acting crazy, too."

"Why? Have you heard something?"

Kathleen sniffed. "There isn't much I don't hear. You think the help doesn't talk to each other? The young ones, like Bridget, that little Irish girl who works for the Fosters? Some of those girls are so scared they lock their bedroom doors at night."

"You mean scared the men might come in?"

"Maybe, but I haven't heard about that. No, it's the goings-on. There's stuff they don't want to see."

"Really? For instance?"

"I don't like to gossip," Kathleen said.

"Kathleen! Everyone likes to gossip. Even novels are a chance to get inside other people's lives."

"I wouldn't know about that, but I'll tell you what Bridget told me, as long as you don't go talking to Mrs. Carter, or any of the other ladies."

Kathleen leaned her small, compact body against the door-post and put a hand up to pat the hair net she wore to keep her fine white hair in place. She made it a habit of never sitting down when she was talking to her employers. "You know that game you and Mr. Arthur played at a party one time, where you hung a sheet in the archway between the living room and dining room?"

"The 'guess whose feet these are' game?"

"That's the one."

The idea was that all the men would stand behind the sheet, so only their feet were showing, and the women had to identify which ones belonged to their husbands. Then the game was reversed, with the women standing behind the sheet. Helen had been surprised that not everyone got it right. There was nothing especially distinctive about Arthur's feet, but she always recognized them. She had a brief, disturbing thought that after their mornings on the porch when they had finished swimming, she would be able to pick out Peter's feet, too.

"Well, Mr. and Mrs. Foster, where Bridget works, had a dinner party last night, and after dinner they played the game."

"That doesn't sound very scary. Bridget must be a mouse."

"That was only the beginning. Next thing, that Mrs. Warden, the tennis champion with the two eyes that are different colors? She says, 'So, Liz, how about the other game you told me you were going to try?' Bridget is coming in with the coffee, and she's back there in the dining room behind the sheet with Mrs. Foster. She doesn't know what to do, so she puts the tray down on the sideboard and waits until she can pass through and serve the guests.

"She's standing there, and she sees Mrs. Foster turn on the light behind the sheet, so it's shining on her, and she calls out to the people in the living room, 'Turn out the lights,' so they do. Bridget is thinking, What is it with these people? We used to play games like this when we were children in Ireland. Aren't they grown-ups? Well, did she get a shock!"

"Don't keep me hanging. Then what?"

"Mrs. Foster starts humming and dancing around like a hoochie-coochie girl in the light, so the people on the other side can see just her outline, her whatcha-call-it?"

"Her silhouette."

"Like those shadow figures Mr. Arthur used to make on the wall for Jack. Then she turns her back to the sheet, but she's facing Bridget, and she motions for her to come over and unzip her dress."

"Uh-oh."

"You said it! So Bridget unzips her, and Mrs. Foster lets her dress fall on the floor. She kicks it over to Bridget, who picks it up and holds it like a grenade. Mrs. Foster twirls around a little, and gets going on her merry widow, which as we all know, is a pain in the you-know-what to get in and out of with those hooks in the back, and the garters holding up the stockings. But she does it herself, bends over, unsnaps the garters, and takes it all off."

"What are the people in the living room doing while this is going on?"

"Quiet as death. Not a peep."

"This is a striptease?"

"Just wait. She gets the merry widow off, and turns so everyone can see her profile. Poor Bridget, brought up in an orphanage by the nuns, wasn't even allowed to take a bath unless she had her shift on her. Now her boss is showing her whole self, even if there is a sheet between her and the company. Bridget is standing there, eyes like saucers."

"Tell me that was the end. Oh dear, poor Liz."

"Poor Bridget. The girl fled back into the kitchen, knocked over the tray with the coffee, and burned her leg. Peered through the crack in the door, and sure enough Mrs. F strips off her panties, does a little bump and boggle, and switches off the light."

"Good Lord. And of all places to do it: Wauregan! What happened next?"

"They clapped, didn't they? What were they supposed to do? And then Mr. Foster said, 'Thank you all for coming. I think the party's over.' From what Bridget heard, he spent the rest of the night holding Mrs. F's head while she upchucked."

"How many years have you been here?"

"Thirty-three this year."

"Have you ever heard about anything like that before?"

"I have not."

"Let's hope you're here another thirty years and that's the last story like that. It was bad of Bridget to tell you. People who work in houses see a lot of things they shouldn't talk about."

"Oh, and the ladies who hire these girls don't talk about them? I hear it in the grocery store. This one says the girl is clumsy. The other one says she's too pretty for her own good. Next thing she'll be coming in holding the breakfast tray over her big belly."

"Thank you for the tea, Kathleen," Helen said, dismissing her. She had been brought up to avoid gossiping with servants. With Arthur away, she had often broken that rule. Kathleen was a special case, but still, the conversation had gone far enough.

The story would be all over the island by the end of the day. Helen was surprised her phone hadn't already rung with someone eager to ask if she "had heard." She knew that Liz Foster was desperate. A few weeks ago, she had asked Helen how she had managed for so long without sex. Helen was flattered that Liz believed she had been faithful, which she had, while others had succumbed to temptation when their husbands were away, and hadn't always been discreet about their flings. She said the best technique was not to think about it.

"Maybe it's easier without a man in your bed, but I think about it all the time," Liz said. "Steve's different since the war. He's like a little boy, sweet, but scared. Have you noticed that when he lights a cigarette, he has to hold the lighter steady with his other hand? He's got a bad case of the shakes. I don't know how he manages to go to work and do his job every day. And sex is just too much for him. He's been back for nearly three years and we haven't really done it once," she said. "We tried at the beginning, but he's given up."

Helen advised her to wait until Steve came to her, rather than attempting to stimulate an impulse that was shut down, but would probably resuscitate itself when he could put the war behind him. "A lot of the men have problems," she said. "Not just sex. People tell me things, maybe because they know about my Red Cross work, and they think I might have some answers. I wish I did. I go to our facility three times a week when we're in the city, and the doctors seem to be making slow progress, even with the less damaged men.

"Our friends are so private, it's hard to know what's going on, but there are more women here than you think who are afraid their husbands have changed, and maybe don't love them anymore. Or it's the other way around: the women have changed and they don't want to fall back into being 'just wives.' Some of us did a lot for the war effort, took jobs, ran our households, brought up our children on our own, paid the bills—things the men used to do. A lot of men feel like they came home to wives who are different from the ones they left, and they're right. None of us talk about our feelings much, and it seems disloyal for a woman who's had an easy war to admit how hard it is to live with someone who's been through hell and can't admit he's still spooked. It must feel open-ended, like living in a dangerous neighborhood with the lock on your door broken, never knowing what might come into your house." Then, thinking about Wauregan, she said, "But being here should help. If anyplace is safe, this is it."

Liz's striptease was not the only divergence from life as it had been known at Wauregan, although it was the least ambiguous. There was a buzzing sexual tension in the air that marked couples who were either having trouble reconnecting, or the fortunate ones who had fallen in love again and were humming with desire. Men and women who had been intimate were rediscovering each others' bodies and feelings. Some husbands and wives found that a partner who had formerly been the embodiment of satisfying sex no longer appealed, while someone else's spouse suddenly looked irresistible. Helen was acutely aware of the low-grade fever infecting the colony because of what she saw and heard, but also because she had noticed her own slide toward a desire for intimacy with both Peter, who was "new," and Frank, who was familiar and safe. She felt as though it was like cheating on Arthur, yet she knew she didn't want her feelings for her possibly imaginary suitors to evaporate. What she wanted to know was if either of them felt the same way.

CHAPTER EIGHT

WHEN Helen and Peter were finishing their second cups of coffee after their morning swim, Jack would usually appear, tousled from bed and not entirely awake. Invariably, he asked if he could have some coffee, "to get myself going," he would say, in as grown-up a tone as a boy whose voice hadn't fully changed could muster. Kathleen poured him a cup of hot milk spiked with a splash of coffee, and Jack sat on the porch floor with his legs crossed, reclaimed Peter from Helen, and the three of them talked about what they might do after Jack had finished painting the wood trim. Helen said he had to work a minimum of two hours a day, and encouraged him by telling him that the house was beginning to look quite fresh. As scraping off the old paint down to the wood was not part of the job, "fresh" was a relative term.

Jack and Peter had quickly developed their own easy friendship. Jack worshipped both Peter and Max, trying to visualize the dangers they had shared in the Pacific, from the newsreels and movies he had seen. Peter had turned over the sand sweeper to one of the summer employees, and he was devoting much of his time to sailing the Judge's boat, fishing, and working on *Red Wing* with Jack. Their time together resonated with his own Wauregan childhood, before the war grabbed him and twisted him into its own shape. He liked Jack's curiosity and his eagerness to work on the catboat, even though he understood that the third "partner" in their project was the invisible, but ever-present Arthur.

Jack had only once mentioned his hope that Arthur would sail the boat again. "Wait till Dad sees what we've done to her," he told Peter. "She'll be spick-and-span and he'll be proud that I can take the tiller." Peter quietly continued caulking the boards and didn't answer.

Helen expected that Peter would fade in importance for Jack after that fall. Then the masters and older boys at his new boarding school would become his role models, but she couldn't imagine how her son could find a replacement for Max. The boy and dog had taken to each other. When Helen and Peter watched them racing on the beach, and saw Jack teaching Max to do tricks, like picking out cards with letters that Jack had made from construction paper, as though the dog could read what was written on them, Peter said, "Sometimes I think Jack's giving Max back his childhood. The war robbed him of the carefree way dogs are until they're really old."

Sometimes Helen allowed Max to spend the night with Jack, and when she checked on them before she went to bed, she would see Jack's arm slung over Max's body, his face turned toward the dog. Even when she kissed her boy, he didn't stir. But when she approached the bed, Max looked up at her with his bright brown eyes, and she felt he was reassuring her that all was well. He made her feel safe and loved, too.

Jack had found a way to turn his relationship with Max and his fascination with war dogs into a project. His new school had assigned the boys a "What I Did on My Summer Vacation" essay to hand in when they arrived. Jack decided to write "My Summer Dog," about Max, and to include war dog history. He bought a notebook at Wauregan's little store, and was quizzing Peter and taking notes. Helen had learned through listening to some of his interviews with Peter that dogs have fought along-side their masters since ancient times; that the Romans fitted dogs with spiked collars and sent them out as the first line of attack; that in other wars, dogs were outfitted in chain mail and plumed helmets; and in the Middle Ages war dogs had their own suits of armor.

"A really bad thing, I don't like to think about it, but I have to put everything important in my paper," Jack told his mother, "was a war between Spain and Morocco, when some of the Moroccans, they were called Rifs and they were part of the Berber tribe, dressed their dogs in the kind of clothes they wore and sent them to the front lines to draw the Spanish fire, so they could find the Spanish gun positions. Peter says sometimes you have to balance the life of a dog against the life of a man who might have a wife and children, and sacrifice the dog. Of course, we didn't do anything like that in our war, but still . . ." he said, and looked thoughtful.

Peter's stories were often historical, rather than of recent vintage. When he talked about the war from which he had just returned, he avoided answering when Jack asked what he meant when he told Sarge that Max had saved his life.

Kathleen did not entirely approve of all the attention Helen and Jack paid to Max. Kathleen liked dogs, but she wasn't "dog mad," which is the way she described the others to herself, then chuckled quietly when she reversed the words to "mad dog." Max showed no signs of being "mad"; his most distinctive qualities were his gentleness, his empathy, and his wolf-like magnificence. His fur was thick enough that Jack could gather a bunch at the back of his neck in his fist without pulling on his skin; his tail was thick and bushy, and he wagged it enthusiastically, sweeping small objects off low tables. Sometimes he showed his affection by leaning against Jack's or Peter's legs. The first time Max leaned on Jack, he toppled over, surprised by the dog's bulk. "I think he's gained a couple of pounds," he told Peter hopefully. "Maybe he's getting rid of those parasites." Peter could hear the vet assigned to their troop say, "They'll kill you just as surely as enemy fire. Just slower. At least the damn bugs don't give you that slimy grin, like the Japs do when they're slicing your insides apart."

Peter was silent. Max was steadily losing weight; Peter had had to adjust his collar, which was getting a little looser each week, and clumps of hair came out when he brushed him. Luckily his fur was so thick Jack hadn't noticed.

Max was a comfort to Helen, too, when her thoughts turned dark, and increasingly, he was a connection to Peter. But nothing could erase the things she knew. One afternoon when she was sitting on the floor with her legs tucked under her, idly scratching Max behind his ears, her mind drifted to the starving Russians who had to eat their pets during the siege of Leningrad; and then, with disgust, to the ugly fox fur scarves with dried heads and desiccated claws that women wore draped around their necks. Even when she was happy, thoughts of death ambushed her. When Max looked at her as though he could feel her distress, she recalled that the Episcopal *Book of Common Prayer* had a service commemorating the death of a beloved pet. She was glad her church seemed to believe that dogs had souls.

Arthur's father had loved his dogs extravagantly, and when one of them died he made its coffin himself and buried the animal on his farm outside St. Paul, after reciting the service. He included a provision in his will for the pair of aging yellow Labs that had accompanied him everywhere for nearly fifteen years. Feeling that they should not suffer from mourning for him, and were too old to form new attachments, he instructed that they be put down and buried next to him in the family graveyard on the farm. When Helen saw that Max could share his love with her and Jack, as well as Peter, she wondered if he had been right.

"His fur is so soft," she said to Peter. "I want to fall asleep burying my face in his neck." An image of tucking her face between Peter's shoulder and his cheek flooded her, and she blushed.

"A heavy coat is a good qualification for a war dog, whether it's assigned to a cold or tropical climate," Peter said, noticing the sudden pink in her cheeks. Feeling self-conscious, he turned to the "lesson mode" he used with Jack. "In the Pacific, Max's coat protected him from the insects and leeches that drove the men crazy when we had to ford rivers. A lot of us got skin rot and sometimes peeled off skin with our T-shirts, but Max could shake himself and keep walking. His feet took the worst beating. On one landing they were cut by coral, and during the long marches through the jungles they were scraped and torn, and got infected. At least the K-9 Corps always had a vet along."

Helen smiled. "The women who were knitting socks for the men in combat could have been making foot protectors for the war dogs," she said, although she couldn't imagine what they would have been made of.

One blazing hot day, when even cooling off in the water didn't look worth transiting the sand, Peter and Jack were sitting in the shade of the Wadsworth porch, and Jack was taking notes for his summer essay. Peter patiently explained, "A war dog has to be physically fit, but he also has to know how to be quiet and stay very still, and when we're scouting, move swiftly and soundlessly. The dogs that were used as couriers to take messages from one handler to another had to race across battle-fields under fire, and withstand the constant racket of guns and explosives, without getting rattled."

"And Max could do all that!" Jack said.

"Not all of it," said Peter. "He wasn't trained as a messenger or a patrol dog. The patrol dogs are the fiercest. When they go out with their handlers they have to hear even the most silent enemy, and on a hand command, go for him, knock him down, and if his handler gives the instruction, kill him."

"Yipes!"

"Max was a scout dog. They went out looking for the enemy with their handlers, but tried not to get engaged. The dogs would sense the enemy long before a human, because their smell and hearing is so strong, and we could launch rockets into the enemy position and wipe out a whole force without ever seeing them. If Max alerted to enemy troops—under the right conditions, he could sometimes pick them out from a thousand yards away—he would freeze, his hackles and his ears would go up, he would get an expression on his face like nothing you've ever seen, eyes hard, chin up, and teeth bared, and he would hold his tail out straight, and point by turning his head in the direction trouble was coming from."

"Then what?"

"Either we'd go after them, or we'd retreat and go back for reinforcements."

Peter said people who had been in combat with dogs often believed the animals had a sixth sense about danger, and told Jack stories he said you wouldn't believe if you hadn't been there.

Helen liked listening to Peter's war dog stories, too. They were a way for her to know him better without asking too many questions. Like Jack, she wanted to know what Peter meant when he had implied to Sarge that Max had saved his life, but she didn't know if he was talking about his survival, his sanity, or both.

She was helping Peter and Jack scrape the peeling paint off *Red Wing* one afternoon, and Max was lying in the shade of a tree with his eyes closed, but his ears up, as though he were listening to their conversation.

"Look at that," Peter said. "His ears feel like velvet, but did you know dogs have eighteen muscles in their ears? That's one of the reasons they can hear so well; they can turn them toward the sound."

For a while, they scraped and sanded quietly, until Jack said, "I think I need one more story for my school paper."

"I've got one that should make a good ending," Peter said. "It's about a dog that saved his master's life when everyone had given him up for dead."

Given him up for dead, Helen thought. Had she done that, too? For the first couple of years after she was informed that Arthur was missing, she had shamelessly used every government contact her family and Arthur's had, mercilessly pressuring the senator from Minnesota who had been a protégé of her father's to find out anything he could. For the last couple of years she had stopped searching until now, when Frank held out hope that he could find something in the CIA files. She wanted to know, but she was afraid if he had died badly, she would always think of him in some torture chamber, or shrinking into a hollow-eyed skull in a concentration camp. She wanted to remember him as he was, here at Wauregan. She stopped herself from thinking about Arthur, and went back to scraping paint and listening to Peter and Jack.

"I don't have my notebook," Jack said, "but I guess I'll remember."

"Sure you will," Peter said. "After a great battle in France, when we beat back the Germans, our medics came out on the field to look for the wounded. Ours, or theirs, we treated anyone who was hurt. One of the soldiers was lying on the field and his dog, a big shepherd like Max, was licking the blood off his face, and trying to wake him up, but when the medics got to him, they couldn't find any vital signs."

"What are vital signs?"

"Signs of life, like heartbeat, breathing, pulse. So they put him on a stretcher and loaded him into the back of a truck with the other dead men, and took him to a field hospital miles away. They unloaded the stretchers and laid out the soldier with the other dead, then went to help the men who were still alive. A couple of hours later, his dog came limping into the hospital area. He had followed the ambulance over rocky ground, and his feet were all cut up. He hobbled over to the stretcher where the soldier was lying, and lay down next to him to keep him warm. It was winter, and one great thing about having a dog on the European front was they slept with their handlers and kept each other from freezing. After a while, the dog stood up and began to paw at the soldier's chest.

"One of the nurses went over to see what was going on. She saw that the man's eyes were flickering, and she hollered for a doctor to come over. They moved him into one of the surgery tents and operated on him."

"What happened to the dog?"

"The vet attached to the unit bandaged his feet, and gave him water and special rations, but the dog paced around the enclosure where they kept the animals, and the bandages kept coming off. Finally, the vet said, 'He wants to see his partner. I think we should let him.' Dogs weren't allowed into the hospital tents, but the vet got permission to take him in for a visit. When the nurse who found him trying to bring his handler back to life saw him, she said, 'Let him stay. He's as good a doctor as any of us.'

"So the dog stayed with his master until they were both well enough to go back into battle. That," Peter said, "is loyalty."

Peter did not tell Jack that he had also heard that the soldier and his dog were killed together in combat within a week of their release from the hospital.

CHAPTER NINE

FRANK Hartman had been thinking about Helen. Immediately after the war, when he was still working for the law firm in New York, he had not seen as much of her and his godson as he knew he should have. It wasn't so much that he felt guilty; he had discovered at Yale, and later in France, that guilt was not a useful quality if he wanted to create the person he had come to believe he was. He had observed that his new friends had a code they insisted they stuck by, and were apt to talk about public service, noblesse oblige, and honor late at night, after drinking the—illegal—bootleg liquor one of their fathers had arranged to have delivered on a regular schedule. But then the conversations would veer off to girls, the ones who were "fast," the "townies" who were easy lays; or the jobs at the family firm they were assured of having after graduation, even as unemployment was surging. By the early 1930s, when Frank was in law school in New Haven, and another Frank— Mr. Roosevelt—was president, his friends were already calling him "a traitor to his class." Frank did not mention that "those people" the president was concerned about were very much like his own family.

His father had been the foreman in an auto parts factory, where Frank worked summers as soon as he was old enough. That was when Smithers Barton, who owned the factory, noticed the boy—he saw him first because of his hair. It was the cornstalk gold his own had been when he was young. He asked Mr. Hartman about his son, and learned that he had skipped two grades and was on track to graduate high school before his sixteenth birthday.

"Bright young fellow," Barton said. "Any plans?"

"I'd be proud if he could do my job one day," Frank's father said.

"Ever think of college?"

"That's not for folks like us."

"Went to Yale myself," Barton said. "You'd be surprised."

Mr. Hartman did not look surprised. He had heard of Yale University and he expected that Mr. Barton would be a graduate of such a place.

"What I mean is, you'd be surprised at who goes there. And makes something of himself. I didn't have to do a darned thing with all that learning," Barton said, wondering why he was talking about this to his foreman. Something about the boy, maybe. "Factory was right here waiting for me."

He began to say, "Might have liked to . . ." when he realized that Frank had come over and was standing quietly behind his father, listening.

"This your boy?" Barton said.

"Frank, shake hands with Mr. Barton. We can thank him

for the bread on our table, and a good job to get up for in the mornings."

Frank gave the boss a strong handshake, and looked him in the eye. "Thank you, sir," he said, and smiled. Barton thought that the boy had a way of making clichés come to life. The smile actually lit up his face. It would be nice if his own son, prepping back east at Groton, was as respectful as this young fellow, and would agree to spend at least one summer working at the plant he would be inheriting. Instead, he was off visiting friends in Newport or in the Berkshires, where he'd heard some tycoons could sleep one hundred in their "cottages." He did not antici-pate that Frank Hartman might come to occupy one of those bedrooms, but he did think he might be worthy of doing more than his father believed was possible.

After that, Barton kept track of him. He learned that the Hartman grandparents had come over from Germany at the turn of the century, and that they spoke German at home—bi-lingual, he thought. Useful. He wondered if the boy could make something of himself.

When the Depression hit the auto industry, Smithers Bar-ton resisted closing the plant that carried his name and that of his father; he could see the red brick factory when he looked down the hill from his house, and he did not think he could bear to stand in the tower that topped his big white Victorian mansion, stare at the empty buildings, and watch the windows go black. It was lucky that he had cashed out of the stock market in early '29 to free up capital; his wife wanted them to build a great camp in one of the summer colonies on the Upper Peninsula in Michigan. When the Crash came, they were still trying to find the perfect site, so the money was sitting in the bank—the conservative bank his family owned, and that was still open.

He'd had to cut back on the charities he and his father had dispensed in the town, and then the plant closed and Frank Hartman's father lost his job. Yet there were still some things he could afford to do: one of them was to send Frank to Yale.

It didn't take long for the bank to go under as well, but by then Frank had earned a scholarship, and then another that took him right through law school. When his mother wrote to tell him that Mr. Barton had had an attack of apoplexy, and was "a vegetable—better dead than like that, poor man," Frank was relieved that he would not have to show his gratitude to someone who knew too much about him.

He graduated from law school before he was twenty-one, too young to take the bar exam, got a job at the law firm owned by the family of one of his new friends, and sent money home. He let his family know that he wasn't coming back to see them because he was working six and seven days a week, and studying for the exam. Like the boys who had befriended him at Yale, he had learned to define "honor" and "guilt" selectively.

And so it was that when Frank returned from France, and Arthur did not, Helen had begun to take the place in his mind that Smithers Barton once had: someone to whom he owed something and whom he did not want to face.

It was only after he left New York, where he could have seen Helen and Jack as often as he or they wanted, and was settled in Washington that he realized there was an aspect of the code he had selectively adopted on which he could act. He could be the kind of godfather that Arthur had hoped he would be. That was when he decided to call Helen and Jack regularly on Sunday nights, and to visit them at Wauregan more often, if Helen would have him. The summer of 1948 was the first opportunity he had to learn if he would be able to fulfill his resolution.

The Sunday night calls had been going on for most of a year when he noticed that the person he really looked forward to talking to was Helen, as their conversations became longer and more intimate. But toward the end of July, he heard a change in her voice. She sounded lighter and happier, and when he commented on her tone, she said, "It's Wauregan. I always feel my best here."

No, Frank thought. It's not only Wauregan. It's that Peter she and Jack are always talking about. He had seen Peter on the July Fourth weekend. The next morning when he was shaving, he had studied himself in the mirror. He had taken his good looks for granted for so long, it had not occurred to him that the few years—to be honest, more like a dozen years—between his age and Peter's had taken a toll.

"Helen," he said, during one of their regular phone calls. "Every summer you admit that you miss Arthur more at Wauregan than anyplace else. Then you say that he's more *present* there, so in a way, you can still feel that you're sharing the summer with him. Which is it?"

"Both," Helen said. "Anyway, it feels different this year."

So? Frank thought. Is Arthur still as "present"?

"As they say, 'Time heals all wounds,'" Helen said, and he heard the smile in her voice. Helen had the kind of husky blues-singer voice that often came from smoking, even though she had never been a smoker.

"You know, when I was at Bryn Mawr, I could have said that in ancient Greek, and now I've forgotten almost everything.

Maybe I should apply to Columbia while we're living in New York and get a master's degree in Classics."

"You're staying in New York?"

"Why go back to St. Paul? I like the East Coast," Helen said.

Yes, Frank thought, and New York is only an hour and a half from New Haven. Jack had told him that the man Frank was beginning to think of as "that Peter" was about to enter graduate school at Yale to study for an architecture degree.

His imagination was making him uneasy. He didn't think Helen was having an affair. Wauregan was no place for that. But she sounded almost sexy. Maybe she was beginning to feel the same attraction to him that he was feeling toward her. Yet nothing in the way she had acted on his last visit indicated that she thought of him as anything more than a friend.

He asked to speak to Jack, but Helen said he was out. "He and Peter and Judge Gavin are having a 'boys' night.' Campfire on the beach. Hot dogs, whatever. Peter said they'd probably be back by dark. Jack's adopted those two—three, since Max is part of the family. The other day Jack told me the Judge is 'sort of like Grandpa used to be.'"

As long as he isn't saying "Peter is like Dad," Frank thought sourly, until Helen changed the subject. "You promised to come up here more often this summer," she said. "Is it too late for you to make it the weekend after next? August 6. It's the first dance of the month."

When Frank hung up, he made another call to cancel the plans he'd made with a woman he had been spending time with recently. Before he went to Wauregan, he would explore the OSS files at the CIA to see what, if anything, they had on the fate of Arthur Wadsworth III. He did not expect to find even as much as he had told Helen, but it wouldn't hurt to be sure.

Frank was not the only person who had noticed that Helen seemed more open.

Her anxiety about Sarge and the sports group had settled down, but late one afternoon, she heard a knock on the wooden frame of her screen door, looked out, and saw Sarge standing on the steps. The light reflected from the sea was dazzling, he was backlit, and when Helen opened the door, she had to shade her eyes to see his face clearly.

She was on the top step, and he looked up at her. He adjusted the bill of his cap and said, "I came to tell you that Jack can rejoin the sports group."

Helen stood straighter and took a deep breath. "I'll ask him, but I'm not sure he's going to have time. He's restoring his father's boat, and doing some sailing with a friend."

"His father's boat. Don't tell me you think his father's coming back."

"I hope so." Helen spoke calmly, but she could feel her face getting hot with anger. She focused on the army emblem on his hat so she didn't have to look him in the face.

"Well, until he 'returns,' you're free to do what you please, right?"

She pressed back against the screen door. "No," she said. "Please leave," and started to turn to go back into the house.

"Not so fast. I have an invitation for you." He moved up a step, put his hand past her shoulder, and leaned on the doorframe, looming over her. When he smiled, she saw that there was a dark gap behind one of his eyeteeth, where a tooth was missing.

He smelled like a man who has been working outside all day, but his sweat smelled sour instead of healthy.

"I thought maybe you and me could make up our differences over dinner on the other side of the bay. I can get the loan of a nice little speedboat. Get you there in ten minutes. I hear the Fish Net has plenty of shedders," he said. Shedders were lobsters that had recently shed their shells and were growing new ones. They were easier to crack open and their meat tasted sweet.

"Dinner?" Helen asked. She caught her breath, and in the firm tone she had learned in the Red Cross when she dealt with the more difficult men who had returned from overseas, she said, "Certainly not."

He moved his arm away and stepped back. "Lost your nerve after, what is it, six years without a man? Sorry about that, Mrs. Wadsworth. But never mind. There are plenty of women here, wives, too, you might be interested to know, who would like to share a couple of lobsters with old Sarge. Forget I asked you. And tell Jack it's fine that he's too busy to finish the job he started in sports group. If you ask me, a boy like that without a father is likely to be a quitter all his life."

"Please go now," Helen said. "Leave me and my son alone."

Across the path, she saw Max standing on the Gavins' porch with his hackles up, growling.

Sarge heard the noise, and in a voice that crawled like a spider, said. "Or what? You'll get that head case Marine captain Peter Gavin and his devil dog after me?"

"No. I'll report you to the Athletics Committee."

"Good luck, lady. I don't think naval captain Daniel Carter, the president of the Wauregan Club, is going to have much time for a woman whose son punched his handpicked sports chief in the gut." He straightened as though he were on parade, turned, and walked briskly away.

Helen started to open the door to go inside, but her hand was so damp she could barely grip the handle. Sarge had frightened her, not just because he had come too close and was in fact a frightening man, but because he had shaken her belief that at Wauregan she was safe from people who behaved that way. Once inside, she headed for the kitchen. Her knees were unsteady and her heart was thudding. She sat down at the scrubbed wooden table and tried to slow her breathing. Kathleen had the kettle on, as she did every afternoon at that hour, regardless of the weather. Helen heard the familiar offer, "How about a cup of good strong Irish tea?" Then Kathleen took a closer look. "You look like you just been out running."

"Thank you, Kathleen," Helen said. "This is just the day for a nice cup of tea."

She considered telling Peter about the encounter. Instead she waited until he and Jack were out sailing on Judge Gavin's boat, as Peter helped Jack hone his skills for the launch of *Red Wing,* and went over to talk to the Judge.

A few days later, when the children were leaving sports group for lunch, Judge Gavin turned up on the athletics field. Sarge could recognize him from a distance. The Judge and his grandson were the tallest men at Wauregan, and even as he approached his eighties, the Judge was lean and taut. His thick white hair still had some bounce and his white moustache drooped like a Mandarin's. He no longer walked with his shoulders back, but his stoop was not pronounced; and while his large, strong hands were knotted with arthritis, if there is such a thing as the prime of old age, he was a good example.

He asked Sarge if he could have a word with him, in the tone he had used when addressing a prosecuting district attorney in his courtroom, or a soldier serving under him during the last war. Sarge said, "Sure." It was all he could do to prevent himself from adding, "Sir," but he was damned if he was going to show the old geezer he was in awe of him.

"I was on my porch the other day when you were talking with Mrs. Wadsworth," the Judge said. "I'm one of the few members of the Association Board who is here during the week, and you might be surprised what comes to the attention of an old man like me." He paused. A little breeze ruffled his hair, and he tipped his head back and examined the sky to see if the weather was changing. Then he turned back.

"A word of advice. I suggest you keep your distance from the women here. I assume you've read the Rule Book. It's clear about employees fraternizing with members of the community."

Sarge dropped his gaze, but when he looked up again, the Judge saw the defiance in his eyes and the set of his mouth. "Got to pick up the sports equipment," he said, and turned away. "These spoiled rotten kids just drop stuff when they're finished and expect me to clean up after them."

"I'll leave you to it," the Judge said, addressing his back. "But understand that I'm serious about this."

In mid-July Dan and Sally Carter were still at odds. Dan treated Sally and their daughter, Louise, who was twelve that summer, as though they were his swabbies. His public behavior was hardly exemplary; he loudly scolded club employees if they didn't respond to his orders promptly, and he was often drunk. When he'd had one too many, he was prone to telling dirty jokes, laughing raucously when others tried to eke out a weak chortle. He had reasons to be distraught. His first ship had been sunk, he and some of his men had been rescued in a sea of fire, and he had been given another command before he had gotten over the shock. Sally knew the basic facts, as she had told Helen at the beginning of the summer, but she was having trouble understanding exactly how the tragedy had turned a man who had been a little too cocky when he left into a sullen, sodden bully. She told Helen that the only time she slept through the night was when her husband was in town. Once, when Dan had a particularly violent dream, he had reached across and backhanded her across the face so hard she could feel the muscles in her neck snapping. No serious damage was done, but Dan was ashamed that he had been out of control. Still, he couldn't give his dream life commands and expect it to obey. Dreams came when they needed to.

"If he didn't have those terrible nightmares, I'd leave him, or kill him," Sally told Helen. "When Arthur gets home, I bet he doesn't act like that."

"You don't have to pretend. There's no evidence that Arthur is coming home. But if he did, I don't see him being nasty or embarrassing, no matter what he's been through. I can't speak to the nightmares. But Dan isn't the only one who's drinking too much and getting the screaming meemies. Will you ever forget George Harwood diving under the table when the rockets went off on July Fourth?"

"Never. I don't have a clue what happened to him in the war, and I bet Jill Harwood doesn't know, either. Do you think any of the husbands have given their wives a lucid, detailed description of their war experiences?"

"Sure. The ones who were in Washington," Helen said, and grinned.

"Why can't we know?"

"The question is why can't they tell? Maybe it was too terrible to describe. Think of the books and poems that came out of the slaughterhouse of the last war. Who would want to bring that back to the world they're so desperate to rejoin?"

"Fine. But that leaves us married to men we don't know anymore."

"And you'll probably have to live with it until they settle down, and what they've experienced drops into the background. Then maybe you'll be able to build something new together."

"You mean like Barbara and Joe Danforth?" Sally said, and laughed.

"Barbara is none of our business. We don't know what it's like behind their bedroom door."

"Oh, don't be so prissy," Sally said, but her voice was friendly. Helen had a mischievous streak, but she could be earnest when it came to gossip. Probably a holdover from the talk about her mother, Sally thought.

Helen smiled back. "Okay," she said. "What about her?"

"Barbara was the fastest girl in my class at Smith and she had a heck of a good time when Joe was away. It doesn't look as though his return has stopped her."

"Has she gone after Dan?"

"Uh-uh. Who would? Everyone's seen what he's like by the

end of the evening. Unless she's looking for someone to take her into the bushes and slap her around, she can do a lot better."

"Don't tell me Dan's hitting you!"

"Yeah, well, I didn't tell you that. I can cope with Dan. What I'm really worried about is that SOB Sarge."

"Not you, too!"

"Yes. He asked me to go over on a boat and have dinner with him when Dan's in town. Of course I turned him down. Now I think he's following me around, standing outside my house at night like a Peeping Tom. What a creep! The worst is, I can't tell Dan, who could do something about it. He's horribly jealous. If I say Sarge is after me, he's likely to accuse me of encouraging him. He's obsessed with who's having sex around here. He even watches Louise like a prison guard. He's already called her a tramp, and she's only twelve."

"Come on! Louise doesn't even have bosoms."

"Apparently he doesn't think she needs them to behave badly. Last Saturday night she came home half an hour late from one of the kids' beach picnics, because she stayed to help clean up. Dan said, 'There's only one thing to do on this island after curfew, and you know what it is. Who were you with?'"

"She was with Jack. Don't tell me Dan thinks Jack and Louise . . ."

"He thinks anyone and Louise. Some of the talks he has with her, I'd hate anyone to hear. One of them starts, 'Only a whore would . . .' and goes on from there."

"Christ!"

"Louise is scared of Sarge, too. She says she doesn't like the way he looks at her, and the other day at swimming lessons, when she came out of the water, he said something about being

able to see through her bathing suit. He told her she's beginning to look like me, and then, according to her, he smirked and
patted her behind. She doesn't want to stay in sports group, but
if she quits, Dan will make her go back."

"Sarge isn't after the children!" Helen thought if she were a
dog, she would be tensed to attack. Lately, she had been thinking about dogs a lot. "This has got to stop!"

"Uh-huh, but it could get ugly. He won't give up. Last night
I was getting ready for bed, putting on my nightgown. I looked
out the window, and he was standing there, looking up at me.
When he realized I saw him, he waved and sort of sauntered
away. For the first time in my life here, I've started locking my
doors. Louise thought she heard him on the porch a couple of
nights back."

"What would he do? He's not going to break in and rape
you."

"No. He's punishing me for refusing his invitation. He's like
Dan; he thinks redheads are 'hot.' He even told me so."

"He asked me out a couple of days ago, too," Helen said. "I
gave him a firm no, and I haven't seen him around my house.
Maybe he'll leave you alone when he realizes he isn't getting
anywhere."

"He isn't hanging around you because Peter and Max and
the Judge could see him from their living room. Our house is
too far off the main path."

"What if I told Peter? Maybe he and Max could patrol your
house a couple of nights. Sit on the porch in the dark, and when
Sarge shows up, give him a scare."

"That's asking for trouble. Haven't you heard that Sarge is
on a mission to get Max off the island? He's almost convinced

Dan that he's a danger to the children. I think Sarge is jealous of Peter, and Max is just an excuse. Look at it from his point of view. There's Peter, handsome as the day, and here all week when the men are in the city. War hero. Member of the community. He doesn't have to work, and he's going back to Yale, which has to be a red flag. I'm surprised the other men aren't on Peter's case, too."

"They may worry, but they aren't going to let on. They wouldn't want anyone to think they don't trust their wives. I don't like to hear that about Max; he's distracting Jack from his obsession with Arthur. I'm crazy about that sweet dog myself. When he comes up and leans against me, and wants me to scratch him behind his ears, I feel as if I've been given a present. If you could see the way he acts with Peter and Jack, it's like the three of them are a pack, and Max is the leader. Whatever happened in the Pacific, Max seems to have gotten over it."

"Well, I wouldn't say no to having Peter sit on my porch a couple of nights this week," Sally said, and gave Helen a teasing look.

"Ah, so you're a member of the Peter Gavin fan club? I gather there's getting to be a nice little group. Quite a few women have asked me about him, presumably because they've seen him and Jack together."

"Or you and Peter together," Sally said, and grinned.

"Never mind about Peter. I'm never with him when Jack or the Judge aren't around. He and Jack have only been working on the boat for two weeks. How does this stuff get inflated?" She did not mention the morning swims, the family dinners with Peter and his grandfather, or her own fantasies.

"Anyway, do you think he'll do it?"

"Do you want me to ask him?'

"Yes, please," Sally said.

The night Peter and Max staked out Sally's house, the sky was overcast, and the stars and moon were behind a heavy cloud cover. Peter sat on a wooden rocking chair against the back wall of the shingled front porch, and Max lay on the floor next to him. It felt strange to be sitting there without a weapon, although Max could be lethal if he gave him the right command. He had to remind himself that his assignment was not to harm Sarge, but to scare him off, so he would leave Sally alone, and drop any further ideas about harassing or, as Sarge might think of it, dating the women in the community.

Helen and Sally couldn't have known how difficult it was for Peter to stand guard with Max, even at Wauregan. It brought back the dark nights when the jungle noises were abruptly overwhelmed by the racket of rockets and gunfire. In the mornings a mess of bodies and body parts would be tossed around the jungle floor, with no meaningful difference between one dead man and another, American or Japanese. When the fighting stopped, the handlers sent their dogs out to see if they could find anyone alive. The First World War procedure of training Red Cross dogs to go out onto the field after a battle and bring back a helmet or another possession of a soldier who was wounded and guide the medics to him was no longer used, but war dogs still often found wounded soldiers and led medics to them.

Operating in war was terrifying, but it was direct. Handling Sarge was more complex. Peter didn't intend to go after him physically, and he was not sure the threat of exposure would be enough to persuade him to leave the women alone.

He suddenly saw movement on the path, and shrank back into the shadows. Most of the lights in the houses were out by then, but Sally had agreed to leave her bedroom light on, so if Sarge turned up, Peter could see him in time to head him off.

The steps didn't sound as heavy as those of a man of Sarge's bulk. For a moment Peter wondered if he were tiptoeing, but as the light from Sally's window shone on the figure coming his way, he saw that it was the Judge.

"Gramps! What are you doing here?" Peter whispered. Max was making a thumping noise, wagging his tail, and Peter gave him the hand motion to be still.

"Came to keep you company. I heard you and Helen talking. I had a word with that fellow myself. He's a rough character. We don't want anything foolish to happen here. You ought to have a witness. Okay if I stick around?"

"Take a pew," Peter said, and pulled a peeling wicker chair back into the shadows against the wall next to him.

For a while the two men and the dog sat quietly in the dark recesses of the porch. The resonance of the war that nagged at Peter was replaced by a feeling of security. When the Judge was around, it was rare that an argument escalated or voices were raised.

Peter was about to whisper something to his grandfather, when they heard someone walking on the path. Sarge appeared and stopped in front of the house. As Peter had expected, he had arrived early enough to be sure Sally was awake and would know he was there. He and the Judge were surprised when Sarge put his hands on his hips and started to whistle a sweetly melodious tune. It would have been touching, but coming from Sarge, it had a menacing quality.

Peter gave Max the signal to stand, and he and the dog walked to the top of the porch stairs, where Sarge could see them.

"Good evening," Peter said. "You've got a nice whistle, but it would be better to save it for a lady who isn't married and would welcome your visit."

Sarge swiveled around and swore. "What the fuck are you doing here?" he spat.

The Judge stood up and revealed himself. "Young man, we discourage language like that in this community."

"Mrs. Carter was feeling uncomfortable about your night-time visits," Peter said. "It would be better if you would leave her alone."

"You threatening me?"

"I'm warning you," Peter said, and Max let out a protective growl.

The Judge stepped forward. "We've already had this conversation. As a member of the Association Board, I'm reminding you of the Wauregan rule that employees are to keep a suitable distance from members of the club."

"What if a member wants to 'fraternize' with the staff?" Sarge said, and smirked.

"Same rule applies," Peter answered. "I hope you're not suggesting that Mrs. Carter has encouraged these visits. You're frightening her, and I'm here to ask you to stop."

"Didn't have the nerve to confront me without your dog, did you?"

"Max usually goes where I go. It doesn't mean anything."

"We'll see about where Max goes," Sarge said. "I'm not having a killing machine around here, baring his fangs, waiting for me to make the wrong move. Mrs. Carter may not be hot for me, but her husband trusts me. Either I can tell him she's been making eyes at me, or I can tell him your dog should be sent off the island. Take your pick."

"Feel free to talk to Mr. Carter about Max," Peter said. "We'll see what comes of that. But leave Mrs. Carter and the other women—and girls, I might add—alone."

"Ah, girls. That little Carter girl's a real cutie. Bet she turns out just like her mom, a nice piece of tail."

Peter snapped. He instantaneously gave Max the "detain" command, and the dog sprang at Sarge, knocked him to the ground, and stood over him with his paws on his chest, panting and drooling into his face.

The Judge spoke sharply. "Peter," he said. "That's enough."

"Sorry, Gramps," Peter said. "Max. Come." The dog obediently turned and walked back to Peter's side.

Sarge, swearing, and swollen with indignant rage, got to his feet and strode over to Peter. With his face only inches away, he said. "That's it for you and your hound. He'll be dog stew pretty soon."

The following weekend, in response to Sarge's complaint about Max, the Sports Committee called a meeting. Neither Peter nor Sarge was invited to make his case, which both had already done privately in conversations with Dan Carter, but Judge Gavin told Dan that as a member of the Wauregan board, he planned to attend. When Sarge's claims had been aired and other members of the committee had expressed their concerns about Max, the Judge spoke up. He said that there had been an unfortunate encounter between Sarge and Peter, which he had witnessed, that Max had reacted the way any dog would if his master were in danger, and that Sarge had not been hurt, unless you wanted to count his dignity. He left out Sally and the incident at the Carter house.

In deference to the Judge, the committee made a compromise. They agreed that Max could remain on the island, but he would have to be leashed and muzzled when he was out and about. At the same time, they drafted a letter to Sarge, reminding him that threatening any member of the community was cause for dismissal.

CHAPTER TEN

LOUISE Carter was surprised when her father didn't raise more objections to her dropping out of sports group. Sally knew the reason, and she was glad Dan hadn't pressed her for an explanation. Louise had told Jack she didn't want to go, although she did not tell him why, and the two of them had concocted a business that would keep them occupied, and meet their parents' approval. Dan grudgingly agreed because he thought it indicated that his daughter was learning to put responsibility before play.

Although the Wadsworths, the Gavins, and the Carters all had telephones, many other homeowners felt it was part of the magic of the place to be out of touch. Those who found it more summerlike to be unavailable walked or bicycled over to the club to pick up any messages the switchboard operator had taken and stuck into flimsy envelopes left over from the war, when paper was in short supply. The operator dropped them into the mail cubbies assigned to each Waureganite, and eventually the recipient would check to see if there was anything in the box. For outgoing calls, there were two stuffy little phone booths with folding glass doors near the switchboard. In an emergency, one of the boys who worked at the club would bicycle a message over to the house where it belonged.

Louise and Jack made an appointment to see the club manager and volunteered to pick up phone messages at noon and at four in the afternoon, and deliver them. They didn't dare ask to be paid, but hoped they might receive tips. The manager checked with the board member in charge of the club, who thought it was a good idea. Within days people without phones began to count on seeing Jack and Louise coming by on their bikes, bearing messages.

"Mrs. Danforth must have a lot of friends," Louise said one afternoon. "Here are two more for her. How many does that make? Eight in three days?"

"Maybe Mr. Danforth calls her a lot. He was away for so long I bet he missed her, and he's making up for it."

Louise didn't say anything, in case Jack was thinking about how long his father had been gone.

They kept the envelopes from flying out of their wicker baskets by holding them down with stones, but one afternoon when Louise's rickety bike, which had belonged to her mother an eon ago, jolted over a heave in the pavement, the envelopes fluttered out. As they carefully extracted them from a thicket of beach plums, they saw that a few were damaged, and one envelope was ripped.

"Hey, that's another for Mrs. Danforth," Louise said. "If we just made the tear a little bigger, we could read it."

"Louise!" Jack said. "Don't!"

"Here goes," Louise said, and with the nail of her first finger, she carefully extracted the folded paper.

"Jeez! What if someone sees us?"

"We'll say we're repairing an envelope that got torn when it fell out of my basket."

They leaned their bikes against a pair of little trees, and Louise read, "Tomorrow, 7 a.m., seaplane will be at ferry landing dock." The message was signed "Pan."

"Pan? Like frying pan?" Jack said, puzzled.

"No, dummy. Like Peter Pan. Someone's coming to fly Mrs. Danforth to Never-Never Land."

"Cut it out. It's probably her nickname for her husband. Or the operator got it wrong, and it was meant to be something like 'Pam.' Don't start trouble."

"Hah! That shows what you know. I heard my mother and Mrs. Clemmons talking about Mrs. Danforth. They've seen her going off in a seaplane and not coming back until the next day, and the pilot is definitely not her husband."

"How about if he's a professional pilot, taking her to meet Mr. Danforth?"

"What if he isn't? That's not what Mom and Mrs. Clemmons think. Good thing the Danforths have Miss Schaller to take care of the kids. She couldn't leave them alone overnight. The baby is, what, six months old?

"And doesn't look one bit like Mr. Danforth, according to my father," Louise said.

"You have a dirty mind. Put that back in the envelope and give it to me."

Jack rubbed the envelope in the sand, to give the impression that it had been damaged by accident, and they delivered it to Barbara Danforth.

She examined the dirty envelope with a puzzled expression, and Jack and Louise did not look at each other.

"I'm sorry it's such a mess," Louise said. "Everything fell out of my bike when I hit a bump."

Mrs. Danforth looked at them and saw regret, but no indication that they had read the message. "Now that the war is over, maybe they'll fix those concrete paths," she said. "They're a real menace." Then she handed them each a generous twenty-five-cent tip, took the envelope, and turned to go back into her house. Jack and Louise exchanged relieved glances, but Jack had noticed that Mrs. Danforth's hand was shaking, and wondered if she suspected something and might report them.

That evening, Helen and Sally brought a picnic supper to the beach, and while they were talking, Louise and Jack sat on a beach towel a little apart, eating their sandwiches. "It would be nice if Mr. Danforth was sending a seaplane for his wife, so they could have some time alone together in New York after all these years," Jack said.

"Shh," Louise said. "I've been thinking about how we can find out. What if we hide by the bay tomorrow morning and watch to see what happens?"

"*No!*" Jack said.

"But you might be right, and then we could do a good deed. I can tell my mother, and she can stop the gossip. That would be excellent."

"Yeah, but can we tell who's in the plane, and whether he's a pilot or a boyfriend?"

"You can tell these things," Louise said, trying to sound mysterious and knowing.

"I'll think about it," Jack said. He didn't want Mr. and Mrs. Danforth to be having problems. He had overheard his mother and Mrs. Carter talking about how hard it was for some of the wives and husbands to get together again after the war. He hoped that when his father came home, it wouldn't be like that. Maybe his parents would have another baby like the Danforths, and he would be practically old enough to be its uncle.

Jack and Louise left their houses before anyone was awake and rode down to the ferry dock. They stashed the bikes in the shrubbery and found a place where they could lie on their stomachs and watch. Louise had brought her father's navy binoculars, which had been made in Germany before the war, and had finely ground lenses.

They didn't have to wait long before Barbara Danforth arrived on foot. She was wearing a full skirt with a flowery pattern, a wide belt, a sleeveless white blouse, and a pair of espadrilles. Her dark hair shone in the morning light, and they saw her push it back behind one ear. Louise, who hated her red hair, wished she could look like Mrs. Danforth when she grew up. She seemed fresh and happy, and distinctively, gloriously, a brunette. Louise thought that one day she could do something about her own hair. She wouldn't be the first woman to change her color. At least she only had another year before her braces came off. She was a natural smiler, and she was apt to flash her braces before she remembered that her mouth was filled with metal, then wish she hadn't displayed the horrible sight.

"Yipes," Jack whispered as he heard the sound of the seaplane coming in, and saw the glint of the metal. The engine slowed to a taxiing speed, and motored along, looking like a plane with two canoes under it. It settled down, rocking on the water on the shallow side of the dock, with its engine buzzing, the pilot pointing into the wind, holding his position until Mrs. Danforth could get in. He opened his window flap, motioned her to come around behind the tail and mount the starboard pontoon. She took off her shoes, held her skirt up above her knees, waded out and stepped onto the pontoon, grasped the wing strut, and put her foot on the step below the door. The pilot leaned over, took her hand firmly, and she maneuvered herself into the passenger seat. The cockpit door was still open when Louise said, "Oh, my gosh!" binoculars tight to her eyes. "You won't believe this."

"What? Give me those!"

"He's kissing her," Louise said. "Look," and handed Jack the binoculars.

The two faces came into focus as though they were only a few feet away. Jack saw Mrs. Danforth with her arms around the man's neck, saw the profile of the kiss, and then the pilot reached across and pulled the cabin door shut. The sound of the engine picked up as he advanced the throttle, the flaps went down, and the plane quickly gained speed. It was almost immediately airborne, climbing at a sharp angle, and Jack and Louise were left staring at each other. The pilot was definitely not Mr. Danforth.

"Okay," Jack said. "Let's make a pact that we'll never tell anyone what we saw."

Louise nodded slightly. Talking about what she thought of

as "romance" was one thing; seeing it was quite different. She was so shocked she could barely move.

"Wait," Jack said. He scrabbled around on the sand until he found a broken shell with a sharp edge. With a quick hard stroke, he scraped it across his middle knuckle until his finger bled, then handed the shell to Louise. She followed his example, and they pressed their bleeding fingers together, mingling their blood.

"Swear?" Jack said.

"Swear."

When Jack returned from his courier job that afternoon with some extra change in his pocket, he found his mother and Kathleen sitting in the kitchen, each with an untouched cup of cooling tea in front of her. His mother was crying.

"Mummy! Did something happen to Dad?" Jack asked in a panicky rush.

"No, sweetie, but there's been an accident, and it's very sad. Mrs. Danforth has been taking flying lessons, and this morning her plane crashed. She and the pilot were both killed," Helen said. "Those poor children. That poor man. Oh dear," she said, and started to cry again.

Some of the women at Wauregan guessed what Barbara Danforth had been doing. They had noticed her disappearances, but had never mentioned them to their husbands. As one woman said, "We wouldn't want to give the men ideas that things are going on here when they're at work."

Barbara Danforth was not buried at Wauregan. Many

people felt it was the place where their souls felt most at home, but creating a cemetery in the sand was against the law. Her husband probably wouldn't have wanted her body brought back there anyway. There was enough speculation about the circumstances of her death. Instead, the children, with their father and their governess, Miss Schaller, dressed in their city clothes, chartered a boat to the mainland. The announcement in the *New York Times* noted "the funeral service will be private."

Jack and Louise only talked about Mrs. Danforth's death once. They had finished a courier run, and were sitting in a spot of shade near the more wooded part of the community on the bay side. "What if we had confessed that we opened her message and read it?" Jack said.

"You're kidding!"

"It would have been honest. And maybe if she knew we found out about her assignation"—a word Jack had learned from listening to his mother and Kathleen talking about the accident—"she wouldn't have gone. She'd still be alive, and her children would have a mother." Jack thumped his fist against a tree trunk, then punched the trunk until his hand hurt.

The next day, they told the club manager they would not be able to continue their messenger service. "I have to finish restoring my father's boat," Jack explained. Louise didn't say anything.

Over the years, the story of the fatal "flying lessons" was regularly recalled when a group of men who worked on Wall Street had a particularly hot mid-August commute, and discussed how convenient it would be to avoid the train and the ferry and share a seaplane to travel to Wauregan from the city. Then they would remind themselves that there were safer, if slower, ways to get there. As for the children, only Jack and Louise knew the truth, and they had made a blood pact never to tell.

CHAPTER ELEVEN

"HOW would you like to go to the movies?" Peter asked Helen. It was morning. The day was already a bright blue and Peter looked boyish and full of energy.

Helen laughed. "What movies? It's Wednesday. The next movie at the casino is on Saturday night. A Disney for the children."

"Nope. The movie I was thinking of is *The Egg and I*. Have you seen it?"

"I read the book."

"Did you like it?"

"I did. Made me laugh. Along with everyone in the English-speaking world, evidently. I hear it's already sold a million copies."

"It's playing on the mainland."

"Were you thinking of swimming over?"

"At the new drive-in theater," Peter went on, teasing.

"As we don't have a powerboat here, or a car on the other side . . ." Helen began.

"Ah, but that's where you're wrong. Bobby Carhart told me to use his Chris-Craft any time. It's such a beauty, I haven't wanted to borrow it, but for a special occasion . . ."

"It's not your birthday?"

Peter shook his head.

"Well, I know it's not mine. So?"

"So."

"The Carharts' boat? The waterborne 'convertible'?"

"That's the one. Built in 1930, just before most people realized they couldn't afford new runabouts."

"Why is he lending it to you? I thought no one except the Carharts were allowed to drive her."

"Sad story. Bobby was at Saipan. A Marine, like me. He was on the cliff opposite the one where whole families threw themselves into the sea so they wouldn't be captured by the Americans. Damned Japs told them if they were caught, we would do unspeakable things to them. Wasn't hard for them to believe, considering what their soldiers did to us."

"What does that have to do with the boat?"

"Watching mothers throw their babies over the cliff did something to Bobby. He says he has nightmares about drowning. As though he's put himself in the place of those little kids. He isn't ready to go out on the water in anything smaller than the Wauregan ferry. Even then, he says, he tries not to look around, just reads the newspaper and pretends he's on dry land."

"Good Lord," Helen said.

"So he told me the *Lux* needs some 'exercise.'"

For nearly two decades everyone at Wauregan had admired

the sleek mahogany Chris-Craft, with a green stripe at the waterline, three sets of green leather bench seats, and shiny chrome fittings, but Helen had never been out on her.

"Okay," she said. "What do we do when we get there? Drive the boat up the highway and park at the drive-in?" Helen giggled, then stopped. She sounded like a sixteen-year-old.

"Gramps's car is at the ferry landing."

Helen nodded. "Were you planning to take Jack on our movie outing?"

"I was thinking of it more as a movie date," Peter said. "So, no. Okay?"

Helen blushed, and felt her cheeks get warmer.

"I can ask Jack to baby-sit for Max; he'd rather do that anyway. What time does the movie start?"

"After dinner. A lobster place I don't think you've been to yet."

Helen did not mention that the last time she was invited out for lobsters was by Sarge.

They left the dock before sunset. The *Lux*, with its inboard motor behind the front bench, was quiet, but there was enough sound as she rushed through the water that Helen did not feel she had to make conversation. She realized that the last time she had been on a date was years earlier, before she and Arthur were engaged. She felt shy and was glad not to have to talk, but could enjoy the wind blowing her hair and watch the sky changing colors. She took off her glasses, which were getting wet from the spray, and saw the colors of strawberries, the insides of conch shells, lavender bushes, spring leaves, campfire smoke, and cotton balls. Nature repeating itself—land, sky, and sea. Shyness gave way to exhilaration, then as the sky faded, to a sweet wistfulness as they pulled into Wauregan's private dock on the mainland.

Peter tied up, jumped onto the dock, and reached out to help her disembark. He held on to her hand a little longer, gave her arm a little swing, and, at a raised eyebrow from her, let go.

"Gramps's car" was a dark gray 1938 Hudson, with an old-fashioned comfortable rounded body, much like an upholstered armchair.

"Too bad he didn't wait a couple of years to buy his Hudson," Peter said. "The '38 was the last one that looked like this. From '39 to '41, the Hudsons were designed by a woman, Betty someone. They were as snappy as Bobby's Chris-Craft—snappier even. Chrome, sleek lines, long hoods, special materials on the seats. The Hudson folks must have liked women; when they introduced a model called the Terraplane in '32, they got Amelia Earhart to christen it. Then in '42, the factory was turned over to make aircraft parts and Oerlikon antiaircraft cannons."

"You don't have to like women to want Amelia Earhart to put her imprimatur on a car called a Terraplane," Helen said. "But I am impressed that you know all that. Only a future architect would notice those details."

"Anyone who's interested in cars notices that stuff. What kind of car do you have?"

"A blue car," Helen said. "We left it back in St. Paul. Don't need it in New York. There's always a taxi."

Peter laughed. "A blue car? Any particular make?"

"Probably, but don't press me."

The lobster place, well hidden up the coast, was not the one Waureganites usually patronized. Peter turned onto a dirt road, and the Hudson's headlights picked out a lean-to with a group of picnic tables under strings of light bulbs. An enormous man wearing a white apron over a bare and hairy chest was carrying platters of lobsters to the diners crowded around one of the tables. In the background, a scratchy radio station was playing the Mills Brothers' version of "Lazy River."

Helen smiled. It had been a long time since she had had an adventure, and in the years she and Arthur had been together at Wauregan, they had never been to this "restaurant," if that's what it was.

"*Semper fi*, brother!" the big man said when he saw Peter.

"*Semper fi* to you, too, you old—"

"Watch it. Ladies here. See you've found one."

"Helen Wadsworth, I'd like you to meet a member of my platoon. Sergeant Harry Dranowski, the Polish lobster-master."

"How do you do, ma'am. Glad to meet you," Harry said, made a swipe at the top of one of the already clean pine tables, and pointed. "Take a seat. Hope you like steamers. My son brought in some good ones this morning. Fresh lobsters today, too."

"I like everything," Helen said.

"Live wire," Peter said under his breath, and grinned at her.

They sat on a bench under the harsh lights. Helen thought they couldn't be very flattering, but Peter was admiring her slight squint lines, the mark of the nearsighted. When they had ordered, Peter asked, "Was Barbara Danforth a good friend?"

"Not really. More the way people at Wauregan just 'know' each other. Her children are younger than Jack, and she grew up in Connecticut and went to Smith. We didn't meet until I started coming to the island. Still, it's shocking to think that she's gone. During the war, when we read about the casualties, even if we knew the men who died, it got to be almost abstract—such huge numbers are hard to take in. But when one person dies in a small place, it feels like it does when there's a hurricane. Everyone is affected."

Peter nodded and tilted his head. "You'd imagine you might get immune to sharing rations with a buddy in the morning, then watching him get blown into such small pieces you can't even find a finger a couple of hours later, when it happens again and again," he said. "You go on, but every time, you're diminished. At least we didn't have the 'Pals Battalions' like they did in England in the last war."

"What were they?"

"A recruitment device. The British army promised that all the men from a village who enlisted would be assigned to the same battalion. Many of those guys had never been any farther from home than the nearest market town, so it made them more comfortable to go off together. You can imagine the leaving scenes at the train stations. Everyone turning out to wave the recruits off, tears, excitement, hugging and kissing, mothers handing their boys packages of their favorite food, the whole damn business. Some of them at home hadn't even received more than a couple of letters from the front when the slaughter started. Sixty thousand killed just on the first day of the

Somme. In a lot of villages, practically all the men old enough to serve were wiped out."

"Christ!" Helen said. "Imagine if that happened at Wauregan! We probably have about the same number of people as they did in a lot of those villages."

Peter nodded somberly.

"Can we not talk about the war?" Helen said. "I'd like to know why you've decided to be an architect."

"It started a long time ago. When I was growing up in New York, we lived in a brownstone, it was dark and vertical, with no windows on the sides because they butted up against other brownstones; kitchen in the basement, dumb waiter to get the food up to the dining room. I thought it was fine—it was home—until 1932, when my father took me to the new Museum of Modern Art to see a show called 'The International Style.' Father liked it—he was an engineer, and he appreciated the way the architects used materials 'honestly,' he said, especially glass. Some of the buildings in the show were almost transparent, and none of them had the kind of ornamentation we were used to seeing. No faux-Adam fireplaces, no seventeenth-century Grinling Gibbons moldings, no Victorian bric-a-brac—you know the drill. Father bought a book about the International Style written by Philip Johnson—did you know he started the Department of Art and Design at the museum? Father and I used to look at it together and talk about what we liked and didn't like.

"Then, when I was in Japan right after the war, I went to Nikko—that's a town with beautiful shrines, although by then they were in bad repair. I stayed in what they call a *ryokan*, a Japanese inn. I couldn't get over it. The walls were covered in woven straw matting; so were the floors. The doors were sliding screens covered in translucent waxed paper, and the beds were like sleeping bags, only much more comfortable, and they rolled up during the day. The rooms were almost empty, except for a couple of low stools and a little niche where there was a scroll with Japanese calligraphy and a small vase with one perfect flower. Outside there was a tiny garden of stones raked in a pattern, one large stone carefully chosen for its beauty, and a little carp pond with some kind of weeping tree hanging over it. I couldn't get over how peaceful I felt there. That was just before I came back to the States. I was in pretty bad shape, but I didn't realize how really bad it was until I got home.

"I guess I could say I fell for a way of living, and I wanted to be part of designing it."

"Gosh," Helen said. The little she had seen of modern architecture seemed cold and uninspired, but she was listening.

A young girl whose skin, hair, and eyelashes were so pale she was almost an albino brought over the clams. Peter interrupted himself long enough to stand up and give her a hug. "Bet you're glad to have your dad back," he said.

"Glad! You said it. Ma and I had some time keeping this place up when he was off there with you 'hee-roes' fighting off Japs, so we wouldn't have to start serving our fish raw. The only lobstermen around here were about a hundred years old. Hope you like your dinner, ma'am," she said to Helen.

"Thank you. I'm sure I will," Helen said warmly.

"When I talk about simple architecture," Peter continued, "I don't mean 'simple' the way we think of it at Wauregan. Those houses are a nightmare. Did you ever hear the expression 'form follows function'?"

"Yes, but I haven't thought about it much. We've always lived the same way, and until the war there were so many servants around, they did all the 'functioning.' Now we're doing so much for ourselves, I'm beginning to get the idea."

"Well, at Wauregan, function is hopeless. Up and down stairs. Beautiful views you can hardly see because the windows are small. Lots of little cut-up spaces. Hideous kitchens. 'Simplicity' on our little island means bare feet and the minimum of comfort."

"Hold on. That's not all. It's also not talking about money, or showing off, and appreciating people because they're good members of the community, and . . . that sort of thing," she said.

Peter dipped a clam in a paper cup filled with broth, dipped it again in a frilled cup of butter, slid the clam into his mouth, chewed, and smiled at her.

"Yup," he said. "That, too."

Helen thought of her house in St. Paul, its heavy lined satin draperies with lace curtains behind them, her English antiques, Georgian silver tea service, and eau de Nil silk-covered bedroom walls. "How are people going to furnish your houses? I don't see my grandmother's Chippendale breakfront in your clean, unadorned spaces; and the kind of draperies we're used to are beautiful, even if they do shut out the light."

"You've heard of Wiener Werkstätte and you certainly know about Art Deco. That furniture is as beautifully made as any antique. It could make you want to auction off everything you've inherited and start fresh."

Helen was not so sure about that. She was quite attached to her grandmother's tea service and she couldn't see how flowered chintz—her favorite—would fit into a steel-and-glass house, but surely there was a compromise. As Peter continued to explain his vision, she realized that he, too, was thinking about comfort. About what he called "a house that doesn't talk back, just does what it's supposed to do, and does it smoothly and with grace."

A few dozen clams and two lobsters later, Harry came over to the table. "Gotta show you something," he said to Helen. "Like to know how to tell the weather?"

"Sure," Helen said.

"Come on then." He led them to the back of the cooking shack, where an old Tabasco sauce bottle was hanging from a wire. Inside the bottle was a clear liquid. "Shark oil," Harry explained. "It gets cloudy? Means there's a storm coming. Better than them instruments the Coast Guard use. They check with me to make sure we're on the same page."

"Gosh," Helen said. She didn't think she'd been much of a date so far. Practically all she had said was "gosh," from the time Peter told her about the Hudson, right through his brief course on modern architecture. Now she was looking at a real example of "simple."

"No kidding," Peter said. "We should call you from Wauregan when we want to know what's coming our way."

"Nah. Island weather's different. You need your own shark oil for that."

Peter asked for the check, explaining they had to get going if they wanted to make it in time for the movie. Harry said, "Dinner's on me. No Marine wounded in action is ever going to have to pay at Harry's Lobsters. House rule." He touched a finger to his forehead—almost a salute—and nodded to Helen. "Same for his lady friend, of course."

• • •

The Egg and I was the story of a young urban couple who move to a "chicken ranch" in the country when the husband decides he longs for the rural life. The sophisticated French-born actress Claudette Colbert managed to portray an appropriately improbable farm wife, and Helen thought her costar, Fred MacMurray, was exactly the sort of husband she would never want to have. In fact, she thought, if someone had even fixed her up with a man like that, she would have wondered if they knew her at all.

This was the first time Helen had been to a drive-in movie, and she found the place, if you could call a big parking lot a "place," at least as interesting as the film. Hundreds of cars were organized in rows facing a huge screen with enormously enlarged actors doing whatever they did. Behind the screen, what seemed to be a patch of woods made a dark and mysterious background. Each driver was given a speaker, so the sound track was broadcast inside the car, creating a strangely disjunctive atmosphere between the intimacy of the voices nearly in their laps, and the action hundreds of feet away on the screen. Helen was as curious about the inhabitants of the other cars as about the setup. She saw convertibles filled with teenagers chewing gum and smoking cigarettes; station wagons with what appeared to be entire families; and cars in which no one was visible—presumably occupied by couples who were prone on the front or backseats. It was odd, Helen thought, to be out among people she had never seen before, and most likely would never see again, after the familiarity of every face at Wauregan. She admitted to herself that the anonymity allowed her to feel as though she was both no particular age and every age she had ever been, free of any definition, aside from "a woman in a car with a man."

She wondered if Peter was going to put his arm around her. Long ago, when she went on dates, while a couple pretended each of them was oblivious to everything except the movie, the boy would slip an arm around the back of the girl's seat, then casually drop his hand onto her shoulder. If he was bold enough, or thought he wouldn't be rebuffed, he would slide his hand over her shoulder, inside her blouse, and curl his hand around her breast. Sometimes he would be able to slip a hand into her bra. The thought of Peter touching her in that way made Helen throb. Surely, she thought, bringing herself back to the film, the characters Claudette and Fred played must have . . . but there they were, in their twin beds, sleeping as separately as two sisters who shared a room.

The closest Peter came to touching her was to move over from behind the steering wheel and sit with his arm and shoulder lined up with hers. That, Helen thought, was quite enough excitement for a maybe-widow.

Her mind wandered, and she had a little conversation with herself. What do we have in common? she asked herself. Wauregan, Jack, Max, the Judge, and Kathleen. Is that enough? Well, we like each other. That counts. Does he wonder if I'm too old to have a baby? No, I am not. How old will I be when he is my age? Uch. Forty-four. And who says he's interested? He only asked me because there isn't anyone else for him to go to the movies with. *This is not going to work.* She directed her attention back to Claudette Colbert, her hundreds of chicks, the kitchen appliance she called Stove, as though it were an animate object, and the husband who didn't care that she had to carry water in a bucket from the stream because they didn't have a well.

On the way back to the boat, she remarked to Peter, "I don't think that's the kind of simple life you were talking about at dinner."

He laughed. "Would it be fair to say that was more a woman's movie?"

"If you mean, no action, no war, no most-decorated American soldier, no Audie Murphy on the cover of *Life*, no cowboys, no crooks . . ."

"Stop! I get the point," Peter said and turned to smile at her, then looked back at the road. "Maybe I should ask if you liked it."

"Actually I liked the book better. It made me laugh out loud. Did you know that Betty MacDonald, who wrote the book, actually moved to a chicken farm with her husband, and left him after something like three years of marriage? That is *not* in the movie," Helen said.

Peter grinned, still looking ahead as they approached the parking place at the ferry dock. "Can you blame her? And no, that's not the kind of simplicity I was talking about at dinner. Although we did learn about one uncomplicated, and I must say inexplicable, appliance: Harry's 'weather station.' I might ask him where he gets his shark oil. It wouldn't be bad to have a little bottle hanging outside Gramps's door."

"Just don't hang it outside my house. By the end of the summer, when people have run out of things to talk about, someone might start a rumor that I'm a witch."

If I were to make a list of the qualities the ideal woman would have, Peter thought, a sense of humor—or is it a kind of benign irony?—would be in the top five. But why am I thinking this way? I'm going to school; she's the mother of a boy on his way to boarding school. She's rich; I'm a student living on a small legacy from my grandmother. I won't be earning anything for who knows how long. I want to have children; she probably doesn't want to start all over again. But, he thought, my God, she's sexy, and she probably doesn't even know it.

By the time they embarked, the moon was bright on the water, and they hardly needed the running light to see their way. Helen thought at first that she was tired, and then realized the feeling was not exhaustion, but an unfamiliar sense of peace. She put her head back, felt the breeze, and smelled the fresh water as it sprayed up around the boat. Peter was watching the compass, although he knew those waters so well he had memorized every rock. They were the only boat out, as the time neared midnight on a Monday. He looked over at Helen, whose eyes were closed, and he pulled back on the throttle until the sound of the motor died away. Helen turned toward him and he pointed to the moonlight making a shimmering path on the water, under the clear starry sky. Peter leaned toward her, she nodded a yes, and he kissed her gently, and then urgently. He pressed her back against the seat and she slid down until he was lying on her, and they were moving together, rocking the boat. He heard her "Mmm," and a little gasp, and then, suddenly, a brilliant searchlight was shining on them and a coast guardsman was drawing alongside and calling from a loudspeaker, "Any problems? Engine give out?"

Peter stood up, holding on to the wheel for balance. "No sir," he said. "Just enjoying a peaceful night on the water. The engine's working just fine."

At that, Helen couldn't hold back her giggles and she turned away, pretended she was sneezing, and choked.

"The lady okay?" the guardsman asked.

"I'd say she's just fine," Peter said. Helen, who had just managed to get her laugher under control, started up again.

"When we see a boat with its running light on, rocking and going nowhere, we check to be sure there hasn't been an accident. Last time, the guy whose boat it was had a heart attack."

Helen was curled up on her seat, shaking with silent laughter.

"Right," Peter said. "I guess we'd better get going. Thanks for stopping, Captain."

"We'll wait until your engine starts," the captain said.

Recovering herself, Helen looked at him and said, "Thank you for your help."

Peter started the engine; the Coast Guard searchlight passed across the bay and flicked off.

Helen started to laugh again. "You really meant it when you said this was a date."

"What did you think I meant?"

"That there wasn't anyone else to go with except Max, Jack, or the Judge?"

"You did not," Peter said, and he was right.

CHAPTER TWELVE

HELEN thought about her evening with Peter for a couple of days, and then called Frank. Barbara Danforth's death and her own uncertainty were nagging at her in ways that crossed back and forth. She wanted to talk to someone—to a man—who was connected to the past as she remembered it; to Arthur; and to the Wauregan that, as its cottagers still wanted to believe, was unchanged and unchanging. When she reached Frank, he noticed that her voice was low, like a trumpet with a mute.

"The whole community is subdued," she told him. "No one knows what to think, but it looks like something was going on between Barbara and the pilot. I hate that this kind of thing is happening here. And now, that sergeant the Athletics Committee hired is going after some of the wives while the men are in town. He's really scary. I wish Arthur were here."

"Since he isn't," Frank said, "I'm glad I'm coming up the weekend after next."

"So am I," Helen said. Then she asked herself if she was really glad, and was not sure.

Her growing attraction to Peter was too impractical, she thought, while Frank was a kind of safety net, and possibly more. "There's the dance Saturday night," she reminded him. "It should be a festive weekend."

Frank thought about Jack and Peter and *Red Wing,* and asked, "Doesn't that boat of Arthur's need a new sail?"

"Yes. The boys are going to borrow one for the launch," Helen said.

"How about I get Jack a new sail and bring it up as a surprise?"

Helen said that Jack would be thrilled. It might also modify his hero worship of Peter. Frank would always be around, and who could guess what would happen when Peter went back to Yale?

Frank was thinking about Peter, too. He had planned to wait for Helen to learn about Arthur's fate from official sources, but decided that, with Peter moving into the Wadsworth family life so quickly, perhaps it was time for him to tell her.

Jack and Peter were working on another project together, a special performance for the annual Wauregan Children's Talent Show, held in the casino on the last Saturday in July. The Wauregan casino was not a place for gambling, which, like the sale of liquor, was forbidden on the island. The big red barn had unfinished wood paneling, exposed rafters, a scarred wooden floor, and a stage. It was used for movies, rainy day activities, dances, amateur theatricals, and the all-island meetings held at the beginning of July and August. Unlike the club, which at least had faded chintzes on its sofas and chairs, the casino was as bare as it could be and still provide shelter.

The first time Jack had been in the talent show, he was five years old. He and Arthur had concocted a Tarzan act that involved Arthur tossing a rope over a beam and holding one end, while Jack grabbed the other, wound his arms and legs around the rope, jumped off the stage, and swung out over the audience like a monkey. Kathleen had sewn leaves on his underpants to create the impression of a jungle loincloth; otherwise he was bare. Jack had won second prize and proudly kept the red ribbon, which was now so faded from its summers pinned on the wooden frame of the mirror in his room that it was almost pink. He hardly noticed it anymore, but when he did, it brought back the memory of the leafy underpants, which he would just as soon not think about.

Fourteen was the age limit for participants, and if it had not been for Max, he wouldn't have thought of entering again. Instead, he and Peter, with Louise as their sidekick, decided to develop an act to display Max's intelligence, gentleness, and, Jack hoped, his lovable personality.

That evening, promptly at six o'clock—Wauregan was casual, but perpetually punctual—the audience gathered. The adults, most of them holding cocktails from their own private stashes, sat on wooden folding chairs set up in rows. The participants would come onstage in order of age, so Jack and Max would be the finale.

The show began with a mother carefully dropping the needle on a Victrola, as three little girls in puffy clamshell headdresses ran across the stage, stopped abruptly, just missing a collision, and launched into a version of Gilbert and Sullivan's "Three Little Maids," with the lyrics changed to "Three little clams in shells are we-ee." They were followed by a girl dressed in a monkey suit, holding what looked like a large banana, but turned out to be her baby brother. She sang a bar of "Yes, we have no bananas, we have no bananas today." Then she held up the infant in his yellow one-piece night suit and pretended to take a bite out of him. Helen imagined the child's mother warning her, "No real bites. He's a baby, not a piece of fruit."

The children's church choir, with the girls wearing flowery Liberty of London smocked dresses and the boys in starched short-sleeved white shirts and blue shorts, marched onstage next, while the choir mistress led them in "Morning Is Coming." After that there was the predictable boy juggling tennis balls and a girl in a pink tutu teetering *en pointe* to the "Dance of the Sugar Plum Fairies." Three girls whose fathers had not come back from the war sang "The Battle Hymn of the Republic"; two boys followed with the army hymn; and finally, in a clear alto, Louise Carter sang the naval anthem for her father.

"What a grown-up voice she has," Helen remarked to the Judge.

"She'll be singing torch songs next," he remarked, leaning over from his great height to whisper in her ear.

The finale was announced by a slightly tipsy father acting as master of ceremonies, as "Jax and Mac," which, when he heard laughter, he corrected to "Jack and Max." As Peter played the Marine Corps anthem on the record player, the boy and the dog, who was unleashed and unmuzzled, marched onto the stage. Jack bowed from the waist, while Max, in the "sit" position, dropped his head, until his nose was between his front legs and his big golden ears stuck forward like little horns.

Jack gave Max the commands to march, halt, and salute, which Max approximated by holding a big soft paw up to his forehead. "At ease," Jack said, and Max sat. "Roll over. Stand. Attention: enemy sighted. Hide!" Max slipped behind Jack, while the audience laughed.

Then Jack announced that he and Max were going to demonstrate a few of the techniques a scout dog learned. "As some of you know," he said, "thousands of war dogs have been retrained to join civilian life. Max is one of them, but he still knows how to follow commands."

A shout erupted, and in the ensuing silence, a man's hoarse, angry voice could be heard. "Get that devil dog off the stage before someone gets hurt!"

Sarge was standing in the open doorway of the casino, pointing at Max. He staggered in and yelled, "What's wrong with you people? That dog's supposed to be muzzled."

Peter, standing behind the curtain, prepared to step out and take over, but Jack reacted swiftly, giving Max the signal to stay and be quiet. The dog stood, ears quivering and hackles bristling. A low, ominous growl came from deep in his throat, but he did not leave Jack's side.

Dan Carter launched himself onto the stage from the front row. He was not entirely sober—Jack could smell the whiskey on his breath—but he spoke clearly, and stood straight. "Sergeant dismissed," he said. "The show will go on."

"Fucking big-shot assholes," Sarge mumbled, loudly enough

that the people seated near the door could hear him. He turned to leave, and as he reached the open door, held on to the frame for balance, then stumbled off, throwing a bottle into the shrubbery.

Jack, shaken but pleased that Max had not responded to the threat, scratched the dog behind his ears and addressed the audience. "You've just seen one of the things a war dog learns: to hold and keep silent in the presence of the enemy. Now we'll demonstrate the kind of situation Max experienced during the war. He and I are the point men for a squad on a jungle island in the Pacific. Behind us, half a dozen men count on him to hear the enemy and warn us. When he points, we realize that we're walking into a trap and retreat so silently the enemy doesn't realize we were there, and we go for reinforcements. Okay, Max, let's begin."

Jack and Max stealthily began to cross the stage, Max in the lead and Jack moving in a low crouch. Louise, hidden behind the curtain, shook the material, and Max immediately alerted. Jack dropped to his stomach and crawled toward the place Max was facing. People sitting in the back stood up to see what would happen next. Jack signaled to retreat, and he and Max crawled back across the stage and disappeared into the wings. This was greeted with applause.

Jack and Max reappeared. "You've had a demonstration of how quiet a war dog can be, and the obedience he shows when his handler instructs him not to go after an enemy. Now, let's see what happens when the enemy is close in."

Louise stepped onto the stage wearing a slicker to protect her arm, brandishing a tennis racket at Max, and yelling, "Come and get me."

"As you can see, this enemy soldier is armed," Jack said.

"Isn't he pushing it?" Helen whispered to the Judge.

"Hope not," the Judge said. "Peter wouldn't . . ."

"We're going to take the enemy soldier prisoner," Jack announced. "But first she has to be persuaded to come with us. That's Max's job." He gave Max the signal to disarm Louise, and Max sprang at her. Louise held her ground, while Max delicately grabbed the tennis racket in his mouth and wrested it away from her, until she held up her hands in surrender. "Notice that there isn't a tooth mark on the prisoner," Jack said.

"Okay, Max. Let's march our captive back to headquarters." With Max herding Louise, and Jack following, holding the tennis racket, they marched offstage.

When Jack and Max came back, Jack announced, "Our last demonstration is chow time." He had a large beef bone in his hand, and he placed it on the stage between himself and the dog. "Pick it up," he said. "Hold it." Max sat with the bone in his mouth until Jack knelt in front of him. "Give me the bone." He put his face close to Max's dark nose, opened his mouth, and Max gently loosened his hold, as Jack took the bone in his teeth.

Helen heard a woman sitting near her whisper, "Ugh. Disgusting."

Jack stood and handed the bone back to Max, while they took a bow, and some in the audience cheered and whistled.

Sally Carter remarked to Dan, "There's your 'dangerous dog.' Feeling a little silly?"

Dan shook his head. "I don't know. Sooner or later that dog . . ." but the rest of his remark was lost in applause as Jack threw a ball as high as he could, Max leapt to an improbable height, retrieved the ball in the air, and mouthed it back.

The judges awarded Jack and Max first place, although one dissenter warned, not unreasonably, that it would give the misleading impression that any child could safely snatch a bone out of a dog's mouth. They agreed that the prize would be awarded with a caveat, praising Jack and Max, but making it clear that under no circumstances was any other child or adult to try the same trick with even a small dog.

After the show, Jack asked Peter if Max could sleep over. "Sure," Peter said. "Gramps and I are having dinner with Mr. and Mrs. Greenwood. They have a daughter my age. We grew up together, and I haven't seen her for years. She's just up for the weekend. You can keep Max from getting lonely."

Helen had been hugging Jack with one arm and patting Max with the other hand when she heard him. She vaguely remembered the "Greenwood girls," hoped it was the one with the rabbity teeth, not the pretty one, who, she had heard, was getting her doctorate in archaeology. "You and Max did a great job up there," she told Jack. "I'm on my way to the Carters' for dinner, but Kathleen has something special cooking for both of you winners. Be sure to tell her all about it."

"Wait till she sees Max's blue ribbon!" Jack said.

"And yours," Helen said.

When Jack and Max headed back to the house, the sun had set and Jack flicked on his flashlight. There were clouds obscuring the moon, and its light didn't penetrate the thick, scrubby bushes on the side of the path. Just out of sight of the casino,

Jack heard a loud rustling and Sarge emerged from a bayberry thicket. He was holding a long stick, and he swiftly thrust it through the spokes of Jack's back wheel, twisting the metal wires, and causing the bike to wobble to a stop. Max halted and waited for instructions. He was fully alert, the hair on his neck was standing up as though it had been electrified, and he barked a warning. Jack, balancing the bike with both feet on the ground, signaled him to be quiet, and, frightened, clenched the handlebars tightly. He and Max were alone on the path with Sarge.

"Hey! What did you do that for?" he asked.

"Think you're such a big deal. Spoiled brat, too much of a baby for girls, falls in love with a dog. Show you who's a man around here," he said. "Where's that ribbon you won?"

"You can't have it. It's mine. Mine and Max's."

Sarge looked at the bicycle basket and saw the blue ribbon pinned there.

"You know dogs can't get medals in the armed forces, not even those famous killers."

"No," Jack said. He wasn't sure he could keep Max from attacking Sarge if he got too close.

"No medals for dogs. Military regulations. Sarge has a ches'ful, though. Bet you didn't know that."

He came closer, and Jack gave Max the signal to stay. Jack's anger was rising in a way he could barely recognize. He was desperate to command Max to rip his teeth into Sarge's hand if he tried to take the ribbon, but the man developing inside the boy restrained him. Later, when he was older and remembered the encounter, he would reflect that was the way wars started: someone wanted someone else's prize.

Engorged with the fearlessness of the deeply drunk, Sarge pulled the ribbon off the basket, held it up triumphantly, then fumbled to pin it on his own shirt. "Show you who's the winner 'round here," he muttered, then turned and walked away unsteadily. The ribbon fell off, and he stamped on it and ground it into the sand on the side of the path. It occurred to Jack that with the exception of the night watchman, the ferry master and hands, and the boys and girls who worked at the club, Sarge was the only person on the island who wore shoes.

Jack's knees felt soft and his hands were shaking. "It's okay, Max," he said, as though it were the dog, not he, who needed to be reassured. "He's ruined it, but never mind. My mother will get us another ribbon tomorrow. Let's go home." The back wheel was too unsteady for him to ride his bike and he walked it back to the house.

Kathleen was waiting to give him dinner. She had prepared a special treat for Max, about whom she was worried. He had been growing thinner, and seemed less robust. He was fine when he was animated, playing with Jack or Peter, but Kathleen knew dogs, and unless one or the other of "the boys," as she thought of them, was around, Max slept, often facing into a corner, as though he were too exhausted to keep his usual vigil. Sometimes she heard him cough weakly, and remembered the way her father had coughed when his lungs were filling up from the smoking, and every cough strained his heart. For this special night, she had prepared a stew with beef and carrots and potatoes for him, better food than she had had as a child in Ireland, she thought. Not that she begrudged it to the dog. That was just the way it was. For Jack, she had a hamburger ready to go into the skillet, a baked potato and peas, and a freshly baked batch of chocolate chip cookies.

When she saw Jack approaching the house on foot, she thought at first that he had lost his flashlight, then she caught a glimpse of his expression, and wondered if the judges hadn't awarded him a prize.

"Dinner's in the kitchen," she said cheerily, and waited to find out what was wrong.

Jack folded himself into a kitchen chair; Max sighed deeply and curled up next to him, and Jack rubbed his back with a bare foot.

"Sarge," he said. "Again. Broke my bike and took the ribbon we won. First prize," he added, perking up.

Kathleen made a clucking sound. "My mother always warned me about bullies," she said. "I could see it myself from a wee girl. If you spent one day where we lived in Ireland those days, you'd know what I mean. Them English landlords called us filthy vermin right to our faces, and they weren't so wrong, because where did we have to take a bath, but in a tin tub on a Saturday night? Some of them was so vicious they knew we'd kill them if we could. One of them, when he had to pay his workers, used to lower a basket out a window on a rope, with the money in the basket. He didn't want to have to touch the dirty Irish and he was scared if he let us get too close we'd tear him into bloody pieces. My aunt worked in his house as a girl, and she said his bedroom door was bolted shut at night with steel bars, like a safe, so he could sleep without fearing someone would cut his throat."

"What did he do?"

"Whatever he could get away with. Took my sister, for one, prettiest of the seventeen of us children, when she was hardly older than you, locked her in his house, and used her until he was finished with her. Then he opened that big heavy front door and pushed her out. She hanged herself the next day."

"Oh, Kathleen. I'm sorry," Jack said, shocked.

"The landlords hated us. That house I was telling you about? It had a dry ditch all around the ground floor, six foot deep, so if any of us Irish had to walk past, gardeners or grooms, or washerwomen and the like, the 'nice' people in the big house didn't even have to see our heads. Sarge is a bad man, but there's only one of him, and I can tell you, because I heard your mother and Mrs. Carter talking, he won't be back next summer. The women have risen up in revolt. The difference, in Ireland there were hundreds of Sarges, and they weren't the hired man, they were the bosses. Be glad you met someone like that when you were young. When you run into another, you'll know what he is and keep out of his way."

"Gee," Jack said. "I guess you're right." He didn't know what else to say.

Then, looking down at Max, who was standing over his empty bowl, licking off the last taste of gravy, he said, "Hey! That's the first time in a while Max has eaten his whole dinner. My mother said she didn't like that he's been such a picky eater. German shepherds are supposed to be gluttons."

"Ha!" Kathleen said, pleased with the results of her cooking. "Want to hear another story from Ireland?"

"You bet!" Jack had grown up hearing about Kathleen's brothers and sisters, and her mother, who made lace and sewed for the gentry, and kept a little shop that supported them all, while their father was "down the pub with those no-good friends of his."

While he ate, Kathleen told him about another dinner long

ago. "That house I was telling you about, they was even stingy with their friends. They used to have parties, and they'd tell the footmen serving at the table not to spend too much time at any one place with those silver platters, so the guests couldn't get more than a morsel before the platters were whisked away. Their dogs was different. They fed them dogs better than the people. Great big hunting dogs they were, with some appetite. One night, a gentleman come from England who didn't know the house so well. He got his scrap of dinner, and after everyone went to bed, he was still hungry. So he crept downstairs and found his way into the pantry. There was a big icebox and he opened it. If he'd gone all the way into the kitchen, he'd 'a seen that the iceboxes with the good stuff were locked with a chain and padlock. Anyway, he opens this icebox, and he sees a big bowl of stew. Looks better than what he got for dinner, and plenty left to make a meal. So he finds himself a wooden spoon, and he starts in on that cold stew and eats it all up. Next morning, the family and the guests are all at breakfast, when the butler comes bustling in, mad as a wet hen, and in a voice you could hear in Dublin, says to the master, "M'lord! Someone ate the dogs' dinner!"

Jack grinned. "Did they ever find out who the thief was?"

"Probably not. Them houses was so big, sometimes they'd fill twenty bedrooms with guests. Could have been anyone, but my aunt knew who it was because she was cleaning up the billiard room after the gentlemen's cigars and brandy and such, and she heard a noise, and saw the man tippy-toeing down the stairs. Now I think of it, they probably fired the boot boy for stealing food, when they practically starved those little fellers. That or they whipped the bejesus out of him.

"Life ain't fair, Jack, and don't you forget it. Just be fair your-self, and choose your friends right. Now you finish your good dinner, and you and Max get off to bed. Be glad you don't have to eat the dog's dinner, although if I say so myself, this was a good one."

Exhausted from the evening's excitement, Jack got under his light summer covers, and Max gracefully leapt up, squirmed until he was comfortable, wrapped his tail around himself, and settled against Jack's body. He made a soft blowing sound as Jack scratched him behind the ears, until the two of them fell asleep. Jack woke up in the night when he heard his mother come home. He was awake just long enough to think of the dogs that stayed in the foxholes guarding their sleeping han-dlers, and knew he was safe.

The next morning, when the children arrived at sports group they found that the mother who was in charge of the athletics program during the war had replaced Sarge. The women who had been on the wartime committee had agreed that for the rest of the summer they would each take a week overseeing the sports program. Sarge had already been shipped off the island by an outraged Association Board.

Jack thought that when he and Louise and other junior counselors had told their parents Sarge was a bully, who scared many of the children in the program, and not only the little ones, they hadn't paid enough attention to do anything about it. They needed to see him themselves—drunk and profane—before they acted. He promised himself that when he was a parent, he would act the way his mother did when Sarge suspended him from sports group: he would find out the truth. He had heard his mother and Kathleen talking about whether two women alone were good enough role models for a growing boy, and he decided they were doing just fine. It was too bad, though, that if his dad wasn't going to turn up anytime soon, Peter and Max couldn't come and live with them.

CHAPTER THIRTEEN

THE first weekend in August, Helen was among the women waiting for the Friday evening ferry. Like the others, she had set her hair and polished her fingernails and toenails in the postwar style of "matching lips and fingertips." Before she and Jack set off for the dock, she caught a glimpse of herself in the clouded mirror over the battered oak table in the front hall. For a moment she saw the college girl who had embarked on the train in Philadelphia's Union Station for New Haven weekends with Arthur. It was then that she first met Frank. He had come a long way since those days, she thought.

The Friday night greeting was marred by the final edge of a storm that slammed into the island. The rain beat down in slanting sheets, and the wind was so strong that every bush and tree and the long sea grasses in the marshes along the bay shivered in the unaccustomed chill.

"Some weather," Helen said.

"Seen a lot worse," Kathleen remarked.

"Like what?" Jack asked.

"Like the Hurricane of '38, when you were four," Helen said. "They called it 'The Long Island Express.' Wauregan was evacuated before it hit, but the winds reached 160 miles an hour, and they ravaged the mainland. In one town across the bay a whole movie theater was carried out to sea. If I remember right, there were something like twenty people inside, watching a matinee. Every one of them drowned. When we came back here after the storm, there was a dead shark washed up in front of the post office, and most of the beachfront houses had been swept away. Our house was one of the few left standing."

"What happened to the people who lost their houses?" Jack asked.

"They built new ones," Helen said. "The houses that used to be in the second row became sea-view property, and there was a rush to build farther back before the next summer."

"Is that why the Carters' house is sort of in the woods on the bay side?"

"No. Mrs. Carter's grandfather built it there because he was a sailor and he wanted to be nearer the bay. But more houses than you'd think are only ten years old. In this climate, it didn't take long for them to look like they've been here forever. Luckily, this isn't hurricane season, but we're going to get sopping wet when we go down to pick up Uncle Frank."

"Too bad you did your hair this afternoon," Kathleen said. "That'll be the end of that."

"Well, it's just Frank," Helen said.

"Then why did you bother?" Jack asked. It had given him an odd feeling to watch his mother getting ready.

"Because sometimes it's fun to primp," Helen said.

The wind was too strong and the rain too heavy for Helen and Jack to ride their bikes to the dock. Jack pulled the wagon as they walked against the slanting rain, stuffed into their foul-weather gear, ducking their heads so they could see the path. They had both taken off their glasses, which were useless in the rain, and their nearsightedness added to the sense that they were walking in a dream. Branches whipped around, and in some places, trees were broken, with limbs hanging or fallen on the ground. When they got to the dock, Helen scanned the collection of families huddled together, waiting for the boat. It was nearly impossible to tell one person from another, with everyone dressed in identical yellow gear. Women who didn't have foul-weather overalls wore bathing suits, and their bare legs stuck out below the hems of their slickers. Wet hair hung out of their hoods in hanks, ruining the afternoon's preparations.

The men on the boat were soaked through their city raincoats. They disembarked looking bedraggled, as they sought their families among the yellow-clad crowd. Helen waved to Frank, and he strode toward her, head up, as though it weren't raining. Helen thought he wasn't a man to hunch over to stay dry, and liked him for it. He kissed her lightly on her wet cheek, and shook Jack's hand.

"You've grown in the month since I was last here," Frank said. "You're almost as tall as I am. You look more like your father every time I see you."

Embarrassed, Jack answered, "Sorry about the weather, sir."

"Never mind," Frank said pleasantly. "I'm looking forward to a weekend indoors playing gin rummy. Your mother tells me you're a whiz, but I bet I can still beat you."

"It's supposed to clear later tonight," Helen said. "The storm's on its way out to sea. Meanwhile, let's get out of here before the wind sweeps us into the bay. How about a hot shower and a cold martini?"

"Great," Frank said heartily. He was immensely glad to see Helen's rain-slick face with her healthy tan and clear eyes. In spite of himself, he reached over and pushed a dripping strand of hair off her forehead and back under the hood of her slicker.

As they crossed the island to the Wadsworths' house, they tilted against the wind blowing off the ocean. Frank took over pulling the wagon, in which his wet suitcase and a large sail bag banged around. Occasionally he put an arm around Jack's shoulders, noticing that he wasn't just taller, he was developing bone and muscle and didn't feel like a little boy anymore. His face had begun to thin out and show the shape that would emerge. Frank could see that his eyes had the light of anticipation that was one of Arthur's appealing qualities. Appealing, but naïve, he reminded himself. He knew that each time Jack saw him he hoped he would be able to tell him something about what had happened to his father. But Frank continued to avoid talking about the war, instead salting his visits with reminiscences of scenes from Arthur's earlier life.

This time would be different. He had a pristine sail for Jack, a way of participating in the boat project that Peter and Jack had been working on together. Frank was not going to let Peter Gavin take over his godson—or Helen. He had decided that this weekend he would tell Helen what she needed to know about Arthur. He hoped it would bring them closer.

• • •

They ate a messy dinner of lobsters and buttered corn on news-papers that Kathleen spread on the big oak table in the rough wood paneled dining room. It was lined with glass cases, filled with Arthur's father's collection of stuffed birds from the region of the Great Bay. As the three of them picked their lobsters apart, Frank told Helen and Jack about the intelligence service he was helping to form. As Jack asked him excited questions, Helen could tell he was working up to the idea that Arthur was a secret agent, and had to stay undercover to protect the United States against the "Communist Threat." She feared that Frank's description of the struggle to establish a permanent intelligence organization strengthened Jack's hope that his father was not actually missing, but was part of the team. She did not entirely discount the possibility, but if he had chosen his country over his wife and child, he couldn't care about them as much as she believed.

By the time they had finished dinner, the wind had blown the storm away and the sky was clear and star-filled. Jack went to bed and Helen and Frank sat upstairs on the semi-circular couch in the captain's room, with the brass binnacle between them. Although the storm had moved on, the breakers were still fierce in its aftermath, and the reflected light from the half-moon streamed on the water in a swath that rippled and widened at the horizon. Helen turned off all but one light so they could see the moonlit scene.

They settled down with a bottle of Scotch and two glasses, and Frank remarked that when he was trained to parachute into France, he learned that it was easier to hide on a full moon night than in the dark.

"How can that be?" Helen said.

"Moonlight casts shadows that make ideal hiding places. In the dark, neither the hunter nor the hunted can see. If you stand still, you may well find that you're in the open," he explained.

Frank's face looked strained, and Helen began to feel uneasy.

"About Arthur," Frank said, fidgeting, on the banquette. "I've found out what happened to him."

Helen could see from his expression that he was not about to tell her that her husband had turned up alive and well. Her heart started to thud and she felt light-headed.

"I'm taking a risk," he began. "I'm not supposed to reveal what I know. Since I joined the CIA I've had access to classified files from the war, and I found the documents about our mission. Until then, I couldn't be sure what happened to Arthur. Frankly, I couldn't imagine how he'd survived, but I didn't want to say anything, in case I was wrong."

Helen's sense of dread increased. "I don't think I'm going to like this," she said. Almost as though Arthur were there, she could just barely hear him telling her, as he had before, "Watch out when someone starts a sentence with 'frankly,' or 'honestly,' it's almost always a tip-off that he's lying."

"No," Frank said. "But this has gone on long enough. It's not right for you to live in suspense, and it's bad for Jack, too."

Helen's breathing was tight and shallow.

"Take a deep breath and have a little more of this," Frank said. He poured some more Scotch into her nearly empty glass with a steady hand, but he didn't look her in the eye.

"Go ahead," Helen said in a low voice. She ignored the drink, crossed her arms, and clasped her elbows tightly.

Frank leaned forward, drained his glass, shook the ice cubes, and poured himself another. The room had begun to feel hot, and he stood and shoved the window all the way up. It squeaked and resisted, the damp wood binding as he forced it open.

"I don't like to talk about the war," he said, "but you have to know what we were doing, and why Arthur isn't home."

Helen sat back against the lumpy blue cushions. She tucked her feet under her, picked up the glass, looked down at the whiskey, and decided she would probably choke if she tried to drink it. Holding the glass against her chest, she made herself as small a target as she could for the onslaught of Frank's information.

"As I've told you, Arthur and I were infiltrated into the southwest, in the vicinity of Saint-Jean-de-Luz, near the Spanish border. Our job was to contact the Resistance, be sure they were supplied through Allied airdrops, and transmit information to help the Allies keep track of German troop movements."

Helen's mind was racing. She heard herself interrupt, "My father took me to Saint-Jean-de-Luz a long time ago. We stayed at a Beaux Arts hotel called the Grand overlooking the sea."

Frank continued as though she hadn't spoken. "When we could kill Germans, we did. Sometimes a couple of them would be in the wrong place at the right time for us. Sometimes, working with the maquis, we'd get a whole patrol. Arthur was the radio operator, as you know, but from time to time, we both went out with the Resistance to blow up trains, knock out lines of communication. Whatever we could do to stop them.

"Occasionally, I'd go on a special mission on my own. Because my grandparents were German immigrants, and I was fluent in the language, I could disguise myself as a German officer passing through. If I was picked up, I could try to make a convincing case that I was secretly working for their side.

"Our other mission was to hide downed Allied airmen and others who were in danger and connect them with guides who could get them over the Pyrenees into Spain. By early '44, the Germans had gotten wise, and it wasn't safe to go over our old routes. The Resistance set up camps in the woods as holding places until the routes were safe, or we could find another way to get them out. We lived with them, but when Arthur had to transmit, we had to go into town. We used a different safe house every time. Saint-Jean is small and it wasn't hard for the Germans to track our signals. They'd turn off the electricity zone by zone, until they found the one we were transmitting from. We managed to keep them off base for six months. Arthur had to get on and off the radio fast, and sometimes even take the transmitter to another place. We always had a backup plan."

The curtains were flapping in the chilly wind off the sea, and the room was getting damp. Frank went back to the window and tried to pull it partway down, but it was stuck. He hammered at the frame with the flat of his hand, but the sash wouldn't budge.

"Never mind," Helen said. "Just go on."

Frank stayed on his feet, pacing.

"For God's sake, sit still," she said.

"Sorry," Frank said, sat, and crossed his legs. One knee was jiggling.

"We got into some tight situations. One time, Arthur was in the train station, dressed like a French businessman, carrying a suitcase with the wireless in it. The Gestapo had set up a checkpoint and he was sure he would be caught, until he noticed a young boy, maybe sixteen years old, right behind him in the crowd. He was dragging a duffel bag so heavy he couldn't lift it. Arthur offered to switch, to give him a break. He knew the Gestapo would never suspect the boy of having a transmitter in his case. They both got through the checkpoint, and on the other side Arthur said the boy looked like he was about to burst into tears. When he gave the boy his bag, he asked what was wrong. '*Vous avez sauvez ma vie*,' he said. Arthur thought, What does he mean, I saved his life? Then the boy told him the duffel bag was filled with pistols. When Arthur got back to camp, we had a good laugh," Frank said with an arid attempt at a chuckle. "Not that anything was really funny. Both of them could have been shot if either of their cases had been opened."

"So you're telling me that Arthur was willing to sacrifice a teenage boy for the cause. That's very interesting," Helen said, "but you're taking a long time getting to the point. *What happened to Arthur?*"

"Let me tell it my way," Frank said. "I want you to be able to picture how we were living with the maquisards, so you'll know what it was like for him."

Helen remembered that she had read an article about the Resistance after the war. The French term *maquis* translated as "thicket," because resistance groups often camped in high ground that was covered with scrub growth and made good hiding places. She felt as though her mind was clogging, as Frank spoke. She wanted to hear what he had to tell her, but her brain was trying to shut him out.

Frank said, "The hills where we set up are so heavily wooded they're nearly impenetrable—it's easy to get lost in them. But partway up we found the remains of an old Roman fortress. The partisans figured if the Romans thought it was relatively safe, it probably was.

"We lived with the Resistance, and the men and women waiting to get out for months. We were supplied by Allied airdrops and sympathetic locals who didn't have much themselves, but were willing to help, usually with food and information. In early 1944, as the time for the invasion at Normandy came closer, we were instructed to make life so difficult that the Nazis had to saturate the area with more and more personnel to suppress the partisan activity. That cut down on the number of troops they could send north to the coast, where they suspected the landing would take place. We did a lot of damage, but it was getting more dangerous."

Frank was reliving those days, and he had drifted away from the finale of his story. He refilled his glass.

"Our major assignment took place in June of '44, after the Allied invasion on D-Day. We destroyed train tracks and bridges, and blew up trains carrying backup German troops and equipment that passed through from Marseille. All along the line, the Resistance slowed the Germans' progress, dramatically depleted their numbers, and destroyed their tanks and vehicles. I've learned that the Resistance, the OSS, and the British secret services reported on the movements of forty-three German trains heading toward Normandy. Our group in Saint-Jean-de-Luz was responsible for three of those trains."

"You could have told me this before," Helen snapped. "All you ever said was that Arthur operated the radio, and you both went out on missions."

"I'm trying to give you a picture of what led up to what you want to know," Frank said. "Why I got out and he didn't, and what happened to him."

"You're making a long story of it," Helen said irritably.

"I know," he said. "I don't want to get to the end. I hoped there was even the slightest chance he'd survived. If he'd been sent to a German prison camp that ended up in the Russian sector, the Russians could have shipped him to one of their work camps. That was the track I'd been following."

Helen shivered. "Are you sure you can't get that window shut?"

He stood up, braced himself, and pushed. This time it slid down. He sat back on the banquette across from Helen and made himself look her in the eye.

"On our last day there, I was on a mission and got picked up by the Gestapo. My papers were in order, but they were suspicious anyway. They gave me a real working over, until I started talking to them in German. Then someone got the idea I might not be as loyal an American as the Resistance thought I was. They asked me a lot of questions about my background, and when I told them my grandparents had immigrated from Germany, and assured them we weren't Jews, I persuaded them that if they'd let me go, I would double and give them some information about the Resistance.

"I knew I'd be out of there before they could use me. There was a group going over the Pyrenees that night, and we were scheduled to be with them. Our mission was over and we had a special assignment, to take two children, the only ones left from a prominent family that had been sent to the camps. The children had been in hiding with their old housekeeper, but she was ill and couldn't care for them, and they had an uncle waiting for them in the States."

Helen was sitting up rigidly. It sounded as though Frank had set up a situation in which he might have been able to save himself and Arthur. But she hadn't been there.

"The Germans let me go after I'd given them a false story that made them think I was leveling with them.

"I got back to camp in pretty bad shape, told Arthur what had happened and that we had to move fast. We were scheduled to go to a safe house in the village, one of two next door to each other that had been abandoned and were boarded up, and we went together. Someone from the Resistance would meet us there with the children, he'd make the transmission and tell our contacts to expect us in Spain, and we'd move out fast and join the group.

"We arrived at the safe house before curfew. I was to keep watch downstairs with the children and Arthur would go to the top floor, where the reception was better. If I saw anything, I'd run upstairs to warn him and the four of us would make our escape through a hidden panel in the pantry that led to a tunnel. That would take us to a bakery across the street. The baker was active in the Resistance, and he knew what to do next. Our backup plan was that if only one of us could get the children out, he had to do it, even if it meant leaving the other behind."

Helen had been holding her breath. Now she inhaled deeply, and her chest heaved. She was trying to visualize the street and the house, but all she could see was a sunlit room with flowery wallpaper, a patterned carpet, and a woman knitting, with a yellow dog curled up at her feet, the ghost of a Vuillard painting. A peaceful domestic scene.

Frank saw that she looked hazy and said, "Helen? Are you with me?"

She nodded. "I'm sorry. I had an image of the house. I wanted to see every detail, but of course I couldn't." She sat up straight, and stared so hard at Frank that he felt as though she could see into his mind. "How old were the children?" she asked, imagining what it would have been like if Jack had been there, waiting for his last chance to escape.

"Young. Around five and seven. Scared, but old enough to follow instructions.

"Now comes the part where luck was against us. In these seaside towns, as you know from Wauregan, when the temperature suddenly drops, the fog rolls in. I was downstairs on watch. Summer. Still light. Good vantage point. The street was clear and I could see for blocks. Then the fog swooped in. Within minutes, even the houses across the street were blotted out. The children had just been left with me, they were paralyzed with fear, and I was seriously worried.

"That's when I heard motors. You know how sounds seem louder in the fog. I was praying that it wasn't the Gestapo, until two black cars emerged like dark shapes in a bad dream, coming directly toward the house. I knew we'd had it. They slowed down and stopped, and when a couple of men rushed out of the car, I realized their listening devices had triangulated Arthur's signal." Frank put a hand on his knee to stop his leg from shaking.

"There was no way to get upstairs to warn Arthur and get the kids out in time. I yelled to him. If he had his headset on he wouldn't have been able to hear me, but he might not have put it on yet, and at least he'd have a chance. There was a window onto the roof he might be able to get out of. In that fog he could have climbed across the rooftops and they probably wouldn't have seen him. The other choice was for him to take his cyanide pill. With the children in tow, I didn't have a choice. I slid open the panel, pushed the kids in front of me, and we dropped through the hatch into the tunnel and made our escape."

Frank had nearly lost her. His voice sounded as though it was coming from a long distance away.

"Since there was never confirmation that Arthur had been killed—and you know what meticulous records the Germans kept—I hoped that by some miracle, he was still alive."

"If he'd survived, he would have come home," Helen said. "But it doesn't make sense that if the OSS knew he was dead, they didn't notify me."

"Damn it, Helen. When Arthur joined up, all the wives were told if they didn't hear from their husbands, not to ask any questions. There was always the possibility that you would never know.

"The Gestapo got him. It's clear from the file I found that they did their worst, but he never talked. When they couldn't break him and the Allies were closing in, they shot him. By then, I would guess it was a blessing."

"How could you save yourself and leave your best friend to be tortured and killed?" Helen said, spitting out the words.

"If it hadn't been for that damned fog, I would have spotted the cars and we all would have escaped. At least I could save the children," Frank rattled on.

"And yourself," Helen said sharply. It might be irrational to be angry with Frank, but she was outraged that he was alive, sitting where Arthur should have been, in Arthur's house, when Arthur had suffered and died.

Her shoulders dropped and she whispered, "My poor love."

"I know," Frank said. "I dream about him all the time, and it's gotten worse since I read his file."

Finally, Helen put her face in her hands and sobbed. Frank moved over to sit next to her and held her while she cried.

She shook him off and stood up, but the whiskey and the shock had hit her hard, and she stumbled and banged her shin. "Shit!' she said, and burst into tears again.

Frank put an arm around her waist and helped her down the hall.

In her room, she sat on the edge of her bed and examined her shin. It was bleeding and the skin was already swelling and turning blue. Frank went into the bathroom and she heard him running the water in the sink. He came back with a warm wet washcloth and carefully patted the blood off her leg. "Do you want some iodine and a Band-Aid?" he asked.

"No," she said. "It's better if it heals in the air." Then she took off her shoes, lay down on her back, with her arms crossed over her chest, and began to cry again. The tears rolled into her hair and her ears, and her head ached. Her teeth had been clenched while Frank was talking, her jaw hurt, and her hands had been clasped so tightly they were cramped.

Frank pulled up a chair next to her bed and took one of her hands, rubbing it, then rubbing the other. "Hang on," he said. "I'll be right back."

He went into her bathroom, rinsed out the washcloth, wet it with cold water, and wrung it out. He gently washed the tears off her face, folded the cloth, and placed it on her forehead.

Exhausted, Helen began to doze off, but "Dead. Dead. Dead" ricocheted around in her mind, and she began to cry again.

When Frank thought she was finally sleeping, he removed the washcloth, pulled up the afghan folded at the foot of the bed and carefully covered her, then kissed her on the forehead and quietly left.

Helen didn't sleep for long. She woke up in the dark, sat up, and shoved off the afghan. Tiptoeing, in case Frank was still awake, she went downstairs and made herself a cup of hot milk and honey, spiked with a generous dollop of dark rum. Then she went back to the room that had once been her mother-in-law's bedroom, and that she and Arthur took over when they inherited the house. She lay on the chaise near the window, sipped her milk, and waited for the dawn. There was something reassuring about that room and that piece of furniture. On many late summer afternoons in the past, she had stretched out there, while her mother-in-law sat on the bed with her feet up, and they talked about Arthur and Jack, and shared wisdom that Helen would remember for the rest of her life. After Mrs. Wadsworth died, Helen left almost everything as it was. In the bedroom Helen would never share with Arthur again, an un-glazed pink chintz with lush roses covered the chaise, and was made into curtains and an upholstered headboard. The bobbles on the white chenille bedspread were gradually falling off, but it was as comforting as a baby's blanket.

As she stroked the frayed fabric on the chaise, Helen wished Mrs. Wadsworth were there, so they could comfort each other. Even in her misery, she smiled as she remembered when she had come to her mother-in-law, upset because Arthur was working nearly every weekend and didn't spend enough time with her and Jack. Mrs. Wadsworth had said, "I've told him if he doesn't pay more attention to you and that darling little boy, he'll lose you both. Well, dear, you can divorce my son if you can't stand him anymore, but you can't divorce me."

Helen's father, the Wadsworths, and Arthur had provided all the stability she had known, even though nothing could fully compensate for her mother's illness, the rages and depressions, or the suicide attempts, when Helen saw her mother being rolled out of the house on a gurney. Once she had gone into her parents' room after her mother was taken away and saw blood splashed over the sheets and big blotchy stains and still-wet bloody footprints on the pale carpet.

One after another, she had lost the few people she could count on as family. The remaining witness to her childhood was Kathleen, who had cared for her as lovingly and as tartly as she had cared for Arthur. Now the only security left was what she could give Jack, and their world at Wauregan. Without Arthur, she was not sure she would ever live in St. Paul again. She had begun a new life in New York, and she was even more determined that, at least for the present, that was where she would stay.

The storm had passed through and Helen watched the sun come up over the horizon in the east, got up stiffly, took a long hot bath, and prepared to face what would come next.

She had begun to form a plan, a last connection to Arthur.

CHAPTER FOURTEEN

HELEN decided to wait to tell Jack and Kathleen what she had learned until the weekend was over, Frank had left, and they were alone.

Depending on Jack's reaction, she was considering asking him if he wanted to leave Wauregan and go to France with her to pay tribute to his father's service. If he agreed, perhaps he would be able to start his life at a new school without feeling the emotional suspense that had haunted them both for so long.

Earlier in the summer she had received a letter from an old school friend, the Countess Pauline de Voubray, an American married to a French count whose château a few kilometers outside of Saint-Jean-de-Luz had been in his family since the fifteenth century. It was the unsuspecting, good-natured count who had unwittingly caused offense when he asked a Wauregan banker what he "did." Their château had been occupied by the Germans during the war, and the de Voubrays had been exiled to the servants' quarters, from which they served the occupying officer and his staff. A great deal of damage had been done to the house and its furnishings during the occupation, and the de Voubrays had just completed an expensive renovation. At Pauline's suggestion, they had decided to open a few suites to personally recommended paying guests, to compensate for the cost of the repairs. Pauline had written to invite Helen to come in August and test their skills as professional hosts.

Helen had not planned to go, as it would have interrupted her last summer at Wauregan with Jack before he left for boarding school. Now it occurred to her that if Jack was willing, they might go to France together to see the place where Arthur had conducted his mission, and from which he had been taken to die. It would be a way of saying good-bye, and the de Voubrays might be able to help Jack understand why the work his father had been doing was important.

When she put on her bathing suit after the night of Frank's revelations, she realized that the one person she wanted to talk to about Arthur was Peter. She headed out to the beach, expecting to see him, but was disappointed to find that he wasn't there. She lingered in the water until her fingers were wrinkled and she was too cold to stay in, but he didn't show up.

Peter was avoiding her. He had seen Frank arrive again, and assumed that he was courting Helen. He was still unsettled enough that he didn't think he had the strength to enter a contest for her affection. Frank, he told himself, was more appropriate in age and experience, and, as Jack's godfather, he was already almost part of the family.

When the Judge came downstairs and saw Peter sitting at

the breakfast table, brooding over a cup of coffee, he asked why he was still inside on a beautiful morning. Peter mumbled that Helen was probably swimming with her houseguest, and he didn't want to be a third wheel.

"There's a reason children learn to ride on three-wheelers," the Judge said. "Balance. Don't make assumptions. Helen told me that Frank was coming to see his godson. She didn't say he was coming to see her. And tonight you and I are sitting with her and Frank at the dance. If she wanted to be alone with him and didn't want you there mucking things up, she would have made other arrangements."

"Mmm," Peter said. "Now look who's making assumptions. We know Arthur has to be dead. I bet Frank does, too, and he's just waiting for the official notification so he can carry her off. I've seen the way he looks at her. Lust," he said grimly.

"As compared to 'love'?" the Judge asked.

Peter hesitated. "I don't know," he admitted. "Arthur must have trusted him, or he wouldn't have asked him to be his son's godfather, but there's something about him that's too perfect. Have you noticed how he always seems to do and say exactly the right thing?"

"I haven't paid much more attention than to register that he's there," the Judge said. "Gotta admit, though, he's a good-looking specimen. Reminds me of those propaganda posters the Germans put up showing the ideal Aryan."

"Uh-huh," Peter said glumly.

"If I were young and I was interested in a woman and had the chance to see her every day," the Judge said, "I wouldn't wait for someone else to step in. Of course, that's only if I were really serious." He looked at Peter questioningly.

"How can I expect Helen, who has a teenage son and has been on her own for all these years, to take me seriously when I'm just about to start graduate school? Anyway, I'm too young for her."

"I notice you didn't say she's too old for you," the Judge said pleasantly.

"Of course not," Peter said. "She's ageless."

"But maybe more mature than you are?"

"I'm not so sure," Peter said. "As you know, when you've been in battle, you grow up in ways you never could have imagined."

The Judge looked at his watch. "Since you've missed your morning swim, I suggest you take the opportunity of the dance to show Helen that you're more than just Jack's buddy."

"I'll think about it," Peter said.

Helen had felt awkward about going to the Wauregan dances after Arthur's departure. She didn't like to attend without a partner, but to stay home would be churlish. Most of the war widows came with groups of friends, and the men took turns dancing with them. In past years, she had sat with Sally and Dan Carter and two other couples, but Dan had been getting drunk earlier in the evening, and he danced too close and pretended it was a joke when he dropped his hand from her waist to her backside. With Frank coming to the island for the second time, she was afraid it would imply that she had invited a date, which was nobody's business except hers. So that he would blend in, she had arranged a table for four, at which she would be the only woman. The others would be Frank, Peter, and the Judge. Let the island figure that one out. After her movie date with Peter, she was quite sure that she was not ready to figure it out herself.

When Helen and her three escorts approached the casino, they could hear the dance music from the end of the path. The band, which had come over from the mainland by water taxi and would return when the party was over, was playing songs from before the war. The tunes created an atmosphere of nostalgia for evenings that had been part of the courtship ritual of Waureganites when they were in their teens and in college. But this dance was for married couples. There would be no stag line two men deep, waiting to cut in on the girls; thankfully, there would not be any wallflowers; and with luck, no women who had drunk too much would be found weeping or throwing up in the ladies' room. The evening might provide a reinvigoration of romance when a man—even the husband a woman knew so well—held out his hand in a gesture of invitation, and his wife stood up, felt his arm around her waist, and rested her palm on his shoulder, while they clasped hands and fox-trotted onto the dance floor, perfectly in step.

At Wauregan, women often wore the same evening dresses from one year to the next, rather than appearing in something new each season, and it was reassuring to see a friend in the frock she'd worn last year, and the year before. With the wartime shortage of fabric, many of the women hadn't bought new clothes for longer than usual, and even after having a baby or two, those who had stayed trim could still fit into dresses they'd owned for a decade or more. Helen wore a long strapless white piqué dress from before the war, with a narrow waist and a full skirt. It had once had a pink sash, but she decided that was too girlish, and had replaced it with a black patent leather belt.

The younger men often still wore dinner jackets they'd had in college. When the evening got late and they were hot from dancing, they hung the jackets over the backs of their chairs, and the inside of the collars showed the embroidered name tags that had enabled one college boy to pick out his own dinner jacket from the others on those long-ago dawns when a party finally ended.

On the crowded dance floor, Helen heard Cindy Dart say to her husband in her sweet voice, "Remember when I wore this to Missy McInnes's party on Long Island? That first time you cut in? I thought I would die, I was so thrilled to see you leave the stag line and come toward me."

Helen remembered nights like that, too, when she and a partner would dance their way onto the balcony of a big country house as the music floated out from the ballroom. Sometimes the boy would tip his head back and look at her, and if he saw that she was willing, would bend his head and kiss her. For the most part, they were gentle kisses, without the urgent expectation that more would follow. Nothing ever did: even before she fully understood it, she was Arthur's girl.

Those days were long past, but seated with her three men, she felt flirtatious and young. She had put grief aside for the night and she was surprised to realize that she was having a good time. Frank, Peter, and the Judge took turns dancing with her, cutting in on each other. As she changed partners, she would brush her hair back, and lift it off her damp neck, thank her partner, and turn into the arms of another man.

When it was Judge Gavin's turn, he danced with her formally, so they were far enough apart to look directly at each other. The Judge asked, in his straightforward way, "Is there something between you and Frank Hartman? He seems like a nice man."

"He was Arthur's roommate in college. We're very old friends."

"Are you sure that's all?"

"What makes you ask?"

"I didn't spend forty years in courtrooms without learning something about reading faces. He's seriously interested in you."

"Maybe worried about me," Helen said. "It's to do with Arthur. Not good news."

"Do you want to tell me?"

"I do," Helen said, "but not tonight."

"Well, then, on the subject of your suitors," the Judge said. "There are two men at that table who are in love with you. I'd be the third if I weren't so darned old. When we get back, you decide if Frank and Peter don't look like a pair of rutting stags, if you'll excuse me, waiting for a chance to lock horns and gore each other."

"Come on," Helen said, disingenuously. "Peter is Jack's friend."

"Either you're faking, or you don't know yourself very well."

"Peter is eight years younger than I am," Helen said gamely, looking away. She told herself that while Peter seemed calmer and more grounded than he had at the beginning of the summer, she wasn't sure he was stable enough to undertake a steady relationship with a woman. He was still sleeping on the porch in the afternoons, and it did not take much for him to snap back into warrior mode. One night, when they went on a supper beach picnic with Jack, they had started home after sunset, and Peter and Max walked ahead of them. Peter looked like the point man on patrol, or a gunslinger in the movies, with his body tense and his arms hanging loosely away from his sides, ready to get to his pistol fast.

"Peter is older than his real age," the Judge said. "He's working through what happened to him in the Pacific, and that's good. You look at the other men around here, you'd think everything was hunky-dory, as though they hadn't seen their friends' guts spilling out, and so much blood even the dirt turned red and soggy. I could tell you stories from the last war that would make you wonder how anyone ever recovered from that butchering. If the men who were in combat don't face what they've seen and done, they'll go through the rest of their lives like floorwalkers in department stores. Dressed crisp as you please, carnation in the buttonhole, manners perfect, 'Madam, can I help you?' but who knows what's underneath? Peter's taking it like a man, facing the nightmare. He's one of the ones who'll get past it."

"I think so, too. That doesn't mean he thinks of me as more than a friend."

"How do you think of him? Better answer quickly. Frank's getting up to cut in."

"I think of him," Helen said softly.

When Frank put his arm around her waist and took her hand, and they began to do the two-step to the music they had danced to dozens of times in their long friendship, Helen asked, "You don't have a crush on me, do you?"

Frank tensed. "Why do you ask?"

"Because the Judge thinks you do."

"I wouldn't exactly call it a crush. I'd say that if you ever want me, I'll be there."

"Gosh. How did I miss that?"

"By the time I met you, it was too late, so I sat back and nursed my wounds."

As they bobbed around to a lively rendition of "Mountain Greenery," Frank said, "I guess you'll officially be declared a widow as soon as the bureaucracy gets around to it. Now maybe we can get to know each other in a different way."

His arm tightened on her waist and he pulled her closer, so they were dancing body to body, and she did not resist. It felt good to be near him, but she had always thought of him as her husband's friend, even in these past years when he had been so attentive. She didn't know if that could change, or if she wanted it to.

He had had more than his usual quotient of liquor, and his mind was jumping around, opening doors he usually kept closed. He hated Arthur and his damned ghost, as he danced with Helen in the Wauregan Casino, and her shiny pageboy brushed his cheek.

The band took a break, and Helen went to the ladies' room, where two women standing at the mirror were complaining that their entire wardrobes were out of style. The current issues of *Vogue* had definitively proven that they would have to go shopping that fall. The pages were filled with dramatic photographs of Christian Dior's "New Look," its narrow sweaterlike tops, small waists, and yards of material, making up skirts so full they would take up most of the backseat of a taxi. Dior, and those who copied him, had instantly made the broad-shouldered jackets and short narrow skirts of Adrian, the popular wartime designer, look outdated. The new shape was available from couture to ready-to-wear, but there were few women at the Wauregan dance that night who looked as though they had read a fashion magazine published later than 1946.

As Helen was applying her lipstick, she saw Sally Carter huddled in a corner in a hushed conversation with two other women. Sally gestured to her to come over. "Wait till you hear this," she said, in a half whisper. "Let me fill her in, girls.

"Molly went outside for a cigarette—they should find a way to make this place fireproof, so we could smoke inside. What fun is a party without a cigarette? Anyway, Molly was having a drag on her ciggie when she heard moans from the bushes."

"Uh-oh," Helen said.

"Umm. But you'll never guess who it was," Molly said.

"I hope it was a happily married couple who couldn't wait to get home and hop into bed, so they did it right here," Helen said primly.

"You're such a Pollyanna," Ginger Ashforth said, and giggled.

"Don't laugh," Molly said. "This isn't funny, and I wish I hadn't seen it. I promise I didn't go snooping to see who was necking back there."

"Go on," Sally said. "Tell her."

Molly had turned pale under her tan. "It was Steve Foster and Ben Alexander," she said. "I saw Ben zipping up his fly."

"You don't think they just went outside to take a leak?" Helen asked.

"Hardly. When Ben had zipped up, he turned to Steve and kissed him on the lips. I dropped my cigarette in the sand pail, and got back in here like a shot."

"That would explain why Liz Foster did her striptease," Sally said. By then, there was hardly any adult on the island who hadn't heard about Liz's performance behind the sheet. "To try to entice Steve back into her bed."

"I know Steve has been having some problems readjusting to married life," Helen said, "but this . . ."

"As though they all haven't," Ginger said. She looked into the mirror of her gold compact and patted powder over her freckles with a down puff. "If that story gets out, it's going to stay alive until Wauregan is swept into the sea."

"Listen to me, you three," Helen said in a clear, cold tone. "If I ever hear about this from anyone else, I'll know one of you squealed, and I'll find out who it was and never speak to you again. Think of Liz and Steve, and Ben and Pam, and their children, and all the other children here, including yours, who are too young to know about things like that. I'm sorry I know it myself."

"I wasn't thinking," Molly said. "Can we all just forget it ever happened?"

"Helen's right," Sally said. "For once, we should keep our mouths shut. Anyway," she added, and put a hand over Helen's fist, which was clenched, as though she was ready to sock someone, "who would want to lose Helen Wadsworth as a friend?"

When Helen went into one of the cubicles, she heard Ginger say, "Whew! The last time anyone talked to me like that was the nun who taught me in first grade."

"Really?" Molly said, raising an eyebrow. "I didn't know you were a Roman. I see you in church here every week."

"Oh no, I never was. My father was sent to a town where

Granddaddy had a mill, to learn to run the business. The only decent school was run by the Catholics. Don't think I didn't consider becoming a nun, though, like every other little girl in the place. Sometimes I wish I'd taken Holy Orders and missed all this."

"Right," Sally said. "In a convent where the sisters aren't allowed to talk?"

"Well, maybe not," Ginger said, and laughed, and Helen heard the door to the ladies' room swing shut.

She shook her head, arranged her dress, and walked over to the sink to look in the mirror. I ought to look heartbroken, she thought, and I am, but I look like a girl who's having the time of her life. How odd. Then she smiled at herself and thought she might as well have some fun before the truth about Arthur sank in. She ran a comb through her hair, which shone from the sun, freshened her lipstick, bared her lips to be sure none was on her teeth, and went back to the party.

As she threaded her way past the band, the piano player looked at her and winked, and she winked back and headed toward her table. Seeing her coming through the crowd, Frank, Peter, and the Judge stood. She was only a few feet away when the casino was plunged into darkness—the joke on the island was that the generator never failed to fail. She took a step toward the table and bumped into a man. It was too dark to see him, but he smelled familiar. By the middle of the evening, most of the men smelled of whiskey and cigarettes, and late at night, some of them reeked of nervous sweat. But there was no cigarette smell on this man. Peter, she thought. Peter didn't smoke; he had told her that the smell of a cigarette could give away the position of an entire troop in the jungle. The men could smoke when they were at base camp, but he quit when he realized that he only really needed a cigarette when he was out on a mission. She leaned toward him, and he stroked her arm, until he found her hand and held it.

"Peter?" Helen whispered.

"Shh," he said. He turned and touched her bare shoulders, and her cheek, and leaned in to kiss her. Helen put her arms around his neck and joined her kiss to his, until she could feel the heat of it throughout her body. Then someone opened the casino doors to let the moonlight in, and they hastily drew apart.

Peter gently put his hands on her shoulders and held her away from him. "Thank you," he whispered. Even after the generator started up again and the lights went on, he was still holding her and they were looking intently at each other.

As the music began again, Peter said, "Meet me later on the beach in front of your house?"

"Yes," she said in a low, hoarse voice.

"Good. One hour after we get home should be safe," Peter said.

The dance floor was filling, and Helen said, "No time is safe, but at least Jack is out for the night." They began to laugh, as though one of them had said something hilariously funny.

"Help," Helen begged; her eyes were streaming and she couldn't stop.

Peter took a deep breath and regained control. "Remember the philosopher William James, who started the pragmatist movement?"

Helen stopped laughing with a snort. "What brings him to mind? Isn't he a little arcane for the dance floor of the casino?"

"I read a lot when I was in the clinic. What made me think of James was something he wrote: 'A sense of humor is just common sense, dancing.'"

"And your common sense tells you we should meet on the beach, and that's funny?" Helen looked up at Peter. Her eyes were bright.

"Something like that," Peter said.

"We'd better save the philosophy for another time. Let's go back to the table before we make more of a spectacle of ourselves than we already have," Helen said, squeezed his hand, then let go.

Frank and the Judge were not the only people who noticed the way Helen and Peter were standing, and in the part-light from the moon coming through the open door, some of them had seen them kissing. Half of Wauregan would hear about it by morning. But as Helen looked at Peter in his black bow tie and white summer dinner jacket, with his shirt crisp against the tan of his face, she didn't care.

The failure of the generator had drawn a line across the evening, and after the lights were restored, the band played "Good Night, Ladies," and the Waureganites went home to talk about the party and each other. Or, for some fortunate couples, to expand upon the romantic feeling that music, a couple of drinks, and a party can ignite.

When Sally and Dan Carter returned from the dance, Louise was awakened by the slamming of the screen door. She heard her mother and father going into the kitchen below her room. She got out of bed and lay on the floor, peering at a sliver of light from downstairs, trying to hear what her parents were saying. Louise was increasingly curious about the adult world, and the atmosphere in her household had been so tense she had gotten into the habit of eavesdropping on her parents in the hope of deciphering their behavior.

"How 'bout one more drinky," she heard her father say.

"Not for me, darling. I got a chill on the way home. It feels more like Labor Day than July," her mother said. "I'm going to make myself a cup of hot milk with honey. Helen's remedy for everything. It should sop up some of that gin. Pour yourself a drink if you want one."

Louise heard her parents moving around the kitchen, but couldn't make out what they were saying, until they settled within earshot at the kitchen table.

"Did you know Peter and Helen were having a thing?" Dan asked.

"Not really. I thought if it was anyone, it would be Frank Hartman. She and Peter have been together a lot, but Jack was usually with them, or the Judge. I thought they were making up a sort of family out of two incomplete households. On the other hand, Helen's been alone for a long time, and Peter is pretty irresistible."

"Just what I want to hear: my wife finds a handsome young ex-Marine head case irresistible. Very nice, Sally," Dan said, slurring slightly. "I used to wonder if I could trust you while I was away. It killed me when I was in the North Sea with U-boats and German subs everywhere, and you were serving coffee and donuts to men on leave at the canteen, with that goddamn red hair of yours like a come-and-get-me beacon."

"It wasn't a canteen. I was at Grand Central Station." They

had had this conversation too many times. "The men were on their way someplace else. I doubt I ever saw any of them for more than ten minutes. Give it a rest. As for Peter, I am not interested. You are my husband. I am faithful to you in thought and deed. Got it yet?"

Dan sighed so loudly that Louise could hear him from upstairs.

"I'm sorry, Sally. I've been wanting to tell you something," he began. "I know I've been cranky lately."

Sally had her back to him, as she poured the hot milk into a cup, and waited to hear what he had to say.

She sat down at the table and put her hands around the cup to warm them. The table was covered with oilcloth in a flow-ered pattern. It reminded her of Dan's family textile company, which had made the special waterproof coating for field jackets and tents and that was now used for raincoats. His was one of the businesses that was still doing well, despite the postwar slump.

"It's not just the war. That was bad for everyone. It's what's happening to the veterans who come in looking for jobs. Even with a couple of thousand employees, we don't have a lot of openings. We've had to let some of the women go so the men who worked for us before can have their jobs back. But every day there's a line of men outside the plants, looking for work. Some of them come in their uniforms, 'fruit salad' all over their chests, hash marks on the sleeves, rank insignias. Enlisted men. Officers. We've hired a few dozen of them, mostly as salesmen, but they don't have any experience in our business, and they say that's what everyone tells them. Remember the movie we saw where the air force captain, genuine hero, comes home and the only job he can get is as a soda jerk in a drugstore? Whoever wrote that wasn't kidding.

"I have you and Louise. I own my company. I have Wauregan; and these guys who did a lot more than I did, fighting so we could live like this, are pumping gas, if they're lucky.

"I know I've been pretty tough to live with and I'm sorry for taking it out on you and Louise. The good news is when we open the new plant in North Carolina, we'll have a couple of hundred new jobs and we'll be able to start hiring again. Meanwhile, guilt can make a guy act ugly, and I apologize."

"Thank you for telling me," Sally said, and reached across the table and stroked the back of his hand.

Louise was relieved. It sounded as though she might get her real father back, instead of the scary, unpredictable man who came home from the war. But what really interested her was that Jack's mother and Peter were, as she thought of it, "in love." When she went back to bed, she decided to get up before her parents were awake and ride her bike over to Jack's to give him the good news. She thought he would be happy to hear that Peter, whom Jack worshipped, might even become his stepfather.

CHAPTER FIFTEEN

THE night of the dance, Jack had been invited to a scavenger hunt, followed by a sleepover party. The hostess, Mary Stamford, was one of the war widows who had chosen not to attend the dance. She was an earnest soul, who had inherited her grandfather's steel fortune, and spent most of her time trying to give it away. She looked like a muffin, but she had a lot of her ancestors' grit, and she had made it clear to her only child, a boy named Andy, that no one deserved to have that much money if he had not earned it. She was determined to raise her son to be motivated, enterprising, competitive, and compassionate. She considered her thrice-married brother a disappointing example of how great wealth can undermine ambition. His principal accomplishment was that he was the president of the Newport beach club—known to its members, and those who would have liked to be invited to join as "the Beach," as though it was the only stretch of sand worth having access to.

Helen liked Mary, although she wished she were a little less earnest. Once, when Helen was joking about the habits of adolescent boys, Mary took umbrage, thinking that she was talking about Andy. It had required a diplomatic explanation for Helen to make it clear that she was just preparing herself, as Mary was, for the awkwardness of being a single mother of a boy growing up without a father.

Mary's husband had been an obstetrician, which, as she remarked in an unexpectedly wry tone, was the wrong specialty for the kind of work he was required to do in the war. After he was killed when his hospital behind the lines in France was bombed, Mary made sure that her brother didn't step in as Andy's surrogate role model. She wanted her son to be tough and self-reliant. In the fall, she was sending him to school in Scotland, which she knew well. Her grandfather had spent many of his later years there, living in a castle, which, she admitted, was undeniably grand, but after all, he had earned the money himself. Some British friends had told her about a new boarding school that was already famous for its Spartan environment. Among its quirks was that the boys were only allowed to take cold showers, as though hot water would melt their spirit.

Mary had explained, "It's all part of the philosophy of *mens sana in corpore sano*—a sound mind in a sound body."

"Right," Helen said. "As first spoken by the Roman philosopher Juvenal. I'm glad I can remember something from school."

"The headmaster was forced to flee Germany in 1933 when he spoke out against the Nazis. What I like is that the school has an international outlook, and teaches independence, responsibility, and community service," Mary said. "The only problem is that Andy is angry that I'm separating him from his friends for the next three years. I probably shouldn't have told him about the cold showers," she said and choked out a laugh.

"So now he's furious with me. He's always been so good-natured and obedient. I'm afraid I've been breaking my own rules and pampering him. That's why I'm giving this scavenger hunt party."

Jack had arrived at the Stamfords' with his sleeping bag, a small suitcase containing his pajamas, bathrobe, toothbrush, and a change of clothes for the next morning—and a sense of relief. As Helen and her escorts prepared to leave for the dance, he felt jealous as he watched his mother smoothing a hand over her pageboy, and checking the top of her strapless dress to be sure it wasn't slipping. Helen had lost weight since Arthur was declared missing, and the dress gapped.

When she was getting dressed, she had called Kathleen in to help her and the two of them tried to pin it on the inside with safety pins, but the stays that held the dress up got in the way, so she was trying to stand up straight in the hope that good posture would keep the dress in place. When Frank came down in his evening jacket, and the Judge and Peter arrived, she looked pretty and flirtatious. Jack didn't like it, even though one of the men was ancient, another was the godfather he'd known all his life, and Peter was as much his friend as Helen's.

As the evening at the Stamfords' progressed, Jack became increasingly uneasy. The scavenger hunt didn't distract him, even when Andy suggested that for "something round" they bring home the rim of one of the used condoms that occasionally washed up on the sand. "It would be perfect," he said. "Mummy would be disgusted." Jack was glad they hadn't been able to find one, dreading that he would have to pick it up. Instead, they collected a dead tennis ball someone had left on the beach, probably after throwing it into the surf for a dog to retrieve.

After dinner and a backgammon tournament, Mary Stamford announced that it was time for bed, and the boys slid into their sleeping bags. They talked for a while, but eventually, the conversation dropped off. Jack lay there, listening to Andy's gerbil going around and around on its squeaky wheel, and the other boys snoring and snuffling and muttering in their sleep, and he worried about what might be going on at home. When he was the only one still awake, he quietly rolled up his sleeping bag, and slipped out of the house in his bathrobe and pajamas. He had brought his suitcase in a wagon trailed behind his bike, but the wheels squealed, so he left the wagon on the Stamfords' porch with his possessions in it, mounted his bike, turned on his flashlight, and rode home. He was preparing to protect his mother from an atmosphere he vaguely remembered from the time when his father was still around. With all those men paying attention to her, he felt he should be on guard.

No one saw him arrive; Helen and Frank had not returned yet, and Kathleen was asleep on the third floor. He got into bed, and lay there, waiting for his mother.

The Wadsworth house was the last one in the front row. To its right was an empty stretch of beach, with dunes that undulated, changing with the wind and the tides. Jack's room was on the corner. The windows on one side faced the sea, and on the other, the bare sand. Even on the hottest nights, the room was airy with the windows open, and it was rare that he had to use the fan that groaned and whirled on his bureau.

At the beginning of the summer, soon after he went to bed, Jack had heard noises coming from the dunes. There was laughter, and then whimpering sounds, like an animal in pain. Wauregan did not have any natural predators that could hurt an animal bigger than a mouse, but Jack had heard some older boys talking about a small yapping poodle with rancid breath and bald patches that belonged to the elderly Mrs. Rheinhold. The boys had been joking about kidnapping it and disposing of it. Even though it was just talk, some of the things they proposed doing were disturbing. Helen had already told Jack that Wauregan was no place for teenagers. There wasn't enough to do to keep them out of trouble, and joking about torturing a dog was definitely a symptom of boredom. He and Helen had been discussing other summer activities off the island he might want to consider, so he would only be at Wauregan for a few weeks each season. "It's not that I don't trust you," Helen said. "I want you to have different experiences. You'll probably be working at Wadsworth Grain in the summers once you go to college, so this is the time to broaden your horizons."

The night Jack heard the animal noises in the dunes, he tiptoed downstairs with his flashlight, and went out onto the porch to investigate, with the idea of saving whatever creature was suffering. The moon was bright enough that he didn't need to turn on the light to see that an older boy and girl had made a nest in a blanket laid in the curve of a dune. The boy was on his knees, bending back, raising his hips to zip his fly; the girl was fastening her bra, adjusting her breasts, then raising her arms to pull on her sweater. Jack hurried back inside, both stimulated and frightened by what he had seen.

On other occasions when he heard similar noises, he did not investigate. He was curious, but he was not ready to see more.

Jack was on alert when he heard his mother come home. She said good night to Peter and the Judge outside the back door, and he heard her and Frank mounting the stairs, talking quietly. He listened until both their doors closed, then sighed in relief. His mother was in her own room, at the opposite corner of the house, with Uncle Frank safely ensconced between her and Jack. He heard Frank's door opening, heard his footsteps heading for the hall bathroom, listened to the water running, the door opening again, and finally, Frank's door closing with a recognizable rattle. When the lights were on in the bedrooms on the sea side of the house, they cast a beam on the sand, and Jack watched until Frank's light went out, and then his mother's.

He was beginning to feel drowsy when he heard a door open again. It sounded like his mother's; she had her own bathroom, but sometimes she got up to make herself a hot drink to help her sleep. There was no sound of Uncle Frank's door opening, so she wasn't going in there, which was good. She wouldn't come into his room, because she thought he was still at Andy's. He was tempted to pop out and show her that he was home, but he didn't want her to ask why he had left the Stamfords'.

He didn't really understand it himself. The best excuse he could come up with was that the gerbil made too much noise, and he didn't think his mother would accept that.

Her tread on the stairs was light, and for a little time, there was silence, until Jack heard the screen door to the porch open with a muted whine. His mother must have been trying to be very quiet, because the door screeched unless it was moved very slowly.

That was enough for him to get out of bed and look out his window. He saw his mother, wrapped in a beach towel, heading for the sea. He thought of all the times she had warned him never to swim alone because even the strongest swimmers can get out of their depth, and he decided to watch to be sure she was safe. Then he saw a man with a towel around his waist come out of the shadows and stride toward her. Jack had a moment of panic, afraid the man was Sarge, or someone else who could harm her, but it was Peter.

Jack saw him approach Helen, put his arms around her waist, and saw her lean her head against him. They stood that way, then turned toward each other. She tipped her face up and Jack saw them kissing. He could feel his own face getting hot with embarrassment and an angry sense of betrayal. He had thought Peter was his friend. Helen wrapped her arms around Peter's neck, her towel fell down around her ankles, and Jack saw that she was not wearing a bathing suit. He wanted to stop looking, but he couldn't move away from the window. They stepped apart, Peter pulled off his towel, took Helen's hand, and as Jack watched, they ran into the water together. Both of them were naked. He couldn't bear to see any more. He turned away from the window, got back into bed, and pulled the sheet over his head.

In the room next to Jack, Frank was stretched out on the window seat, watching the light from the moon rippling over the water, and thinking about his options. He had seen the aftermath of Helen and Peter's kiss at the dance, and had been seized by jealousy and desire, but he decided that whatever was going on between them was unlikely to outlast the summer. Now he saw them on the beach, naked and holding hands, as they ran into the sea.

He was annoyed at himself for not having realized earlier that Helen, who had just learned that Arthur was dead, might need to feel more alive herself. During the war, he had seen how often sex was the antidote to death. If he had been more assertive, maybe he, instead of Peter, could have been with her.

Feeling queasy, he stood up, paced around the room, then returned to the window seat. Hating himself, Peter, Arthur, and even Helen, he lay there, propped on one elbow, with his hand under his chin, and watched. The next morning he would notice when he was shaving that he had scratched his face in anguish as he saw Helen and Peter come together in the water.

Upstairs, Kathleen was sleeping in her single bed, which she had pushed against the wall under the window so she could enjoy watching the night sky in solitude. As the moon crossed the sky, a strong beam shone on her face, and she woke up and looked out. At first she thought she was dreaming, but what she saw brought her fully awake. Peter and Helen were standing in the waves, neither of them with a stitch on, and Helen had her legs wrapped around Peter's waist. Kathleen's experience of sex was minimal; she had come to America to train as a children's nurse when she was eighteen years old, and her strict Catholic upbringing had put the fear of God in her when it came to men. She was barely twenty, living with a family and taking care of a baby and a three-year-old, when she went to one of the Irish dances on her night off, met Jimmy Corrigan, a handsome young cop whose ears stuck out, reminding her of one of her brothers, and the next thing she knew, they were courting. They had married suddenly because Jimmy was going overseas to fight in the Great War. The family she worked for gave her two weeks for a honeymoon, and she and Jimmy drove to Niagara Falls.

Jimmy was a devout Catholic boy, and she was his first woman. Between them, they figured out the basics, but when Kathleen thought back on those nights, what stayed with her was how soft his skin was, and how young he felt when she held him. Less than a month later, he was shipped overseas. He had just turned twenty-one when he was killed in the mud of Flanders. Kathleen had never had another man, nor wanted one.

Nevertheless, she told herself, you didn't need a lot of experience to recognize that Helen and Peter were making love. "Good," she said aloud. "It's about time," then turned over and went back to sleep.

When they emerged from the sea, Peter couldn't tell if the water streaking down Helen's cheeks was seawater or tears. They walked quietly back to the place on the sand where they had left their towels, and Peter held up the towel she had tossed on the sand, wrapped it around her, and held her close.

"Can we talk?" Peter asked. "Or are you too cold?"

"Freezing. Come on up to the porch and I'll get a couple of blankets."

When they were each snug in warm wool, huddled together on the wicker couch, Peter turned to face her, and they spoke of love, with Peter entreating her, and Helen crying silently.

"I know you still hope Arthur is alive," Peter said. "I don't blame you. He's your husband. But you have to know how slim the chances are. Pretty much everyone who made it through the war has been accounted for. So have most of the ones who didn't. I don't know where that leaves us."

"No," she said. "Last night Frank told me Arthur is dead."

"Is he sure?" Peter asked.

"Yes. He read his file. It's classified, but now Frank's in the CIA, he can get at stuff. He thinks I'll be notified pretty soon."

"Oh, Helen," Peter said. "I'm sorry."

"I'm devastated, but I'm relieved," she said. "I wanted to believe he was alive, but it seemed so unlikely. I've been in love with the idea of Arthur all this time, but it's been six years since he went overseas with the OSS, and I've almost forgotten what he looks like, except in pictures, or in dreams. He hasn't seemed real to me for a while. Maybe that's why I could do what we just did. Or maybe it was a way of pushing death away. Feeling alive. I've been faithful to him until tonight.

"But let's be realistic. This has to be a one-time adventure. Think about it. When you're a virile fifty-year-old, I'll be closing on sixty."

"No," Peter said. "Let's think about now. You don't seem to be any age to me. I can't imagine that will ever change."

"About you and me?" Helen said. "In a way, I knew Arthur wasn't coming back, but now that I'm sure, it's different. Meanwhile the whole island saw us kissing at the dance. I don't want to be paired up before I'm ready."

"No one saw us. It was dark."

"Remember, someone opened the doors? Anyway, we looked like we'd been kissing and I was on my way back from the ladies' room. I'd just reapplied my lipstick."

"I don't get it about lipstick. Is it supposed to keep men away from women they're not supposed to kiss, because it leaves a telltale smear?"

"No, Peter. It's supposed to make us look like movie stars. Don't change the subject. If Jack hears about what happened at the dance and confronts me, I'm going to say that when the generator quit, you were holding on to me to be sure I didn't trip in the dark, and the Wauregan gossips made it into something else. Will you back me up?"

"Of course," Peter said. "Could we go back to what Frank told you? How come he got out, and Arthur—his partner—didn't?"

"Something to do with fog and a surprise raid by the Gestapo," Helen said. "Arthur and Frank were supposed to take two children out over the Pyrenees that night, and he said there was no way both of them could escape and save the children, too."

Peter nodded. Maybe Frank could have saved Arthur, and maybe not. And maybe the reason he was suspicious was that Frank was too close to Helen.

"Don't tell even your grandfather about Arthur. Frank found out by snooping in some CIA files he wasn't supposed to see. I'm going to tell Jack and Kathleen when the weekend is over, but even they can't say anything until we get official notification.

"When you go back to Yale, you should stop thinking about the older woman you thought you cared about the summer you recovered your equilibrium after the war. Can you do that?"

"No," Peter said. "I want to meet you on the beach every night for the rest of the summer and make love to you."

"That's what I want, too," Helen said and he could see her smile, white in the moonlight. "Let's hope we don't get much rain."

Fortunately, for the next couple of weeks the weather was dry.

CHAPTER SIXTEEN

LOUISE arrived at the Wadsworths' before seven o'clock on Sunday morning. Kathleen had just come down to the kitchen, and Louise asked if she could go upstairs and wake up Jack. "It's such a beautiful day," she said disingenuously, showing her braces in what was meant to look like an innocent smile.

"Didn't you know? Jack had a sleepover at Andy's house last night," Kathleen said.

"His bike's in the rack," Louise said. "Maybe he came home early."

"You can go and see if he's in his room," Kathleen said, "but bike or no bike, I doubt it."

As Louise mounted the stairs, she was thinking it was good that Peter had replaced Mr. Wadsworth at the helm of the catboat, since Mr. Wadsworth was almost certainly dead. She discounted Jack's persistent, but in her opinion, hopeless dream that one day his father would step off the ferry, drop his briefcase into the red wagon Jack had pulled down to the dock, kiss his mother, and give Jack a manly hug.

Louise was not the first visitor to the Wadsworths' that morning. Just after dawn, Max had pushed the back door open with his nose and trotted upstairs to Jack's room. Hearing him scratching at the door, Jack woke up and let him in. He was idly stroking the dog as the two of them lay in bed, and trying to memorize the way Max looked. After the summer, it would be a long time before he saw him again. He was admiring his big furry paws and his mixtures of colors, blacks and brown and that reddish gold. Good for camouflage, he thought. As he rubbed Max, the dog stood and stretched with his hindquarters in the air and his tail high, then subsided again, lying nearly flat with his head between his paws, looking at Jack with his golden-brown eyes. Jack noticed that he had lost more patches of hair. Peter said it was one of the symptoms that he was still suffering from the parasites that infested him in the jungles, and they had to be careful not to exhaust him, as it was hard to recover from the organisms that had invaded his body.

Jack had been excited about working on *Red Wing* that afternoon, especially now that they had Uncle Frank's sail for the upcoming launch. Peter believed she was nearly seaworthy, but Jack didn't even want to see Peter after last night. Before he had to decide, there was breakfast, and then church. While he was balancing Peter's treachery against his desire to finish *Red Wing*, Louise perfunctorily knocked on his door, opened it, and walked in.

"I told Kathleen you were here," Louise said. "How come you left Andy's?"

"That gerbil of his was squeaking around on its wheel and I couldn't sleep," Jack said. "Anyway, I don't like Andy much this summer. He's always looking for trouble. What time is it?"

"Early," Louise said. "Seven?"

"What are you doing here?" Jack had been sleeping in his pajamas, and he could feel his morning erection poking out of the gap in the front where the pajama bottoms tied. He sat up and crossed his legs Indian style, and bunched the light blanket over his waist, holding the covers until his erection settled down. It had nothing to do with Louise, he told himself. It was just the way he woke up, even if no one was in the room.

"I have news," Louise said. "About your mother."

"What kind of news?"

"Good news. I think she's in love!"

"I hate girls. All you ever think about is love. You should get rid of those stupid romance magazines before they twist your mind, and before your mother finds them. My mother is in love with my father, and that is not news for *True Confessions* magazine."

"Listen to me. Last night at the dance? I heard my parents talking when they got home. The lights went out at the casino, that old generator again, and when they went on again, guess who was kissing who?"

"I don't want to know. That's girl stuff."

"Everyone in this place is going to know by the end of church this morning, so you might as well hear it first. It was Peter. Your mother was kissing Peter."

"Of course she was. She always kisses Peter and the Judge. They're friends."

"Not like that, dummy. Really kissing him. 'By the light,

by the light of the silvery moon . . .'" she sang. "This is really exciting. You might get Peter for a stepfather, and think how nice that would be."

"Louise," Jack said sharply. "I have a father. If my mother was kissing Peter, it was just a friendly kiss. Get out of my room. I want to get dressed."

Louise was startled. She had never seen Jack so upset, not even when Sarge kicked him out of sports group. She could not imagine a better stepfather than Peter, and the fact that Max was part of the package made it practically perfect. Very few real fathers, certainly not her own, spent as much time with their children as Peter had spent with Jack that summer. He was definitely good dad material.

She pulled herself together and walked out of the room. It didn't take a genius to understand that Jack was stricken at the idea of Peter and his mother getting together. If that happened, he would know his mother had given up hope that his father would come home.

Jack lay down, spread himself over Max's big, comforting body, and hugged him until the dog squirmed to get free. He had vowed that he would believe that his dad was alive until there was undeniable proof that he had been killed. He abruptly decided he would never sail *Red Wing* with anyone except his father. What he had seen last night was awful enough. If the whole island was going to be talking about his mother and Peter, it was a disaster.

He went into the hall bathroom and washed his face in cold water and rubbed it hard with a dry towel until the skin was pink and the place on his nose that was peeling from the sun was nearly raw. Then he dressed in long pants and a white shirt for church, and went down the hall to knock on his mother's door. Sleepily, Helen called out, "Who is it?"

"Me," Jack said. "Can I come in?"

Helen looked at the clock by her bedside, a Tiffany traveling clock that had been a wedding present, and had the date of her marriage engraved on the silver frame. "What are you doing home? I thought you were at Andy's," she said sleepily. She felt both languid and tingly after her night with Peter.

"I was," he said. "I left."

"Can you tell me why later?" Helen asked. "If it isn't catastrophic, how about going back to bed until the sun's really up?"

"No!" Jack said. "The sun *is* up. I want to talk to you."

Helen slid upright on her elbows, pulled the sheet under her arms, and said, "Okay, come in."

She patted the bed, inviting Jack to sit down, but he stood defiantly just inside the doorway. He didn't want to get too close to his mother, who had been kissing a naked man a few hours earlier. Max stood alertly at his side, sensing the tension.

"I'm not working on *Red Wing* with Peter anymore," Jack said.

"What are you talking about?"

"I'm talking about my father. It's Dad's boat. I want to wait and sail it with him," Jack said, his voice cracking.

"It wasn't Dad who's been helping you restore it all summer."

"I don't care. It isn't Peter's boat. Peter's around here too much, anyway. I heard about you and him at the dance, and I'm ashamed to be your son if you act that way when Dad may be in a prison camp somewhere, or doing a secret job for the government. If I don't see Peter, can Max still come over? Max is okay, aren't you, old boy? Anyway, we've almost fixed

Red Wing, and Dad and I can finish her when he comes back."

"And if he doesn't?" Helen asked. She was considering whether she should tell him what she had learned. At least it would explain that, whatever he had heard, she was not being unfaithful to his father. But before she could decide, Jack turned away and closed the door behind him.

When Helen went downstairs for breakfast, she found Jack and Frank already at the table. Frank liked to linger over what Kathleen called "a good Irish breakfast" of sausages, crisp bacon and scrambled eggs, toast with the jelly Kathleen made from the island's beach plums, fresh squeezed orange juice, and multiple cups of strong coffee. He appreciated breakfast more than he could have imagined before he lived with the partisans in the woods, where even squirrel meat was precious. Jack was making toast soldiers and dipping them in his soft-boiled eggs, then sucking the egg off the end of the toast, purposely ignoring Kathleen's reminder that he should bite off the eggy bit and eat it tidily. When Helen came in, Frank internally flinched before he stood and said good morning. Jack didn't look up, but continued to dip his toast.

Helen sat down, unfolded her napkin, and prepared to lie. "I haven't even had breakfast," she said, "and Jack has already told me there's a rumor that Peter and I were kissing at the dance, and now he doesn't want to work on *Red Wing* with him anymore. Wauregan is a small place. We all see so much of each other, we get tired of the same old stories, and anything that sounds possible gets made into a big deal. Last night when the generator went out, I was coming back from the ladies' room and I bumped into Peter. He held on to me to keep me from wandering away from the table, and so I wouldn't trip. People saw us and drew the wrong conclusions. You were there, Frank. Can you tell Jack that the rumor is false?"

Frank took a sip of his coffee, looked Jack in the eye, and said, "Your mother is telling the truth. Small communities breed gossip. I've been looking forward to coming back one more time before the end of the summer when *Red Wing* is finished, to see you and Peter set sail on her. I hope you'll change your mind."

"Why can't I sail her with you instead?"

"Because I didn't restore her with you. Peter did," Frank said. His coffee tasted bitter, and he pushed away the plate with his half-finished breakfast.

"Mother?" Jack said.

Helen thought that Frank had lied with remarkable ease, considering that he was likely to be jealous. It was harder for her. "I'm looking forward to seeing you out on the water," she said. "I'm sure your father would be proud of all the work you've done."

"Okay," Jack said. He knew his mother and Frank were lying, and that kissing was only part of the story, but his dedication to *Red Wing* overcame his disgust at the adult behavior he wanted to forget, and his guilt at having seen something meant to be private.

Many Waureganites were not particularly religious during the winter, except for the requisite Christmas pageants and Easter services, but they were devoted to their summer church. It was a "low" church, where Communion wasn't served. Members of the colony described it as "non-denominational Christian." Regular Sunday attendance was part of the bond Wauregan created, reminding the colonists that their shared values were spiritual as well as secular. Sunday morning church had had a central place in the weekly schedule since the founding of the association. Families bicycled over, the men in ties and jackets, the women in colorful light dresses, the girls with sashes tied in fat bows, and the boys in freshly pressed shorts and shirts— and everyone wore shoes. They parked their bikes in the racks outside, and followed the music from the small organ into a world where personal likes and dislikes were set aside, and at least for an hour they could feel as though they were part of a synchronous whole.

Like the other buildings, the church was clad in weathered shingles. The ceiling and beams were constructed like the inside of a boat, and the podium and pews were in the Arts and Crafts style that was considered suitably unpretentious when the church was built. With the exception of a stained glass window behind the chancel, which showed the infant Christ with Mary, all the other windows were clear.

Although the colony's clerics were usually retired from their regular parishes and had their summers free to spend in the colony's parish house, they still had plenty of preaching left in them. Some returned long enough to conduct the marriage service for a child they had christened. One long-term minister was succeeded by his son, Dr. John Waters, who was preaching that morning.

The children's choir was an intrinsic part of the proceedings. Adults who had grown up at Wauregan watched the boys and girls filing into the chancel and remembered how serious and proud they had been when they were young, and sang hymns for the whole congregation. Choir practice was held every Wednesday afternoon, after which the choristers were rewarded with ice cream cones from the general store. The older children were part of the bell ringers' chorus, and the pure chime of the bells was a sound they only heard in summer. The more sentimental members of the congregation thought that their children's voices and the bells must sound the way the angels did when they were at their most carefree.

A Wauregan tradition was the Sermon for the Children, aimed at boys and girls under ten. It took place early in the service, before the children got restless. The children liked being called up to the altar when the minister asked them to gather around, and sometimes he picked a couple of them to participate in a demonstration of his theme.

On the Sunday morning after the dance, when the children had trotted down the aisle and drawn together around Dr. Waters, he asked for two volunteers. Hands shot up, and he chose a boy and girl as his assistants. Then he held out a new tube of toothpaste, unscrewed the top, and gave the tube to the little girl. He instructed the boy to hold out his hand, and asked the girl to squeeze the tube onto the boy's palm. "Not too hard," he said. When some toothpaste spurted out, he said, "Good work! Now put the toothpaste back into the tube."

The girl looked at him, puzzled. "How?"

"As Julie and Alex have demonstrated, once the toothpaste is out of the tube, you can't get it back in," the minister told the children. He retrieved the tube, replaced the cap, and produced a large white handkerchief to wipe Alex's hand.

"Now, is this about toothpaste?"

"Noooo," the children answered brightly.

"That's right. It's about words. Once we've said something, we can't take it back. Sometimes our words can make messes, like the one I cleaned off Alex's hand: angry words, lies, gossip that will hurt someone, or secrets you've promised to keep, but tell anyway. The toothpaste you can't put back in the tube reminds us that if we say something we will be sorry for afterwards, we can apologize, but we can't unsay it."

After the children left for Sunday school in the parish hall, he addressed the adults. "I'd like to elaborate on the toothpaste sermon for the older members of this congregation. You might be surprised what a minister hears. You can't be in a place as small as Wauregan and not know what's going on. Last night's dance was a good example of a feeding trough for gossip. That's likely to be true whenever men and women get together, have a few drinks, and some of them get carried away. Add to that the fact that for a few minutes we were plunged into the dark, a lively imagination can get busy. I've already heard a few stories, and they didn't make me feel as though the party was an unqualified success.

"I'm not going to end on a negative note, but before I turn to something more inspiring, I should say that this has been the worst season for harmful gossip I can remember. When we suffered the death of a wife and mother, instead of bringing out the best in this community, the tragedy led to a spate of salacious rumors, although I'd wager that no one here today knows the truth.

"When we leave this blessed place, I ask all of you to follow the example of our Lord Jesus Christ, and exercise your Christian charity. Don't pass along stories that can hurt others. As my mother used to warn me, 'If you don't have something nice to say, don't say anything.' Let's attempt to find something good to say about each other, or hold our tongues.

"Remember the words of the Prophet, from Ecclesiastes 3:1–8, 'To everything there is a season, and a time to every purpose under heaven.' It is good to keep in mind that the last two lines are 'a time of war; and a time of peace.' Thanks to God and the efforts of millions of people of courage and goodwill, some of whom are here today, and others who have lost their lives, we are in a time of peace again. May we cherish it, and leave this morning with hearts filled with gratitude for the beauties of nature, and the traditions of camaraderie and loyalty that were established here in 1898 at the end of another conflict, the Spanish-American war. Let us bow our heads and say a silent prayer of thanks to the founders of Wauregan, who had the wisdom and foresight to establish a sanctuary that nourishes the body and the spirit."

As Helen, Frank, and Jack left church, Helen glimpsed Peter and the Judge. Peter winked at her so quickly she wondered if she had imagined it, and then she imagined some other things.

Jack seemed sobered by what he had heard. Instead of joining his friends, he quietly mounted his bike and slowly rode home on his own.

"The boy's growing up," Frank said.

"I know. This summer, I've felt him drawing away from me. I used to worry that without Arthur around, he'd become a mama's boy, but I don't think that's in the cards. I'm glad for him, but I miss the little fellow who held my hand so trustingly, and came to me with his treasures and his troubles. I always thought I'd have at least two children, and Arthur and I used to talk about having four, in two sets: the big ones and the little ones. Now I know Jack is the only child I'll ever have, and he's on the brink of not being a child anymore."

"Just be thankful he isn't still holding your hand," Frank said, and smiled.

His kindness and common sense made her feel guilty about Peter, and she wondered whether what was happening between them would be over when Labor Day came. If it was, she knew she could count on Frank to be waiting for her.

CHAPTER SEVENTEEN

JACK spent Monday morning in bed with a summer cold. He was glad he didn't have to see anyone except Kathleen and his mother, and he didn't want to see Peter.

When Helen brought a tray with a cup of bouillon and a chicken sandwich up to his room, she was prepared to tell him about Arthur. She would talk to Kathleen later, when they were alone.

Helen slowly mounted the stairs to find Jack. He was dozing, with Max snoring at the foot of the bed. A reprieve, she thought, and brought the tray back to the kitchen. A couple of hours later, she was back, carrying the reheated soup. Jack was sitting up reading. Max didn't raise his head, and she thought again that he had become uncharacteristically lethargic as the weeks went by.

She straightened the bedcovers and set the tray on Jack's lap.

"Mmm," he said, "I'm beginning to be hungry again."

"Good. Can we talk while you eat?"

"Sure," he said.

"There's something I need to discuss with you," she began.

"Mother. If you're going to start about sex, it's too late."

"Oh," Helen said, momentarily distracted. She looked at him, and saw a slim, handsome fourteen-year-old, nearly six feet tall, with clear skin, clear eyes behind horn-rimmed glasses, and light brown hair cut short enough that when it flopped over his brow, it didn't quite reach his eyebrows. Over the summer he had outgrown the gangly stage. How was she to know if he was ready? Most of her friends had heard about the mother-and-daughter team in New York whose trade was to initiate prep school boys.

"*Were* you going to give me a sex talk?"

"No. This is about your father."

Jack pushed the tray aside, got up, and walked over to the window. It was the same window from which he had seen his mother and Peter "necking" as he thought of it, and he frowned. "Did Uncle Frank find out something?"

"Yes," she said. "The Gestapo caught your father while he was transmitting. He and Frank were going to escape from France that night, taking two little children whose parents were in the camps, and whose lives were in danger. Frank and the children got away, but Dad was captured and killed in a German prison."

"Why didn't the OSS tell us?" Jack said. He bit his lower lip to try to keep his chin from wobbling.

"I don't know," she said. "They've probably been keeping a lot of what happened under wraps so as not to compromise people who worked for them in the Resistance. That's the only reason I can think of. Uncle Frank expects we're going to be getting official notification soon."

"How did he find out?"

"He got a look at your father's file when he joined the CIA," Helen said. "He was pretty sure your father hadn't made it, but once he knew for sure, he thought he should tell us as soon as possible, so we wouldn't keep hoping."

"How come Uncle Frank got out and Dad didn't?" Jack asked angrily.

"He says he was downstairs on lookout with the children. Then a fog rolled in, thick, like we have here, and he couldn't see the Gestapo coming until it was too late to get upstairs to warn your father. He says his only choice was to get himself and the little boy and girl out through a secret passage, and hope your father heard the Germans in time to climb out a window and escape over the rooftops. Unfortunately, that's not what happened."

Jack inhaled deeply, trying not to cry. *"Unfortunately?"* he said. "How about tragically? Desperately. *Horribly?* Please, Mother, leave me alone."

Helen went over to try to comfort him, but he put out a hand to hold her off. "No," he said and then, with a howl, "No! No! No!"

Max, alarmed, jumped off the bed and Jack sat on the floor and sobbed into the fur on his neck.

"Go away," he cried. "You could have made Father stay with us. It's your fault he's dead."

Helen heard him sobbing most of the afternoon and left him to grieve, with Max to console him. At dusk he came downstairs, dressed, but with his hair sticking up. His glasses helped mask his red and swollen eyes. Max was pressing against his leg as they walked.

"I'm going over to Peter's," he said. "Did you tell him?"

"Yes."

"Before you told me!"

"I wanted to wait to talk to you until Uncle Frank left, so we could be alone."

Jack shook his head. "Can I ask Peter if Max can stay with us a few more days?"

"I'd like that, too," Helen said.

After Jack went out, Kathleen and Helen sat at the kitchen table and talked about Arthur. In all the years she had known Kathleen, Helen had never seen her cry, but as the tears ran down her face, she didn't bother to wipe them off, just kept talking about her "little boy," as though the grown-up Arthur who had gone to war was someone else entirely. Helen was glad Jack had gone out. She was sure Kathleen would never let a child see her cry, and it was a kindness that she did not have to hide her anguish.

Jack still wasn't back at dinnertime, but the light on the Judge's porch was on. Helen could see Peter and Jack sitting forward on the old sofa, in almost the same position: elbows on their knees, heads down, each cupping his cheeks in his palms. Whenever she looked, it seemed they hadn't moved.

Helen and Jack talked about Arthur all week, and sometimes Kathleen joined in with something she remembered from his childhood that neither of them could have known. More than once, Jack asked why Frank had escaped and Arthur had not.

"We can only know what Uncle Frank told us," Helen said each time.

"What do you think happened to the children he took over the mountains?"

"I think they were safe. He would have said if they didn't make it. I understood that they had an uncle here, in the States."

Toward the end of that sad week, Jack was sitting in the living room, turning the pages of an old *Life* magazine, wondering whether his father had still been alive when the magazine was published.

Helen hadn't been feeling well, and he still didn't feel so great himself. It could make anyone sick to think about the Nazis catching a person, and what they probably did to him.

He decided to take a walk on the beach, empty at that hour except for beach boys closing umbrellas, folding chairs, and picking up the toys children had left behind. The waves were breaking gently and the sun was low on the horizon, slipping in and out of the clouds. Suddenly determined, he picked up speed and started back to the house. Helen's address book was next to the phone under the stairs, the only phone in the house. He turned to the letter "H," found Frank's home number, and asked the operator to put through a long-distance call. When Frank answered, Jack got right to the point.

"I want to know what really happened to my Dad," he said.

Frank was more than a match for a grieving fourteen-year-old. "It's just as I told your mother, and I understand she explained to you. When we took on a perilous mission we both knew we might never come back. Your father was a brave man. I couldn't save him when the Gestapo turned up."

"But why could you save yourself? I don't understand. When you went through the tunnel to the bakery across the street, why didn't you get caught there? The Nazis must have looked in all the houses on the block."

"The Resistance was very efficient. There was always a backup plan."

"Except for my father."

"Except in cases where there was nothing they could do. Your father died, but thanks to the work he did in France, a lot of people were saved. When the Gestapo found him, they must have thought he was alone. That was a big help for the group scheduled to leave for Spain. Probably the reason we were able to get out."

Jack kicked at the wall under the stairs and started to whistle tonelessly. "Okay," he said. "What happened to the children you were saving?"

"The children? I turned them over to the people who were going to take them to their family."

"Were they coming here? To America?"

"That's what I was told."

"Could you find them now if you wanted to?"

"I don't know. I never learned their real last name, or the name of the uncle who was adopting them."

"I want you to find them," Jack said. "My father gave his life for them, didn't he?"

"Yes, you could say that he did."

"That makes us almost related."

Frank smiled at the way a teenager thought. It was true that he didn't know where they were, or how to contact them, but he said he would see what he could do.

"Am I right that *Red Wing* is going in the water soon?" he asked.

"Yes sir," Jack said. "Are you coming to see us take her out?"

"I haven't talked to your mother about it, but if you'd like, I'll be there. I want to be sure your new sail does her job."

"I'll ask Mummy—Mother—if it's okay. She's always happy when you're around," Jack said. "I guess you remind her of the old days with Dad."

That wasn't what Frank had in mind, but there wasn't much he could do about it, at least not at the moment.

Helen told Jack she was glad he had called Frank and had asked him to explain some of the things he didn't understand about Arthur's capture and death. She said she would be happy to have Frank visit them again, as it was too late to retract the invitation, and Jack told Peter that "Uncle Frank" was coming back for the great event. Peter found that somewhat puzzling. He had expected that the just-past weekend of the dance was likely to be the last time he would see Frank Hartman that summer.

CHAPTER EIGHTEEN

PETER and Helen enjoyed themselves and the good weather for the next ten days, until Peter had to leave the island to find a place to live in New Haven. He called Helen every evening, and Jack began to be accustomed to hearing his mother talking animatedly on the phone, sometimes whispering or laughing. He started to think it wouldn't be so bad if his mother and Peter got together. He couldn't remember his father very well. Mostly he replayed small memories and stories his mother and Kathleen had told him, but he had been doing that for half of his life. The very aliveness of Peter was a relief. He was looking forward to seeing him on Friday afternoon, and he and his mother agreed to surprise him and go down to meet him at the ferry.

Peter had told Helen he would be bringing a friend for the weekend, one of the architects he was planning to work with. They had a plan, which he would tell her more about when he saw her. The partner who was coming was putting up the capital. "And has plenty of talent," Peter added. "It could be exciting." Helen was pleased at the prospect of being included in Peter's planning session. It gave her a sense of being more settled than she had felt for a while. She had avoided looking ahead for so many years that the idea had a novel appeal.

Once again, on Friday night, Helen, Jack, and Max, who had been their houseguest all week, were standing on the dock as the ferry pulled in. When Peter disembarked, Helen saw that he was with a woman; she was young, tall, and lithe, and her long glossy brown hair was tied in a single braid that hung down her back. It was a warm night and she was wearing a remarkably unwrinkled linen blouse and a wide skirt with a belt that emphasized her narrow waist. Helen was so shocked she felt ill.

Peter waved at her and came over. Max jumped up to greet the woman, whom he evidently knew, and she bent over and kissed him on the nose. "Sweet Maximilian," she said, before she stood up and put out her hand for Helen to shake. It took a great deal of self-restraint for Helen to look her in the eye and shake her hand. Her eyes were green, she thought, or maybe the color called hazel, and her name was Melinda.

"I've been looking forward to meeting you," she said to Helen. "Peter has told me all about you and," looking at Jack, "you, too. How is he as a partner? I hope you've gotten him into practice, since he and I will be partners soon, too."

"In what?" Jack asked, just this side of rudely.

"In designing houses," she said. "This week we started making plans for a brownstone we've bought in New York. Office and residence. Enough room for all," she said, looking at Helen in a friendly way.

Helen was stunned. It would be more than agreeable to think that "all" included her, but Peter hadn't mentioned the house. She was afraid that what Melinda was referring to was that Peter's "friend" Helen might visit them from time to time.

Having come this far, she and Jack walked Peter and Melinda back across the island. At home, Helen collapsed onto the living room couch, and Jack sat in a fat armchair across from her. "What was that all about?" she said, as though to herself.

"What was what about? That's the architect Peter's going to be working with," Jack said, although the atmosphere on the way home had struck him as practically sinister. His mother had been excited to be meeting Peter, but when she saw him she seemed awfully chilly. And he definitely didn't like it that Max seemed so fond of whatever-her-name-was. Dogs should be more discriminating about whom they make friends with.

After dinner Helen called Sally.

"Tomorrow," she said. "Can we have lunch at the club? Just the two of us? It's urgent."

"Sure. Dan's going fishing, so he can't come anyway, but why urgent?"

"Peter's here with a date," Helen said, too miserable to make up an excuse.

She heard Sally let out a low whistle at the other end of the phone. "Okay," she said. "What time?"

"Twelve-thirty?"

"That's fine, but why would you want to be there if Peter and his 'lady friend,' or whatever she is, might be there?"

"I want to show my face, so everyone who's been gossiping

about me can see there's nothing to it, and that I don't care who he has here for the weekend."

"Ah, you finally admit that you've been the subject of a certain amount of animated speculation."

"Not funny," Helen said. "Just meet me there."

"You think you can carry it off?"

"Probably not," Helen said, and laughed shakily.

"You know what they say about curiosity?"

"I know what they say about a lot of things. Just because something's a cliché doesn't mean it's true."

"Well, if you're sure. It's my turn to watch your back," Sally said. "Like you've been watching mine all summer."

Late the next morning, Helen was about to open her screen door when Peter strode out of his house, with Melinda behind him. She was dressed in a sleeveless white blouse with the collar turned up and another colorful cotton skirt. As she mounted the Judge's bike, a breeze caught her skirt and it billowed around her. Definitely not dressed for the beach, Helen thought. So it must be the club. Well, she told herself, if I can take Arthur's death and Frank's somewhat mysterious explanation of what happened, I can take this. How long have I known Peter anyway? Damn it, she thought, I feel like I've never *not* known him.

At lunch, Helen was unnaturally lively, turning to chat with three women at the next table, and laughing here and there, the laughs like cheery little punctuation marks. Peter had come over to say hello, leaving Melinda at the table. Helen noticed that she had the long neck and elegant carriage of a dancer.

She straightened her spine in an approximation of the other woman's posture.

When Peter bent over to greet her, she gave him a patently false, but apparently enthusiastic "welcome back" greeting, and asked whether Max missed Jack, now that he had returned— for the most part—to the Gavins'.

Peter was about to ask if Helen would like to come over later that afternoon to hear more about the plans he and his partner were developing, but she turned away to order a Bloody Mary before he could deliver his message, and, confused, he backed off.

"Why don't we *all* have Bloody Marys?" Helen proposed, including the women at the next table. "My treat. It's almost the end of summer. Let's toast August." Sally thought that was a bad sign. Helen never drank at lunch.

Helen gulped her drink, ordered a tuna salad, then pushed the plate away. Peter and Melinda were leaning toward each other, talking intensely.

"Oh God," she said. "I think I'm going to be sick. Excuse me. I have to get home." She shoved her chair back, stood up shakily, and walked away. Sally watched her take her bike out of the rack and set off.

"What happened?" one of the women at the next table asked Sally.

"There's been a stomach bug going around," Sally lied. "It comes on suddenly. Anyone want to play tennis this afternoon? I've reserved a court for four o'clock, but Dan's out on a fishing boat, and he'll never be back in time."

"Who's that beautiful young girl with Peter Gavin?" another of the women asked.

"Oh, her," Sally said. "We met her earlier. They're working on some kind of architecture project. You know he's going to get his degree at Yale. The Judge probably wanted to see who he's planning to work with. Always very protective of his 'boy.'" Realizing that she was babbling, Sally stopped talking.

"Since you've lost your lunch date, why don't you join us," the third woman said. "And we can catch up on everything that's been going on."

Recognizing that as another kind of fishing, Sally confirmed that one of the three of them would meet her at the tennis courts a few minutes before four, finished half her sandwich, and signed the bill.

Close call, she thought, as she left. She considered going over to Helen's but decided to leave her to sort things out on her own, and went back to her house to read until it was time to change into her tennis whites.

When Kathleen saw Helen's face, pale under her suntan, she said, "Jeez, Mrs. W? You look like you been poisoned. Bet you ate something with mayonnaise that went bad in the heat."

"No," Helen said. "Peter has a date."

"I saw her," Kathleen said. "Just because she's a woman doesn't mean she's a 'date.' Why would he do that to you?"

"I don't know," Helen said. "I'm going upstairs to bed. When Jack comes home, tell him I'm sick."

"Want me to bring a bucket upstairs in case you whoops?" Kathleen asked.

Helen shook her head and slowly climbed the stairs. She went into the bathroom and inspected her face in the mirror. It was, she told herself, a middle-aged face. She was a fool to have thought anything else.

Kathleen heard her come down again, go into the dining room, and take a bottle out of the liquor cupboard. "Hmm," Kathleen muttered. She had been afraid that when Jack went to boarding school Helen would take to the drink. She'd seen enough of that at home in Ireland to know the signs, but Mrs. W had never been one to hit the bottle. For sure it wasn't spoiled mayonnaise that had done her in.

In the morning, when Helen made her way downstairs, she looked blurred and tired. She came into the kitchen, holding an empty bottle by the neck, and threw it hard into the trash. "Watch out you don't cut yourself when you take out the garbage," she said to Kathleen. "I'm glad I asked Frank to come again next weekend, and that dratted catboat is finally going to be launched."

On Monday, when Peter went down to the beach for an early swim, Helen wasn't there. When the lights were out in her house that night, he made his way to the place where they had been meeting, but she didn't come. When he stopped by the house on Tuesday, Kathleen told him she hadn't been feeling well, but he had seen her riding her bike to the market, and Sally's bike had been in and out of the Wadsworths' rack.

He asked Jack if his mother was better, but Jack was evasive. He didn't know what was going on, only that Helen had made some unintelligible, at least to him, comments about leaving Wauregan early and going to France. As she hadn't elaborated, he let the subject simmer in the back of his mind until something more emerged, if it ever did. What confused him most was that there had been considerable evidence that Helen and Peter would get together after they learned his father was not coming back. He had started to think of it that way: "not coming back" sounded less terrifying than "dead." But how could he tell what was going on between two adults? He was fourteen years old and he had never had a girlfriend. Now he had begun to think that if this was what Louise had called "romance," they, whoever "they" were, could count him out.

Over at the Gavins', Peter and the Judge were having a conference. Peter admitted that he could not understand what was wrong with Helen, and why she wouldn't see him.

"Whatever it is, Jack and Kathleen are in on it, too," he said. "And this is the weekend Jack and I are launching *Red Wing*. Worse yet, Jack told me Frank Hartman is coming again, to watch the launch, he says. What business is it of his? Nothing to do with him."

"Maybe it is, and maybe it isn't. Why don't you just walk in and ask her?"

But Peter did not "just walk in." He stayed close to the house, and worried.

By Wednesday, when Helen hadn't seen him, she decided that maybe he had gone back to New Haven.

That afternoon Helen was dragging a full wagon home from the grocery store. The load was too heavy to pull behind her bike, and she was trudging along, switching arms, and hoping she wouldn't hit too many bumps and that the groceries wouldn't fall out. The prospect of standing on the path, collecting one orange after another, and trying to figure out what to do about sticky broken eggs was more than she could bear.

The Judge spotted her and walked casually down the steps of his house to meet her.

"Next time I decide to stock up, I'm doing it in two trips. This is like hauling rocks," she said.

"Haven't seen you much the past few days. I hear you weren't feeling well. Better now?"

"Better enough," she said wanly.

"Just wait until you get old. You can't imagine how often you only feel 'better enough.' And now it's time for my next birthday."

"I didn't know your birthday was in the summer."

"It isn't," the Judge said and chuckled. "It's two weeks after Christmas, gloomy January. When I was a boy, my mother told me I could choose any day of the year to celebrate my birthday, as long as it was at least six months away from Christmas. So I chose August, when we'd be here, in the place I liked best. I've let it slip for a while. During the war I had my mind on other things, with my boy away."

"I've been meaning to ask. How come you call Peter your boy? What about his parents?"

"They're good people. Good parents. My son's a retired engineer, moved down to Charleston. Spends his days playing golf now, even though he tells me there's an alligator living in the water hazard on the seventh hole. The other thing he does is paint. He's gotten quite good at landscapes, although I can't say I specially like that swampy scenery with all the dead moss hanging from the trees. I don't know why they call it 'live moss.' Peter's mother is a garden designer, nice for her, they have a long growing season.

"To answer your question, Peter started coming to us here when he was seven, after my wife and I lost our other son. Peter is my *summer* boy."

"What happened to Peter's uncle? Do you mind my asking?"

"No. It was a long time ago. He got his driver's license, and a week later he was killed in a car crash. The other driver was drunk. After that my wife was nervous about even riding in a car. She was pretty much of a shut-in, except at Wauregan. Peter's father was older, and already married. I thought it would help my wife to have a child to take care of, and it would be good for Peter to be on the island. We started having him for a couple of weeks, but he loved it, and after a while he came for the whole summer. It was okay with his parents, and it turned out fine. When Peter came, my wife started cooking again and going out. She taught Peter to bake, did you know that? I'm a darned fool for cakes."

"What's your favorite?"

"Coconut cake with lemon curd filling. Three layers."

"Whew," Helen said, shaking out a hand that was sore from dragging the wagon. "Thank goodness I'm home. Why not celebrate this year? Kathleen and I could organize a festive dinner. Isn't Peter off island? You shouldn't be alone. How about tomorrow?"

"Tomorrow it is. Peter has been here all week. Working on his portfolio for his first classes. I wouldn't want to do it without him." The Judge looked at her sideways. "I think I can speak for him. We'd both like to come to dinner."

Helen swallowed. "Well, good," she said.

"I'll see that Peter makes that coconut cake," the Judge said. "Any other gustatory requests?"

"Since you ask, how about fried chicken and those lacy corn fritters of Kathleen's? No green vegetables. No string beans. No peas. No spinach. It's my birthday party and I'm not eating anything green. You can have all the vegetables you like."

"Maybe a nice tomato aspic, if it's not too hot, so it won't melt. I'll chop up some cucumbers to put in it. Then you'll have something healthy. Seven o'clock okay?"

"Thank you, Helen. I'll look forward to it." Judge Gavin turned away and strolled back to his house before Helen could see that he was grinning like a boy who had just put a frog in someone's bed.

When Peter arrived, he was carrying a cake plate with a glass dome that covered a tall coconut cake with at least an inch of white icing and a thick sprinkling of coconut flakes on top. He gave the cake to Kathleen, fished in his pocket, and handed her three candles. "Yesterday, today, and one to grow on," he said.

Then he kissed Helen on the cheek. It was a guest-hostess kiss, as impersonal as a handshake.

The Judge had brought his trumpet and announced he was going over to the casino after dinner. "The teenagers are having a dance. They put together their own band, and asked me to be the trumpet player. Imagine that!" the Judge said. "Me and the sixteen-year-olds."

The conversation was stilted at first, and the silence between Helen and Peter was notable. Finally, Helen said formally, "I expect you're looking forward to getting to New Haven and starting your design life."

"Yes," Peter said. "As I told you the night we went to the movies, it's time for some changes in the way we live. I want to take the traditional design principles based on symmetry and balance, and open them up, get rid of clutter, let in more light, so rooms flow into each other instead of being a series of closed boxes.

"There's an emotional lockdown in the country since the war, and our houses reflect it. The pretense that being in combat has barely affected those of us who fought is just plain false. I'm sick of watching guys act as though it's unmanly to show fear or uncertainty, and who can't admit something inside them has been broken and may never be fixed. Wauregan's particularly bad that way."

"I know," Helen said, warming up slightly. "I hear it from the women. I'm not saying this place needs a spotlight, but even a metaphorical flashlight under the covers might help some families. Fathers and mothers and children, shut off from each other, as though it would be bad manners to get too close."

The Judge interrupted. "I'd call it constipated," he said. "Sorry if that offends you, Helen. What can you do? It's not like prune juice is going to solve the problem."

Helen and Peter both laughed.

"We're getting started," Peter continued. "Melinda, the woman who was just here, and the other partner are engaged to be married. They've already bought our first house, a brownstone in New York like the one I grew up in. Melinda and Michael—that's her fiancé—are going to live there while it's under construction, and I'll spend weekends in New York, working with them. We're going to knock down walls and open up the little rooms to make spaces where people can breathe, and can't shut themselves off from each other. We'll put in skylights and get rid of the outside stairs, so you can walk in off the street and the ground floor won't be like a cave. We're thinking of making a kitchen with a place for dining—not just a 'nook'—and French doors opening into the garden." Peter's enthusiasm was overcoming the uncertainty he had felt since the Judge told him Helen had invited them for dinner.

"The other two are already practicing architects, but I expect I'll learn a lot by helping. I'm hoping I won't be too far behind when we're ready to take on real clients."

Helen realized she had been holding her breath, and exhaled. "Engaged to be married," she thought.

"What are you going to use for money, before you get started?" the Judge asked.

"Sell coconut cakes," Peter said and grinned. "Just kidding. I'm planning to take a drafting course first thing, and do freelance drafting. It won't bring in much, but a bachelor doesn't need a lot."

Peter went into the kitchen, gave Kathleen a kiss, much to her surprise, and brought out the pencil and pad of paper Helen used for her grocery lists. Then he began to draw. "Grandpa has already seen this, so it won't be a surprise to him. Here's what I'd like to do to our house here, when I have the skills and the wherewithal to do it," he said. He showed Helen and Jack the places where walls would come down, and new windows would go in, and explained that the dark woodwork would be painted white and the floors would get a coat of white deck paint.

When they sat down for dinner, the Judge noticed that as

they talked about the resuscitation of his house, when his grandson got excited, he touched Helen's arm, and once she put her
hand over his. Judge Gavin was pleased with his night's work.

After dinner, as the Judge prepared to head off for the casino, he said to Jack, "I know this is for the older kids, but I don't
think they'll throw you out if you're with me. Want to come?"
Jack nodded enthusiastically. "May I go?" he asked Helen.

"Sure, if they'll let you in," she said.

"Have fun, you two," Peter said. "I'd like to stay awhile and
talk with Helen. It's time for us to catch up." He looked at
Helen. "Okay with you?"

Judge Gavin kept his face expressionless, and with a wave to
Kathleen to thank her for dinner, he and Jack set off. The Judge
was humming, with his flashlight showing the path before him,
and his trumpet under his arm.

"Where shall we go?" Peter asked Helen, when his grandfather had left.

"I don't know."

"It's not that you don't want to talk?"

"I do, if you do," Helen said.

"How about coming over to our porch?"

"Good idea," Helen said. She told Kathleen she would be out
and thanked her for dinner. Kathleen made a shooing motion
with her dishcloth, and turned back to the sink. Since Helen had
told her about Arthur, she was mourning the boy she had helped
bring up. It made her sad to think Mrs. W might be starting
again with someone else, even though she knew how unhappy
she had been. Mr. Frank could come to Wauregan every weekend, and Kathleen would bet he wouldn't catch Mrs. Helen, but
Peter Gavin was another matter. As she washed the dishes, Kath-

leen, who hadn't heard the discussion in the dining room about the architecture partnership, hoped Peter wasn't planning to tell Helen about the girl with the braid. If that's what it was, she was afraid Mrs. W would come home and drag herself upstairs like a sad old lady again. On the other hand, maybe she wouldn't come home at all, which, Kathleen admitted, would not be a bad thing.

Damn that Mr. Arthur, she thought. I'm sorry for swearing, Holy Mary, Mother of God, but he should never have gone away. He was too old; he didn't have to go, and now they can't even tell us where that sweet boy is buried.

On the Judge's porch, the sofa springs creaked as Helen and Peter sat down.

"How could you sleep on this thing?" Helen asked.

"I'm not doing that anymore. When I was in New Haven I worked so hard on my portfolio for architecture school that I just collapsed in bed around midnight and fell right asleep."

"Dreams?" Helen asked.

"Not too bad. I think the worst is over."

They sat there quietly, listening to the cicadas until Helen asked, "Was there something you wanted to talk to me about?"

"I'd like to know if you and Frank Hartman are keeping company."

"Not the way you mean," Helen said. "He'd like to get closer, but I still mainly think of him as Arthur's friend."

Peter caught his breath in a long, indrawn sigh, and then let it out.

"How about you?" she asked. "I thought Melinda was your girlfriend. When I saw you together, you looked like you were having so much fun. I felt so sick I went home and got into bed. Is there anyone else? Someone more your age?" Her mouth was dry and she couldn't swallow.

"I asked Melinda here because it was hot and muggy in the city, her fiancé was away, and I thought it would be nice for her to have a weekend at the beach. We're friends. If we were more than that, what difference would it make? You told me you were too old for me. If it helps, I'm doing my best to catch up with you." He bent his head. "See? I'm getting gray." That was hardly the case. His curly brown hair was tipped with bronze from his days in the sun, but Helen didn't see any silver strands. She wanted to touch his hair so badly she sat on her hands.

He straightened up, the springs squeaked again, and he pressed down on the cushion as though he could make the sofa shut up. "I need to ask how you feel about us being together. I think about you all the time."

"I'm glad," Helen said. "I wondered if our nights on the beach were more than you were ready for."

"Is that why you pushed me away?"

"No. It was Melinda. I figured all along you were going to find someone more your own age, and I should back off."

"Bad call," Peter said. "Why do you think we're sitting here?"

Helen took a deep breath, sighed contentedly, and Peter put an arm around her.

"I have something I have to do before I move ahead," she said. "I've decided to take Jack to France, so we can say good-bye to Arthur properly."

"When are you leaving?"

"The week before Labor Day. I've told Jack, but I haven't made much of it until the Wadsworth office confirms that we have reservations on the *Ile de France*. She's just back in the water, and she's heavily booked, but she's sailing the middle of the week after next—it's a Wednesday, the last day in August. I have a school friend who married a Frenchman. Their château is only a few kilometers from Saint-Jean-de-Luz, where Arthur was caught. They've invited me to stay, and if we can get there and back before Jack starts school the third week in September, we'll go.

"It's rather odd. I told Frank, and he's been trying to talk me out of it. He says there's nothing to see, and it will just upset Jack. Then, when he realized I was determined to go, he announced that he was going to meet us in Paris for a weekend after we leave Saint-Jean. He says he has business there. CIA business. Who knows what that means? I think it's just an excuse. But don't draw any conclusions. Separate rooms, and no romance."

Peter took her chin in his hand and kissed her gently.

"Umm," she said, wanting him to kiss her again, and he did.

He drew back and asked, "Why can't I go with you, instead of Frank?"

"Because he asked first," she said, with a little mischief in her voice.

"Can I kiss you some more before you disappear across the Atlantic?" Peter said.

"You can do more than kiss me," Helen said. "It's a perfect night for the beach."

CHAPTER NINETEEN

IT was raining hard on Friday. Helen was stretched out on the couch in the living room, reading *Forever Amber,* the historical novel that had been on the best-seller list two years in a row, when Sally blew in. She was dripping water in streams from her slicker.

"You have to love your friends to visit them in weather like this," Sally said as she discarded her outerwear and shook her red hair like a dog shaking its fur. "This is a real stinker."

"Sure is," Helen said. "I'm glad to see you. It was looking like a long day. Jack is in his room, writing the final draft of his essay about Max. He told me not to interrupt him, and I'm getting tired of my book."

"Pretty steamy stuff," Sally said. "Make you want to enter the sex arena again?"

"Not in a bodice and gosh knows how many layers of clothing," Helen said, and grinned. "Want to stay for lunch?"

"Can't. Louise is at the house, as bored as the rest of us, and I promised we'd have a baking afternoon. You can expect a delivery of waterlogged brownies around dinnertime. I'd love a cup of coffee, though."

"Let me put on a fresh pot," Helen said. "Come on into the kitchen." She swung her legs over the side of the couch and stood up.

"You have the longest legs," Sally said. "Every woman at Wauregan is jealous of your legs."

"Thanks," Helen said. "Everyone always thinks someone else is prettier, or has something she doesn't have. Ever notice that? A long time ago, I decided I wanted to stay out of the competition. That's why I always wear my glasses. When we were going to coming-out parties, my mother begged me to leave them in my handbag. She said if I wore them, men would think I wasn't interested in anything except books. That was one of her saner periods. As for my legs, when I first went to dancing class, they were a positive deterrent. The boys were so short, they didn't want to dance with me. My mother's advice? She said if I felt awkward dancing with one of the shrimps, I should think about how I could eat crackers off his head. That was supposed to make me feel better."

"You're kidding!"

"I know. Don't ask! Actually, wearing glasses was helpful at parties. I could spot who was coming from the stag line, and if I didn't want to dance with him, I could ask my partner to steer me away. Anyway, glasses are part of me. A security blanket, or maybe a barricade. I don't usually like people to get in too close."

"Just what I wanted to talk to you about," Sally said.

"Can we get the coffee going first?" Helen said. "I have the feeling you've got something on your mind."

Sally laughed. "Ever hear the expression 'You can't make new old friends'?"

"A few times. And you're establishing your bona fides as an *old* old friend, before you give me a lecture," Helen said.

"You have the slowest coffeepot," Sally said. "Drip, drip, drip."

"I've been meaning to make a fire to dispel the damp," Helen said. "How does that sound? Then we can wrap a couple of camp blankets around ourselves, drink our coffee in front of the fire, and you can tell me whatever it is."

Soon they were seated cross-legged in front of a nice blaze, with ancient rough gray blankets over their shoulders, sipping coffee. Helen had unearthed some oatmeal cookies she had made the day before, but they were so soggy from the damp they curled instead of crunched. "All we need is marshmallows on sticks," Helen said.

"Oh, gosh, did I tell you what happened the other night at the Stamfords'?" Sally asked. "Mary went off-island and left Andy with that old bat who's supposed to be taking care of him. She went to bed, and Andy invited a bunch of kids over. Someone got hold of beer, and they had a party. Mary found out about it when she discovered the bottles in the trash, along with the remains of a box of marshmallows. "Marshmallows and beer!" Sally said. "Only a teenage boy would think that was a good combination."

"I'm glad Jack wasn't there," Helen said. "He's not crazy about Andy this summer. He says he's mad all the time, always trying to think of ways to irritate his mother."

"Happily, Louise was too young to be invited. I'm going to send her to camp next year."

"Jack, too. Maybe a ranch out West," Helen said.

The two women were quiet, while Helen waited for Sally to unburden herself. She hoped it wasn't more bad news about Dan's behavior. Then, spontaneously, she decided to share her news about Arthur with her closest friend.

"Sally," she said. "There's something I want to tell you, but you can't let on that you know. Don't tell Dan. Or anyone. Promise?"

"Swear," Sally said.

"Arthur was caught by the Gestapo in Saint-Jean-de-Luz the day he and Frank were supposed to leave France for Spain. Frank told me he's finally learned what happened. They tried to make him talk, but when they couldn't get anything out of him, they shot him. I've known for a while he had to be dead, but I didn't want it to be true. Now it's confirmed, it's been very strange. I don't want to tell anyone here because I'm not supposed to know. Frank found out by looking for Arthur's OSS file, which apparently he can access through the CIA."

"I'm so sorry," Sally said. "Does Jack know?"

Helen nodded. "He was devastated. I've never seen him cry like that, even when he was little. Since then, he's been sticking close to me. At first Jack couldn't understand why Frank escaped and Arthur didn't, but he called Frank, and I think he's accepted his explanation. I suspect Jack had an image of Frank and Arthur standing back to back, shooting the Gestapo as they came through the doors, like cowboys in a shoot-out. Frank said when he comes tomorrow, he'll draw him a floor plan of the house they were in to show him how impossible it was. Arthur was upstairs transmitting, while Frank was on lookout close to some kind of secret exit, and

Arthur couldn't get down in time. Jack asked Frank if he could keep the sketch.

"I got a call from Arthur's secretary this morning. We're booked to sail to France next week so Jack can see the place for himself. It was my idea, but Jack says he wants to 'pay homage'—his words—to his father. Jack's excited, which is great. The end of the summer here is always depressing.

"Frank was against it. Said it would open wounds. But when I told him I was determined to go, he asked if he could meet us in Paris, 'to start fresh,' he said."

"Why not in Saint-Jean? Surely he can find the house more easily than you can. Are you going to see him in Paris?"

"Yes. Jack's never been abroad. If we're going to France, he should have at least a couple of days in Paris."

"Now we get to the point," Sally said. "I came over to talk to you about Frank. Dan is worried about you. He and Frank were in the same entry in the freshman quad at Yale. As you probably know, Frank was assigned to Arthur's suite, with a couple of boys from St. Mark's and that guy Ray Garner from Texas. They stayed together for four years, and were in the same college as Dan.

"Frank was on scholarship. Came from a family of German immigrants. His grandparents' last name was Hauptmann, which his parents Americanized, but when he arrived at Yale, he was still called Fritz. Blue collar all the way. When Ray saw him—even in clothes that were probably ordered from Montgomery Ward, or maybe even homemade—he decided he looked like he came from a long line of aristocrats. Texans think they can do anything, and there's nothing they like better than to put one over on New Englanders. He got the idea that if Frank had the right clothes and the right introductions and exposure, he'd be a fast learner. So Ray decided to do a Henry Higgins and transform him into a perfect facsimile of a boy from a distinguished midwestern family. Frank didn't resist for a minute. Ray took him to Brooks Brothers and bought him a new wardrobe. Then he started in on his accent—he used to have that kind of flat 'a' that's a dead giveaway. Dan says he ate it up. Next, he got him to call himself Frank instead of Fritz. When Ray thought he was almost ready, he fixed him up with some of the less popular rich girls from our set, who would be safe to practice on because they'd be thrilled to have such a handsome date.

"Dan was in the room one night when Ray and Frank were pretty drunk—Ray was teaching him about wine—and he said, 'Now, Frank, don't disappoint me. I'm setting you up to marry the richest, most beautiful girl I know, and you'll be fixed for life.' That was when you and Arthur were still just friends, before you'd realized that you were in love. Arthur had had you up to Yale a couple of times and Ray Garner picked you out as the perfect candidate."

"That's not true!"

"Listen to me, Helen. Dan may have problems, but he cares about you and he's a shrewd judge of people."

"Yeah. Like Sarge?"

"Okay, that was a mistake, but the whole committee thought Sarge was a great choice, so it wasn't just Dan. Anyway, the point is that when Dan heard that Frank is coming back here again tomorrow, he told me to warn you. He doesn't have a problem that Frank realized the American dream, going to Yale and working in Donovan's office with the white-shoe boys.

Dan's all for that. It's one of the things I like about him. But Dan thinks Frank is after you because he can't keep working for the government at what they pay unless he has a rich wife."

"He could go back to Donovan's law firm if he wanted to make more money," Helen said. "Anyway, he's been very good to us. As you said, it's the American dream to rise up and make it to the top."

"But pretense isn't part of it. Look at Eddy Duchin. He married a society girl from Newport, but he never pretended he came from anything but a poor Jewish family. Same for Benny Goodman, who married a Vanderbilt. Remember, she divorced some Brit to marry him about six years ago? I can think of plenty more. Tom Lamont, the senior partner at J. P. Morgan, probably the most distinguished man on Wall Street, was the son of a poor itinerant preacher. Then he got scholarships to Exeter and Harvard. He's proud of his background. Ever hear Frank talk about his family?"

"No," Helen admitted. "But Arthur was one of the roommates. If he thought Frank was a phony, why would he have chosen him to be Jack's godfather?"

"If you'll excuse my saying so, Arthur led a sheltered life. His parents were decent people and he was brought up to be trusting."

"And to believe that in America, anyone, given a chance, can realize his potential," Helen added. "It was only two generations ago that Arthur's family and mine made their fortunes. My grandfather started out in a log cabin in Canada, and walked three miles back and forth to school every day, mostly in deep snow. It wasn't until he was in his forties that he built the railroad. And Arthur's grandfather was a wheat farmer before he became 'the Grain King' and started brokering all the wheat in the Midwest."

"Dan's not at his best these days," Sally said. "But he has a nose for a fake, and he's not a snob."

"Funny, you should be telling me this. Earlier this summer, I think it was over July Fourth weekend, after Frank had been sweet-talking Kathleen, she said, 'Did you ever notice Mr. Frank walks like Mr. Arthur, he dresses like him, and talks like him? Almost like he copied everything Mr. Arthur did. Where's his own personality?'"

"Kathleen's no fool," Sally said. "Now, having conveyed Dan's message, I admit that the war changed a lot of men, some for the better. Frank and Arthur volunteered for dangerous duty, and as far as we know, they made a real difference. And since he's been here this summer, I've gotten to know him, and I like him. He's been great with Jack, and if you think he's the man for you, maybe he is. I'm just sorry that it didn't work out with Peter. Now *he* is the real thing. Faced up to his problems, dealt with them, and knows what he wants to do with his life. I could have sworn he was in love with you until that woman turned up."

"Actually, it turns out she's engaged to be married to someone else. She really is just a partner in the architecture firm Peter's going to join. But once he goes back to New Haven, there's still a chance that he'll meet someone else who's his age, and who doesn't have a teenage son. Frank has been a terrific friend, and heaven knows, he is handsome as the day. It's a pleasure just to look at him. He even smells good when he comes off the tennis court. I don't think he sweats."

Sally laughed. "See what I mean? Cool as a cucumber. Anyway, be careful before you give away your trust." Then she said soberly, "I am sorry about Arthur. I'll miss him all my life."

Helen wiped a finger under her eyes to hold back the tears. She started to speak, but choked up, and Sally put her arms around her and they both cried.

CHAPTER TWENTY

F RANK arrived the next day on the early morning ferry for *Red Wing*'s launch. When he came downstairs after changing into a pair of white linen trousers and a blue button-down shirt with the sleeves rolled up, Kathleen thought he looked like a movie star, and frowned. Life was getting too complicated around here. She had a presentiment that it would only get worse, after what seemed to her to be Helen's sudden and ill-considered decision to take Jack to France.

Peter and Jack had agreed to sail *Red Wing* after lunch, but early that morning, Peter had stopped by the house to ask if anyone had seen his rigging knife.

"I don't like to go out without it, and I haven't been able to find it," he said.

"You had it a couple of days ago when we went out on the Judge's boat," Jack said. "Maybe you left it aboard."

Max had followed Peter into the house, smelled the leftovers from breakfast, and was on his way into the kitchen in the hope of a handout from Kathleen. "Are you going to take him out with you?" Helen asked.

She and Peter shared a brief, complicit look that had nothing to do with the dog, and smiled at each other with a heat only a fourteen-year-old with other matters on his mind could have missed. Frank saw, and decided to ignore it. Peter would not be coming to Paris.

"Of course!" Jack said.

"I think it's fine. He's used to a slightly bigger boat, but catboats are steady," Peter said.

When Peter and Jack sailed together in the Judge's boat, they always brought Max along. *Red Wing* was similar enough to the larger boat that Peter was confident he wouldn't have any trouble getting used to her. The main difference was that the catboat tended to ship water when pressed hard, Max might slip around a bit, and Jack would have to work the bilge pump to keep the bottom dry.

After lunch, the sky that had been clear that morning began to be streaked with low gray clouds, and the wind picked up. When Peter and the Judge arrived at the Wadsworths', the Judge reported that he had been keeping an eye on the weather. Peter had not established a "shark oil weather station," but even if he had, after close to eighty years on the island, the Judge was as good at predicting the weather as anyone at Wauregan.

"There's a chance there'll be a blow later this afternoon," he said. "We should get going before it starts. The weather on the bay can change fast, but if you boys stay close to shore, you should be able to beat anything that's coming. Wear your foul-weather gear. You'll get good and wet if there's a squall."

The prospect of the sail reminded Peter of the day when his

grandfather's boat was first delivered. He wasn't even as old as Jack. The Judge had taken him out when the boat arrived, and he would never forget the thrill of feeling her under him, and the sense that as long as his grandfather was around he was in safe hands. Now he felt younger than he had since he went into combat. He was in love, and he was about to take the boat he and his lover's son had been working on all summer for her first sail. The gray sky couldn't dampen his elation. He had hoped that a Wauregan summer would help him complete his cure, but he couldn't have imagined how new he would feel.

Helen, Frank, Peter, Jack, and the Judge set off. Frank rode Arthur's bike, and even the Judge, who was less enthusiastic about cycling as he aged, rode his beat-up old Schwinn. In his euphoria, Peter decided he'd had enough of muzzling and leashing Max. He let the dog run loose, and Max trotted along beside him, tail up and ears pricked, attuned to Peter's joy.

When they arrived at the yacht club, the wind was whistling and whitecaps were snapping against the gray-green water. Helen looked questioningly at the Judge, but he nodded, and they settled on the old wooden rocking chairs on the porch, where they had a wide view of the bay. Frank helped Peter and Jack push the dolly down the ramp into the water until the boat floated. They untied the bowline, and Frank hauled the dolly ashore, and joined the others to watch. Peter vaulted into the cockpit, and Jack and Max jumped aboard together, rocking the boat so Peter had to put out a hand to steady himself.

Peter dropped the centerboard, signaled Jack to hoist the sail, and they headed off the wind, with Peter at the tiller. They could hear Helen, Frank, and Judge Gavin clapping as they began to make way. Man and boy leaned on the broad rails in the open cockpit, since the small boat lacked thwarts. As the sail filled with wind, Peter took hold of a line to help Jack trim her. *Red Wing* heeled nicely to starboard and picked up speed, as they headed offshore on a comfortable reach.

"Let's have a nice straight sail out, with the wind behind us," Peter said. "Head over to that buoy about a half mile down, come around it, and see how we're doing. We'll leave the nun to port and if the weather kicks up, we shouldn't have any trouble getting home. Let's see how close we can cut it when we tack."

"Sort of like racing against ourselves," Jack said gleefully.

Sailing in easy sight of land, they attained the buoy. The catboat was doing nicely, although she was a little wet because it was the first time she'd been in the water since her restoration, and her planks had dried out. With water starting to leak into the bilge, Peter realized that he should have let her stand at mooring for a couple of days to let the seams tighten up.

"Get the bilge pump," he called to Jack, "and pump out some of this water while we're under way." Jack reached under the bow and extracted a big metal tube with a spout, and a plunger with a mop on the bottom. He placed it in the hole beneath the floorboards in the bilge compartment and pumped, but as he depressed the plunger, he turned the spout the wrong way, and it poured the water back into the boat, splashing Max, who moved behind Peter and tried to get his balance, his nails ticking on the floorboards as the boat sailed into increasingly rough water.

"Hey!" Peter said. "Watch what you're doing."

Jack rotated the pump so the spout was pointing over the side, and the water spurted out, but no matter how energetically he pumped, the bilge kept sloshing. He looked at Peter and pointed down at their wet feet, but Peter said, "That's normal. We have to pump her out every so often. When a boat's been in dry dock so long, the water hasn't had a chance to swell the wood and the seams are a little open."

The breeze had freshened, and Peter decided to come about and head straight for home, but as they rounded the buoy, the wind stiffened sharply. Peter estimated some of the gusts at twenty to twenty-five knots, too strong for a twelve-foot catboat. The bay was kicking up swells that produced a flurry of whitecaps, and Peter called out over the wind, "Time to go back." The boat was heeling hard, and Max was sliding and scratching across the deck, trying to get to the higher side when the rail dipped into the water.

Jack was holding the sail line, but he was no match for the wind, which was jerking it out of his hands. He already had a rope burn on the inside of his index and middle fingers, when a big gust shot the rope through his hand. Peter said, "I'll take that," and reached over to grab the line. As Jack turned it over to Peter, he felt less connected to the boat and more frightened, and he grabbed Max's collar and held him close, as the sea slapped over the side.

They had boiled around the buoy and come around onto the port tack, when *Red Wing*'s attitude shifted sharply. She heeled over hard and Peter and Jack strained to put their weight onto the windward side as a counterbalance, to keep the boat as flat as possible. Sailing *Red Wing* for the first time didn't seem like an adventure anymore. It felt like a life-or-death race for home.

They beat into the wind, as increasingly high waves smashed into the little vessel. On the big gusts, the catboat buried her nose in the surf, lifting the stern and leaving only the smallest amount of rudder in the water to steer with. The bay had built up some big rollers and Peter had to fight to keep the boat on a steady course. The windward stays were pulled hard and tight, but with the rudder unable to counteract the force of the wind, Peter felt himself losing the battle. He transferred his weight as far back in the stern as he could, and crisply ordered Jack to join him, in an effort to level her out. By then, they had tacked several times, and although they were hard over, she was side-slipping a good deal. Peter reefed in the sail as he began to reach the limit of his ability to control the boat.

On shore, the Judge had taken out his binoculars. It wasn't looking good, but he would put his money on Peter's ability to get *Red Wing* back safely. After all, he had taught him to sail, and unless Jack panicked and did something stupid, they should be all right.

"Can I see?" Helen asked, reaching for the binoculars.

"Not sure you want to look. It's rough out there," the Judge said. "They'll be fine, but it can be a little too exciting to watch."

"Please," Helen said.

He handed the field glasses to her, and she tried to see what was happening, but the waves were smacking so hard at the boat that it kept disappearing from sight. Just as she thought they must be swamped, the boat would pop up again.

"Is there something we should do?" she asked anxiously, and handed the glasses to Frank.

"Not much we can do," the Judge said.

"I'm beginning to wish I hadn't given Jack that sail," Frank said.

"Wouldn't have mattered; they'd already arranged to borrow one," the Judge said. "I might give a call to a friend, who owns the big powerboat anchored over there. If it gets any worse, they're going to need help, but for now, I'm trusting that they can make it on their own."

Out on the water, Peter and Jack saw that the rain was approaching from the far shore. As it drove toward them, the surface of the bay turned an ugly, dark gray. The rain hit hard and the new canvas sail sucked up the water. Normally the added weight of the wet sail would be no concern, but Peter knew the boat was already too hard pressed by the gusting wind. He considered tacking again, but thought changing course would increase the chance of rolling. He decided to minimize the number of tacks, attempting to sail as far as he could on each leg before coming about to regain the harbor. He guessed he could manage to keep the boat from capsizing if the squall passed by quickly, the normal pattern of these fast summer dustups. But this was no squall; it was a full-fledged storm. In a powerful burst, the wind drove the sail down, a wave broke over the side, lifting the stern so that the rudder was out of contact with the water, and any attempt to steer became useless.

This was the worst weather Peter had contended with in all his years of sailing. They had one life preserver aboard, which Jack was already wearing. He told Jack to take charge of the centerboard, which was rising in its casing whenever the waves hit and the boat rolled. "Keep pushing it down," Peter called out, and Jack tried, but it continued to pop up, banging about, leaving nothing under the boat to resist the roll.

In the heavy rain, the visibility was poor, and when Peter

heard what sounded like a horn he squinted through the curtain of water to see if something was coming at them. Off to the starboard side, surprisingly close, some 150 yards away, he could just spot the stern of the Long Island ferry, steaming along in the ferry lane, moving in the same direction as *Red Wing*, which, pushed off course, was too close to the lane for safety. Within minutes the big vessel's wake hit, dramatically increasing the size and strength of the waves they were fighting.

With *Red Wing* barely balanced, a giant roller rushed under her, creating a bigger wave than anything that had walloped them so far. The wind buried her bow, the centerboard popped up, the boat lost its balance, and a big gust whipped the line out of Peter's hand, burning his skin. *Red Wing* heeled hard to port, the hull rose as the roller passed under her, and the lee rail sank under water.

Instantly, the boat's open cockpit filled with water. The heavy canvas sail sank beneath the roiling waves, and the rudder and tiller floated away. Lines whipped around everywhere and Peter, Jack, and Max were hurled into the whitecaps. Seconds later, *Red Wing* was swamped, lying on her side. There was no way to right her.

Peter surfaced, and frantically looked for Jack until he spotted him in his lifejacket. He was floating face up, but he wasn't trying to swim back to the overturned boat so he could hang on to her. Peter struggled over to him, with every wave pressing him back, yelling, "Are you all right?" but Jack didn't respond. His head was bleeding and streams of blood were snaking into the water. He gasped weakly, "The boom. Struck me when we went over."

Peter firmly gripped his lifejacket and called over the

screaming wind, "Got to swim to the boat. Too far to shore. Can you do it?"

"I think so," Jack said, and coughed as water sloshed into his mouth. He felt very small and young.

"Let's go!" Peter yelled.

They swam together, each using all his strength to fight the waves. When they at last reached the boat, Peter treaded water, holding on with one hand, and using the other to push Jack up onto the hull. "Lie down, straddle her, and hang on to the keelson," Peter called. "I'm going to look for Max. Can you see him from up there?"

"No. He was forward when we rolled."

"Okay," Peter said. "I'm going to dive for him. Hang on and don't move." Peter stripped off his slicker to free himself, and plunged below the turbulent waters.

The accident had happened too suddenly for Jack to take it in properly. He had been certain that with Peter in charge, they would make it. Now that he was out of the water, he was hopeful that when his mother, Frank, and the Judge saw the weather change they would have called for help. Nevertheless, he was shivering with cold, and dazed from the blow to his head. Thinking about Peter in the water looking for Max distracted him from focusing on how alone they were, and the danger they were in. He had a thought that briefly brightened his outlook: in a way, this was like being in battle with Peter— or his father.

Peter dove under the hull and saw Max. His head was just above water, and he was struggling weakly. One of the lines was coiled around a hind leg, and he could paddle, but he couldn't get free. Peter began to reach for his knife, then remembered he hadn't been able to find it that morning and had gone off without it. There was enough air under the hull that he could stay down, and he concentrated on trying to untangle the line that was restraining Max, but it was wet and the snag was tight. He surfaced and called up to Jack, "I've got him. Do you have a knife?"

Jack shook his head. He wasn't allowed to carry a knife.

A wave sloshed water into Peter's mouth and he choked, then took in a long breath, and went down again. He fumbled, desperately trying to detach Max from the stubborn line, but it was too tight, the water was rising, and there was less and less air. He had gotten one part of the coil unwound, when he saw that Max had stopped paddling. Peter couldn't tell if he was still moving on his own, or if it was only that the waves were rocking him.

He surfaced again and shook his head at Jack, who was wiping blood off his face and looking confused. Peter dove once more, but Max was no longer struggling. His eyes were open but there was only a tiny spark of life in them. The man and the dog looked at each other, and Peter put an arm around Max's neck and pulled him toward him. Max gave a cough, almost like a sigh, and his eyes glazed over. Peter kicked up to get air, and went down again, fighting to bring Max's body out from under the sail. His eyes were streaming with tears, but they mixed with the saltwater, and Jack couldn't tell that he was crying.

Straddling the hull, Jack thought if Peter was still diving, the dog might make it. After the stories he had heard about war dogs, he had come to believe Max was nearly immortal.

Peter finally managed to pull Max free, grasped his limp body with one arm, and swimming with the other, dragged him to the side of the boat. He tried to push him up onto the hull. Jack, who didn't realize Max was dead, reached down to grab his collar, but the wet dog was too heavy for the exhausted sailors. Instead, Peter caught a line that was floating in the water, tied it behind Max's front legs, and pulled himself up onto the pitching hull. It took them a long time, but they managed to drag the dog up by the rope. Although Max's tongue was lolling out and he wasn't breathing, Peter bent over him, trying to pump the water out of his lungs. At last he gave up. "My fucking knife," he said. "If I'd had my knife . . ." And then he was silent, his face drained of color and his expression stony, set, and frightening. Without his slicker, he was deathly cold, shaking worse than Jack, and they huddled together in the wind, rain, and spray, hoping that help would come soon.

The three spectators at the yacht club had become increasingly uneasy as the weather turned ugly, and when the rain erupted, the boat was no longer visible. "I don't like this," the Judge said. "*Red Wing* can't take this kind of weather."

"Dear God," Helen said.

"What's the emergency procedure here?" Frank asked.

"Call my friend with that big power boat," the Judge said. "Goddamnit. I should have done it before." He was already dialing three digits on the wall phone inside the small yacht club building.

In minutes, Jim McDermott, a small stocky man in his mid-forties who had been winning races on the bay all his life, and whose house was near the yacht club, arrived on his bike, pedaling at top speed. His powerboat, *Sarinda*, was rocking wildly on its mooring. Frank pushed the yacht club's big row-boat into the water, and he, McDermott, and the Judge got in. As Frank rowed her out to the speedboat, he asked Judge Gavin if he could get the rowboat back to shore on his own, while he went out with McDermott. If they needed to bring Peter, Jack, and Max aboard, there wouldn't be room for anyone else. The Judge remarked that he still had a couple of functioning muscles, and despite the wind and the sheeting rain, he could make it back through the shallower water. He wanted to be part of the rescue, but the younger men's strength was critical. He resigned himself to staying with Helen, while Frank and Jim went out to hunt for *Red Wing*.

With the sea kicking up, McDermott had to keep his speed down. "Not much time for introductions," he said. "I'm Jim, and you're Frank, right? Jack's godfather?"

"Yup. What's your bet? This is a whopper of a storm."

"Where did you see them last?"

"Going around the buoy."

Jim plowed through the water toward the buoy, and cut a couple of big circles to get a 360-degree view. As he started the second circle, he saw something white on the surface of the water and his heart sank. He caught the wheel, straightened it out, and powered over for a closer look.

"I think that's it," Frank said. "Swamped!"

"Christ," Jim exclaimed. "They're practically in the ferry lane."

As they got closer, the men recognized *Red Wing*, and saw that there was a body lying on top of her. "Jack!" Frank yelled, but his voice was yanked away by the wind.

"Do you see Peter?" Jim asked Frank, yelling over the noise

of the storm. Then he realized that Peter had been pitched off and was in the water, clinging to the boat. Jim told Frank, "I'll hold the wheel; you're younger and stronger than I am. Let's see what we can do." He tossed a life ring to Peter, who seized it, while Frank pulled him in and over the side of the powerboat, which was being thrown around in the sea. Then he called to Jack, and threw the ring out again. Jack sat up, as Frank yelled at him to jump off and grab the ring. Jack slid off the hull, struggled into the ring, and Frank pulled him through the roiling sea.

As Jack got closer to the boat, Frank saw that Jack was leaving coils of blood in the water, and more blood was dripping down his face. "Head wound?" he asked Peter.

"Not serious," Peter gasped. "Maybe a few stitches."

When Jack was in the boat, Jim sent him below, out of the weather, and told him to wrap himself in a blanket and stay there.

"Looks bad for *Red Wing*," McDermott said. "Good thing the Judge called me and I had fuel in this thing. Let's head back; we'll see if we can save the boat when the storm is over."

Peter erupted. "We can't go back yet! We can't leave Max."

That was when Frank and Jim noticed the dog bobbing under water, and back to the surface again, on the end of a line.

"We don't leave our dead on the battlefield," Peter shouted. He snatched up the boat hook, used it to pick up the line he had tied around Max, and dragged the dog into the boat. Shivering in the wet and cold, he carefully placed Max on the deck, and sat next to him, leaning against Max's body, cradling his head, as though he could keep him safe.

"He all right?" Jim asked dubiously.

"Mourning. Let him be," Frank said.

As they turned back toward the yacht club, Jack stuck his head out of the hatch, and cried out, "What about *Red Wing*? She's my father's boat."

Jim answered as he struggled to hold the wheel steady. "Sorry, son. We can't tow her in the way she is; she has to be upright. We can come back for her when this lets up. If I can get the sail off, she'll right herself, but I've got to get you back to your mother."

When they reached the mooring and Jim cut the engine, they didn't wait for the Judge to row out for them, but jumped overboard and swam the short distance to shore. Peter was towing Max behind him. Helen ran down to the edge of the bay, and with water pouring off her hair and down her neck, she grabbed Jack and held him close, then tried to catch Peter's eye, but he didn't look at her. He took a wagon that had been left at the yacht club, and lifted Max's limp body into it. Then pulling the wagon behind him, he cycled home in the rain.

The Judge and Helen thanked Jim McDermott, and he nodded. "I'm glad you got your boys back. It's lucky I was home—always nice to have a chance to help."

The rain was already slowing when the Judge, Helen, Frank, and Jack rode their bicycles back across the island. Jack was still wearing the bulky oversized life jacket, but he didn't notice.

As soon as Kathleen had run him a hot bath and bandaged the cut on his forehead, and he'd had a bowl of her homemade chicken soup with rice, Jack went up to his room. He lay on his bed and stared at the ceiling. It was dark, but he was still awake when he heard the mournful sound of the bugle from across the path. The Judge was playing taps for Max.

CHAPTER TWENTY-ONE

HELEN saw Frank off on the Sunday night ferry, then biked back to the house and went up to Jack's room. She found him lying on his bed, pale and exhausted. He looked at her beseechingly, his eyes glittering with tears, as though she could undo the tragedies of the weekend. For a moment, it seemed that he was peering behind her, automatically looking to see if Max was following. Helen waited for him to say something, but he didn't speak and she picked up a stack of laundry Kathleen had left on his bureau and opened the top drawer to put it away.

"Sweetie," she started, but he burst out, "No!" She pulled out the next drawer, where Jack had crammed his sweaters, tumbled in any which way. She took them out and dumped them on the bed.

"Why don't we fold these together and talk about what happened," she said. As the sweaters fell in a heap, she noticed a gleam of metal. She and Jack reached for it at the same time.

Jack got it first, and tried to stuff it under the covers.

"What's that?" she asked.

"Nothing. A knife."

"Where did you get it?"

Jack looked down, and didn't answer.

"Jack?"

"It's Peter's."

"Did he give it to you?"

Jack shook his head and stared at the foot rail of the bed. "No."

"Did you take it?"

He nodded.

"Is this the boat knife you said you hadn't seen this morning, before you went sailing?"

"Yes."

"Look at me," Helen said angrily. "Peter's your friend. How could you have taken his knife?"

"I wanted something of his to keep. When am I ever going to see him again? He told me, next year he expects he'll be working, and he'll only be able to come back for a weekend here and there. He said this was the last summer of his boyhood."

At the thought that Peter might only be an occasional visitor in their lives, Helen felt as though her heart had dropped into her stomach. "Of course he'll be back. He loves his grandfather, and he loves it here. The Judge would be alone if Peter wasn't around," she said, reassuring herself. She was thinking, Peter will be in New York on weekends this winter, the war will begin to fade into the background, maybe we can work something out.

"Okay," she said firmly. "It's early and Peter and the Judge will still be up. I want you to go over there, give Peter back his knife, and apologize."

"Peter won't talk to me."

"Sure he will."

"No. That's the way he gets when he's upset. He told me once when I went over it wasn't a good time to visit. He said it wasn't me; sometimes he has to be alone to hear the voices of his friends from the war."

Helen imagined the "voice" he was listening to was Max's.

"Just go over there, Jack," she said. "Do it now."

Peter was in the dim living room of his grandfather's house, sitting in a rocking chair, pushing himself back and forth with his feet. Everything at the Gavins' was dark; the walls were paneled with pine that had been cured by the smoke from the fireplace, and hung with faded watercolors of sailing scenes, and every piece of furniture was covered in green cotton with dingy white trim. The floors were scattered with rag rugs, lying crookedly where they had slid around. Peter didn't acknowledge Jack until he walked over and held out the knife.

"I took it," Jack said. "I'm sorry."

Peter accepted the knife and put it down on a pine table next to the chair. Jack saw that Max's collar, with its tags, were on the table.

"Why?" Peter asked.

"I wanted something of yours. I thought you would go away and I wouldn't see you again."

"Like your father?"

Jack nodded, unable to speak.

"You already have something from me, and you gave me something to keep, too. All the good memories of this summer."

"If you had the knife, you could have cut Max loose and he'd be here now," Jack said, and put out his hand, as though to touch the top of the dog's head.

"Maybe, but he'd been under a long time when I got to him."

"There would have been a chance."

"Possibly, but there's something you need to know about Max. Sit down and stop hovering."

Jack perched on the edge of the nearest chair.

"I've told you that when we were in the Pacific a lot of the dogs and men got parasites, little organisms that you swallow in the water, or get under your skin. If you have enough of them, or the wrong kind, they can kill you. For a dog, heartworm is one of the worst, because there's no cure. Max had a bunch of parasites, but the bad news was that he had heartworm. The vet told me it would be kinder to put him down before he started to suffer. But I wanted to give him one great summer, not just for him; for me, too. Maybe you didn't notice, because he was so happy when he was with us, but he was getting weaker. He slept nearly all the time when we weren't doing things outside, and you saw yourself that he wasn't eating much. That panting he was doing? It wasn't just the heat. The worms get into the heart and the lungs and make it hard to breathe.

"Max wouldn't have been here next summer; I doubt he would have made it more than a couple more months. This way, he was scared for a few minutes, but he went fast and painlessly. That's not to say that you did the right thing by stealing my knife."

Jack flinched at the word "stealing." He had tried to persuade himself that he'd just "borrowed" something from a friend.

"But the person you really wronged was yourself. Do you understand that?"

"I guess so, but it was your knife, and I took it. I'm sorry. Where's Max now?"

"In the big freezer downstairs. We're going to take him back to Gramps's farm, I'm going to make him a casket, and we're going to bury him under a big oak tree."

"Why not at your house?"

"I don't have a house. I was away for three years, and while I was gone my parents sold the house I grew up in, and moved to South Carolina."

"Where are you going to live when we leave here?"

"I've told you. Yale University, New Haven, Connecticut."

"About the knife?"

"Yeah?"

"Is it okay?"

"It's not okay that you took it. But it's okay between us. I've been thinking of giving you something to remember this summer, and Max. I was going to wait until he was gone, and write you at school, but I'd like to give it to you now."

Peter picked the collar off the table and detached one of the tags. "I'm going to bury Max with his army ID, but this is his civilian name tag. I thought you might like it to remember him by."

"I won't ever forget him. You should have it."

"I'll always have Max with me. I don't need anything to remind me, but you didn't know him very long."

"Will you be here next year?"

"On weekends, when I can. I'd miss Gramps and this place, and you, and your mother, and Kathleen. I'm going to want to hear how your first year at boarding school goes. I'll drop you a line once in a while, and maybe you'll answer and let me know how you're doing. I might even be around when you come back to New York for vacations," he said, and hoped that was true.

Peter leaned back in his chair. "For now, though, I'm pretty tired. Thank you for bringing my knife back. I've had it for a long time." He stood and held his hand out steadily, and they shook hands like two men acknowledging that they had been through a life-and-death experience together, and survived.

As Jack headed home, he wondered what would have happened if he'd been sailing with his father, and whether Arthur would have agreed to put *Red Wing* in the water when the weather was taking a nasty turn. He imagined his father might have said, "Son, I know you'll be disappointed, but this is no weather to be out in a small boat. Don't worry; we'll have many more summers to sail her together," but he couldn't remember what his father sounded like.

After Jack went to bed, Helen looked across the path and saw Peter sitting on the screened porch, bent over, with his head in his hands, and decided to go over to offer whatever comfort she could.

She opened the door, and he looked up. "Would you like to take a walk?" she asked. "It's a beautiful night."

He shook his head, but then he stood up. "Okay. Why not?"

They walked toward the beach, and Helen felt a chill; Peter was keeping his distance from her, as though he were alone.

They had reached the far end of the front row of houses, when he finally spoke. "I want to tell you something I haven't told anyone, not even my grandfather, about what happened in the Pacific," he said. "Do you remember I mentioned that Max saved my life?"

"Of course."

"You need a pretty strong stomach to hear about it, but when I was thinking about you today," he said, "I thought if you knew what happened in the Pacific, it might help you understand why it took me a while to recover. Do you want me to tell you?"

"Please," Helen said.

"Okay. As you know, Max's handler was killed, and I took him over temporarily, even though I was an officer. No one else knew how to do it, but I'd worked a lot with bird dogs, which gave me a leg up, and we needed him. We'd landed on an island and I was leading a scouting party—we were called 'fire teams'—of six men in the jungle, when Max alerted. Usually, he sensed the presence of the enemy before they saw us, and we could get in position to fight, or go back for reinforcements, but someone behind me coughed. The Japanese were on us in an instant, two to one, so fast all we could do was raise our arms and surrender. Luckily, I had just enough time to give Max the signal to lie down and stay, so they didn't see him. What happened next is probably going to make you feel a little sick. Want to sit while I tell the rest?"

"No. Let's keep walking." Helen thought it might be easier for him to talk if they were both looking ahead, rather than at each other.

"Instead of taking us prisoners, wasting time to march us

back to their camp, then come back for an attack, they figured out a way to get rid of us, and use it as a warning to our men when they found us. They showed us that they wanted us to use our entrenching tools to dig vertical holes wide and deep enough for each of us to stand in. When we finished, they motioned to us to climb into the holes. Then they filled in the dirt around us, so just our heads were sticking out. I saw the other heads, and thought how I had let my men down. With Max there, the Japs probably wouldn't have found us if one of our men hadn't had walking pneumonia. The guy should never have come out. That cough gave us away.

"Once the Japs had planted us in the ground like cabbages, they started hitting our heads with the butts of their rifles, and a couple of them unbuttoned their trousers and urinated on our faces. One sadist cut the eyeballs out of one of our men. That was the worst thing they did. They were laughing and shouting, and all we could do was try to think ourselves into some other state, like we'd been taught, in case we were captured and tortured. I'd never had to try it before, and frankly, I didn't have what it takes.

"I was one of the lucky ones; the guy who took me on kept slapping my face back and forth, until I could feel my head swelling up. I thought my skin was going to burst. My lip was split, and my nose was bleeding, but that wasn't enough for him. He took his fist and slammed it into my nose until it was practically flattened out. Then the Jap in charge gave an order and they gave our heads a couple of extra kicks—I'm almost deaf in one ear from one of those kicks—and they slipped off into the jungle, leaving us to die. It didn't take any time for the flies and the ants to start in on our faces."

Helen was sickened, but she was afraid to speak. It was as though Peter was under a spell, keeping his voice steady, so he could tell the story.

"Here's where Max comes in. When I gave him the 'down' command, the Japanese didn't see him—they were too busy with us—and he knew to lie very still. But as soon as the violence began, he crawled back through the brush. After he was a safe distance away, he raced back to base camp. When he arrived without us, the colonel in charge pulled a squad together. Max led them straight to the burying ground, and they dug us out and brought us into the medics' tent, and the doctors got to work. The guy whose eyes were gouged out died that night; he'd gotten a concussion from being battered by a gun stock, and an aneurism killed him, which was probably better than the life he would have had—not just being blind, but remembering what it felt like to have his eyes scooped out like melon balls. The medics did a good enough job on my nose so I could get back into action, but it was hard to breathe, and when the war was over, they rebroke it and set it, so it's pretty straight now."

"What happened to Max after the war, when you were being rehabilitated?"

"That's a nice word, but it wasn't 'rehabilitation.' I was in a place where they treat the worst cases. Some guys there will never get out. I was in pretty bad shape when I arrived, but as it turned out I mostly needed a good rest and a psychiatrist who could help me put what happened in a box and shut the lid. The doctor told me that when the bad memories start, I should allow myself to think about them for five minutes a day, and then put them aside. There was no point pretending the images wouldn't come back, but he said the five-minute system keeps a lot of the sick stuff under control. Then he said I should think about something that made me feel calm and at peace, to replace the terrifying memories."

"Does it work?"

"Sometimes. I think about Wauregan, sailing on the bay with my grandfather. I try to hear the sound of the wind in the sails, and remember the way the air and the water smells. That's one of the reasons I'm spending the summer here.

"While I was in the hospital, Max went to the K-9 Corps program where they retrain war dogs so they can be returned to civilian life. The ones that didn't make it had to be put down, but Max has such a great soul, and he's instinctively sociable. There's nothing vicious about him, and since his job was scouting, he only had a couple of encounters when we took a prisoner and he had to go on the attack.

"I guess some of my men heard I was in bad shape and thought Max would help, so they sent him to me. Did Jack tell you what I told him about Max yesterday, after he brought the knife back?"

"You didn't tell him about the Japanese and the holes?"

"No. You're the only one who wasn't there who knows, except the doctors at the hospital. I told him that Max was dying. The vet who saw him before we came over at the beginning of the summer said he'd be lucky to make it to Labor Day. Max had heartworm, and God knows what other parasites. The jungles are lethal that way. A lot of dogs died, not in combat, but because of what we drank and walked through, and what bit us. Jack had a great time with Max this summer, but he would never have seen him again. I gave him one of his tags to remember him by."

Helen was crying silently. "Thank you for telling me," she said. She could see the battered heads in her mind, and the flies feasting on the blood. She was profoundly touched that Peter had confided in her. She had heard some bad stories from the men she worked with in the Red Cross program, but she'd taught herself to put them aside when she went home. These images would stay with her for the rest of her life.

"Maybe telling you was a pledge from me to you that we can tell each other anything," Peter said. "Most of those stories don't get around. Even soldiers don't talk to each other much about what they went through. It's hard to come back and be the person you were before the war."

"Are you the same person you used to be?"

"I think I am, in the ways that count. I have the idea that all our lives, right until the end, we're all the people we've ever been. A couple of nightmare years in combat are bad, but when everyone around you is in the same situation, it starts to seem almost normal. It doesn't have to turn you into someone else."

CHAPTER TWENTY-TWO

HELEN and Jack had left the island, and Judge Gavin crossed the path to visit Kathleen.

"How're you doing on your own over here?" he said. "If you need anything, you know where I am."

"Mmm-hmm," Kathleen said.

"What's this about Helen taking Jack to France all of a sudden?" the Judge asked.

"Going to say good-bye to Mr. Arthur, so they says."

"How come Frank Hartman is going to meet them in Paris?"

"I'd call that 'wait and see pudding.'"

"What's that?"

"What I always told the children when they asked what was for dessert. Mr. Arthur, and Jack, too.

"I know what's going on with Mrs. Helen and your grandson, and I'm not sorry, but it's hard to be glad when the only reason those two look like they might be getting together is because Mr. Arthur is dead and gone. I loved that boy like he was my own son. Same with Jack. I say a prayer to the Holy Mother for my Arthur every night. I hope he didn't suffer too much."

"I hope so, too," the Judge said.

Jack was thrilled to be going to France with his mother. After his encounters with Sarge, the sinking of *Red Wing,* and Max's drowning, sometimes he didn't feel any older than when his father went away.

What he didn't understand was why Frank wasn't coming to Saint-Jean with them, but was going to meet them later in Paris.

"A lot of the men who were in the war can't talk about it, and even Uncle Frank, who is going on with his life, probably doesn't want to relive that night by going back to the house, or even the village where it happened. Your father was his best friend, and he probably feels guilty that he survived and your dad didn't, even though it wasn't his fault," Helen explained.

Jack looked at his mother. "Oh," he said. "But I still don't get it. If he's coming all the way to France, why can't he show us where Dad was taken? He was there."

"I showed you the map he drew for us. Saint-Jean is a small place. We should be able to find it on our own. The house is across the street from a bakery. You can't believe what French croissants smell like when they've just come out of the oven."

"What's a croissant?"

"Something between a roll and a cake. Flaky and buttery. Yummy."

"That doesn't sound so special."

"All of France is special. If I can't go there with your dad, there's no one I'd rather be there with than you," Helen said.

The Wadsworth office had reserved the same cabins on the recently restored *Ile de France* that Helen and Arthur had when they sailed on her in the 1930s.

When they boarded and toured the ship, Peter, who had come to see them off, explained to Jack that the *Ile* was the first ship decorated in the Art Deco style. "It was inspired by the 1925 Paris Exposition des Arts Décoratifs et Industriels Modernes," he said in a reasonably good accent. "The exhibition changed the way the fashionable world looked at decoration. Before, there was a movement called Art Nouveau, which was full of curlicues, and lots of details, gussied up and fancy. This was a reaction. It was simple, and it also paid a kind of reverence to the machine age, so the furniture and some of the art had a streamlined quality."

"I think I know what you mean," Jack said. "It's sort of like what you told us about at Wauregan."

"I thought the *Ile* was finished after the war broke out in Europe in '39," Peter said before he had to disembark when the festive farewells that accompanied a sailing were over. "She wasn't going to be doing any more passenger trips, but luckily she was berthed in New York. The British Admiralty used her as a war supply ship for five years. After the war, the French took her back to the shipyard where she was built and restored her."

The *Ile* was still popular with the cream of the social, business, and Hollywood worlds, so there were a few famous faces in the first class dining salon. Jack was hardly so sophisticated that he was above being impressed. Most evenings after dinner, Helen went back to her cabin to read, and Jack set off for second class, where the younger travelers flirted shyly. Even though Jack was only fourteen, they cheerfully included him. He overheard one girl say to another, "Take a look at that one. Give him a couple of years, and he'll be a heartbreaker." He was embarrassed, but extremely pleased.

When Helen was in her cabin, she wished she had chosen any other ship. She hadn't known what vivid memories she had stored of the last time she and Arthur crossed on the *Ile* early in their marriage. One evening when she unlocked the door to her stateroom, she had an eerie feeling before she turned on the light that Arthur was sitting on one of the beds waiting for her. After that, she left a light on when she went to dinner. She didn't want to return to a room inhabited by her ghosts.

At Cherbourg, Helen and Jack boarded a train for the overnight trip to the southwest of France. Much of the French railway system hadn't been restored yet. Helen explained that France and England had exhausted their financial resources during the war, and it would be years before they were back to normal. Nevertheless, there were still sleeping compartments, shabby, but private, and Jack was excited to sleep on a train and wake up in the French countryside. They passed through villages and territory that looked decidedly foreign. They also passed through burned-out towns, but the train traveled fast enough and the route was circuitous enough that they barely saw them before they were gone. At last, around lunchtime, they arrived at the station nearest Saint-Jean-de-Luz. The de Voubrays had sent a driver to pick them up in their prewar Citroën, and he piled their luggage on the roof, tied it down, and set off. A few kilometers out of town, they turned onto a narrow country road, reached an open wrought iron gate, passed along an allée of cypress trees, and at last arrived in a circular pale gravel courtyard, surrounded by urns overflowing with flowers. A fountain splashed vigorously in the center; the water spouting from the trunk of a sizable bronze elephant, posed on one leg, as though it were dancing.

The Count and Countess de Voubray's château was a large mellowed cream stone house with sun-faded red shutters and brick towers at all four corners, each topped with a slate roof that looked like half an onion. Ivy grew up the old stone walls. Helen had told Jack that members of the de Voubray family had lived on this land since the 1300s, and the château had been built in 1660. Time had given the building the kind of character that was the architectural equivalent of what the French called wrinkles: *rides d'expression.*

The staff, some of whom remembered Helen from before the war, were lined up on the steps to greet them, although they were fewer in number than they had been in the 1930s. Pauline, slim and chic in linen trousers and a narrow fisherman's jersey, flew down the stairs to embrace Helen. Jack approached more slowly, waiting for the excitement to subside. Pauline stood back and inspected him before kissing him warmly on both cheeks. It always surprised people who had known Arthur that Jack looked so much like him. "Did you enjoy your adventure on our broken-down trains?" she asked. "It will be a while before we can restore what was lost during the war."

They were escorted upstairs by two footmen in striped waistcoats, where they found their luggage already in their rooms and a maid unpacking Helen's suitcase and putting her clothes away. Pauline had discreetly put her in a different room from the one she had shared with Arthur in the past. This room was freshly covered in a blue and white toile—walls, ceiling, curtains, and bed hangings—and had a pair of doors leading onto a small balcony dripping with flowers. Jack's room, across the hall, was paneled in limed wood with windows that overlooked lush gardens.

When they had changed out of their traveling clothes, they made their way to the terrace. It was hot and peaceful, with a churring of crickets in the lavender fields beyond the lawn. Pauline was sitting under a green and white awning, gazing at the rows of olive trees, and in the far distance, a thin sliver of sea. She asked Jack if he would prefer it if they spoke in English. So she wouldn't make him feel self-conscious, she said, "It's been so long since I've used my own language, I could use some practice."

"I'm taking French in school, but I'm not very good yet," he said, "so that would be great."

The butler came in and quietly conferred with the countess. "My husband is just washing up," she said. "He'll be with us soon, and we can have lunch."

When Louis-Arnaud de Voubray came out onto the terrace, Helen was shocked at the change in his appearance. He was only in his early fifties, but he looked like an old man. He was emaciated, almost entirely bald, his skin was an unhealthy greenish-yellow, and he walked with a limp. He had been a good-looking man of his type: upright, of medium height, with a finely drawn face that might have seemed ascetic if it hadn't been for his obvious delight in life. Helen would not have known him in his own house if he had not greeted her with such affection.

"My dear," he said. "I am sorry for the loss of your Arthur. As you may notice, the war was something of a nuisance to me as well."

"Louis-Arnaud was sent to a labor camp in Germany after the Germans did something quite inexcusable to our house, and he protested," Pauline said. "They beat him, and shoved him into a car and drove away. I didn't know where he was until our friends in the Resistance learned his location. Herr Hitler was not kind to his slave laborers. He didn't feed them enough to keep a picky cat alive, worked them until they couldn't stand, and they died where they fell, or were shot. Louis-Arnaud was lucky. He was strong when he left here, but he was forced to use the last of his reserves to survive."

"You see what I look like after a few years of peace," the count said. "You can imagine what my dear Pauline saw when I came home."

"He weighed eighty-one pounds."

"Ha! That single pound made the difference. If I had dropped to eighty, it would have been the end. And so, as you can imagine, I enjoy my food." Helen saw that the greatly reduced Louis-Arnaud had developed a little potbelly.

"How awful!" Jack exclaimed, shocked. The grown-ups seemed to be taking the count's near-death lightly, but he was sure he had already weighed eighty pounds when he was ten.

"Others endured far worse," the count said.

"How extraordinary that Arthur was so near us and we

never knew it," Pauline said. "I carried some messages to the Resistance, but I only had one contact. They had cutouts, so each of us knew as few people who were involved as possible. Then if we were caught, even under torture, we couldn't give away what we didn't know."

"I didn't realize that you were alone when the Germans were in the house. I assumed Louis-Arnaud was here, too," Helen said.

"Correct. I was here until I wasn't," Louis-Arnaud explained. "Now, what have we?"

The butler in his white cotton jacket and a maid in a gray uniform with a white apron and cap had arrived on the terrace carrying trays holding a tureen of lobster bisque and a beautifully arranged *salade composée*. "A light lunch, so you may enjoy our cheeses at the end," Louis-Arnaud said as they seated themselves at the table.

Helen and Jack spent the afternoon with Pauline, lounging around the swimming pool surrounded by tall cypress trees, with a distant view of the rocky coast and beyond it, the sparkling sea.

"This is paradise," Helen said languidly. "The water here is so different from Wauregan. It's the most amazing blue."

"Uncle Frank has eyes that color," Jack remarked.

"And who might that be?" Pauline asked.

"Jack's godfather, and Arthur's partner in the OSS. They apparently operated nearby, out of Saint-Jean. He's meeting us in Paris."

"Why didn't he come here?"

"Jack asked the same question. A lot of men never want to see the places where they fought again," Helen said. "I expect he's one of them. Even for us, we plan to make one trip to the village to see the house where Arthur was taken away, and otherwise, I hope you don't mind if we leave most of our sightseeing for Paris."

The first full day they were there, Helen and Pauline caught up, and Jack sat apart in the garden or by the pool, reading and listening to the women, hoping to learn something about the way his father had been when the countess knew him. He discovered that the château had been given to an ancestor of the count's by a king of France. He was glad he had written his summer composition about war dogs, but he was storing up information about France in case he had another assignment. He learned that the French king, Louis XI, had stayed in that very house—perhaps even in the room where he was sleeping—in 1463, and that after Louis XIV was married to Princess Marie-Thérèse of Austria, the wedding took place in the town. It was then that Louis XIV ennobled the de Voubray family. That was why Louis-Arnaud and Pauline were called the count and countess. What's more, the Duke of Wellington had stayed there during the Napoleonic wars. Jack was sure there was a lot more to learn, if he could ask the right questions without seeming to snoop.

During one of their conversations, Helen remarked to Pauline, "I remember that big stone-floored room where you set up bridge tables after dinner when you had parties. Wasn't it originally part of another building an ancestor of Louis-Arnaud's tore down to build this lovely house? Do you still invite the neighbors around for an evening of bridge?"

"No," Pauline said abruptly. "That's a little museum the Germans left us. You and Jack should see it."

They had been sitting by a pair of open French doors in the drawing room, with the scents of the garden blowing through, and Pauline got up. Some stray rose petals had come in on the breeze and she brushed them off her skirt, and gestured to them to follow her.

They walked through a long passage until they reached a heavy wooden door with iron hardware. There was a key in the lock and when Pauline turned it, opened the door, and stepped back, Helen gasped. The stucco walls had been defaced by graffiti—swastikas, rudely painted sketches of men and women in contorted sexual positions, caricatures of Jewish men with beaked noses, who were holding babies by the legs and bashing them against a wall. The ceiling was riddled with bullet holes, and Pauline pointed to a corner where the floor was stained a yellowish gray. "Their urinal," she said.

"But why?" Helen asked.

Pauline raised her eyebrows and her mouth turned down scornfully. "Letting off steam, maybe," she said. "It must have been strange for them to be living in a place where they were hated. Louis-Arnaud and I have talked about it, and that's all we can think of, aside from pure bestiality. Which there was plenty of, as well.

"We were never allowed in this room when the Germans were here, until one evening the commanding officer told Louis-Arnaud to bring the men a tray of schnapps. When my husband saw what they had done, he lost his temper. In fault-less German, he told them that they were pigs, and worse. I was standing in the back of the passage," she said and pointed behind her. "I was in the shadows, and they didn't notice me. I could see what was happening, but there was nothing I could do. One of them grabbed the tray and they forced him to drink every glass of schnapps until he was reeling. Then they beat him, and that night they took him away. Later, the commandant told me he hadn't realized my husband understood German, and he had heard too much. He was a danger to them, and he had to go. He didn't ask if I spoke their language. Of course, I would have lied. Thanks to our Fraulein Elsa, who practically brought us up, we learned German in the nursery.

"I'll never forget that week in August. The sky was so clear I could see every star, and each night I went outside and wondered where Louis-Arnaud was and if he was looking at the same stars. I especially remember it because I heard there was supposed to be an Allied airdrop and someone had alerted the Germans. When the parachutes floated down, every man was shot in the air. Members of the Resistance were waiting for them, but they were outnumbered by the Germans. Most of them were caught and shot where they stood. Only one or two escaped to tell the story."

"Do you remember exactly when that was?" Helen asked.

"Of course. It was the most beautiful month I can remember. Not a drop of rain, and never that fog that comes off the sea sometimes. The only good news was that there was a group going over the mountains into Spain, and from what I heard, they made it."

"Wasn't that when Dad was caught?" Jack asked Helen.

"That's what Frank said. He told me he escaped the end of the first week in August, but the way he remembered it, there was a lot of fog that night."

"Perhaps it was a different year," Pauline said.

"It was the summer of 1944."

"Then perhaps he has forgotten what beautiful weather we had."

"Mmm," Helen said. "About this room. Why didn't you get rid of every trace of what the Germans did?"

"Louis-Arnaud said this place had seen many things in five hundred years, and this is part of its history. If we restored it, we would be pretending that these horrible things hadn't happened. We keep this room to remember the filth people can stoop to, and be sure to act before evil prevails."

"You're not going to show it to your guests when you open your little hotel, are you?"

"Certainly not! We've carved out a nice apartment for ourselves so we will have some privacy. That, and this room will be locked."

Helen and Jack walked to the center of the room, slowly turned around, and looked at the images on the walls.

"I'm sorry," Helen said. "I've never seen anything like this. Maybe in the South, where they have the Ku Klux Klan and lynchings and burn crosses on the lawns of respectable Negroes who dare to move into white neighborhoods. But where we live, never. You were brave to leave it."

"In even the most beautiful garden, a poisonous snake can crawl out from under a rock and bite you," Pauline said in a matter-of-fact tone. "You may recover, but the next time, you will be careful where you step."

CHAPTER TWENTY-THREE

HELEN and Jack waited another day, gathering their courage, until they were ready to drive into Saint-Jean-de-Luz, and the de Voubrays' car was available.

"Are you ready?" Helen asked Jack.

"Sort of," Jack said.

It wasn't hard to find the place using Frank's map, and, as promised, the bakery faced the house across a narrow street.

The house looked like every other in the neighborhood. No longer boarded up, it had been freshly painted a soft creamy color. There was nothing to indicate that a man had been dragged to his death from the upper floor, where one window was open, and a sheer white curtain billowed in the slight breeze.

"This is it?" Jack said.

"It must be," Helen said, trying to imagine it as it had been four years earlier.

"Have you seen enough?"

"I guess so," he said unconvincingly. "At least we came." He had expected to feel grief or fear, but instead felt oddly blank. This place didn't seem to have anything to do with him, or with his father.

Next door, a woman came out of her house carrying a wicker shopping basket. She was approaching middle age and was still quite pretty, with nearly black curls and lightly tanned skin. As she started to walk, Helen saw that her gait was stiff and clumsy. One of her legs was artificial, encased in a flesh-colored stocking, and she was wearing black tie-up shoes.

"Mother?" Jack asked, tilting his head toward the woman.

"The war, I suspect," Helen said. "I told Pauline since we'd be in town, we'd have lunch at a restaurant near the harbor where Grandpa took me long ago. It was very simple, but the fish was from the morning's catch, and they grilled it over a wood fire. And I'd like you to see some of the village. There's a lot more to Saint-Jean than the de Voubrays' château. I hope I can remember how to find the restaurant."

At the corner, two taxi drivers were leaning against their cars, smoking strong-smelling Gauloises cigarettes. "They must know the town backwards and forwards," Helen said. "Let's test my French."

The drivers were talking languidly, holding their cigarettes between their thumbs and first fingers. They were bulky and swarthy, and one had a luxuriant gray moustache. The men looked at each other. "Est-ce-que vous cherchez quelqu'un à cette maison?" one of them asked. Are you looking for someone at that house?

She told them about their mission and that they had come to see where her husband had been taken away by the Gestapo.

The man with the moustache asked if her husband had been a radio operator working with the underground, and if he had

had a partner, blond and blue-eyed, who looked like a German.

"Exactement," Helen said.

"What are they saying?" Jack said, and Helen translated.

"How did they know?"

"Maybe they were in the Resistance, but I don't think I can ask them."

"Condoléances sincères, madame," the older man said. His mouth turned down, so the ends of his moustache looked like parentheses. Then he asked her if she knew what had happened to the other man.

He had taken off his cap and was running his hand through thick black hair streaked with gray.

Helen explained that her husband's OSS partner was in Paris and that they planned to meet him there in a couple of days. Had they known him?

"Je ne sais pas," the man said—I don't know. He and the other driver glanced at each other quickly, and he jammed his cap back on his head.

They gave her directions to the restaurant, which was open and run by the same owners. Wishing her a good day, the drivers turned back to each other. They were gesturing animatedly and speaking so fast Helen couldn't have understood them if she had tried.

"Weren't they nice," Helen said, as she and Jack walked toward the harbor. "And what fun it will be to take you for lunch where I ate with Grandpa."

"I didn't think they were so nice," Jack said. "I thought they were scary."

Helen could see what he meant, but she intended to give Jack the best afternoon she could, and didn't answer.

• • •

That night after dinner, Jack came into Helen's room.

"How can you sleep in here? Little blue and white lambs and shepherds everywhere. What is this stuff? Don't you wake up and wonder where the walls stop and the ceiling starts?" Jack asked.

"It's called toile," Helen said. "And the room feels cozy. If I need a break from the 'lambs and shepherds,' I can look out at the beautiful view."

Jack sat in a plump toile-upholstered armchair, and Helen settled on a matching chair with her feet on a needlepoint footstool.

"About Dad," Jack said. "For years, I hoped he was alive. Now he's dead, and I can't really remember him."

"Did it help to come here?"

"Yes, but it wasn't seeing that house in the town. It was the room the Nazis wrecked. It showed me why Dad was fighting. It made me proud of him."

"Me, too," Helen said.

"But you know what was weird? Remember when the countess said she remembered the week the count was taken away? She said that the sky was clear every night."

"Mmm-hmm," Helen said carefully.

"But Uncle Frank told you that it was foggy when he escaped. Wasn't it the same month?"

"I'm pretty sure it was. I was touched when Pauline said she had gone out every night to look at the sky and the moon, and wonder if the count was seeing the same moon, wherever they had taken him."

"Why would Uncle Frank have said it was too foggy to see, if it wasn't?"

"At first, I thought it must have been a different time. But I asked Pauline later, and she insisted that was the week of the Allied airdrop, just as Frank said. I do know that the airdrops always took place when the moon was full. Sometimes, if the weather was bad, the pilots would have to wait another month to try again. Uncle Frank didn't tell me the partisans on the ground had been blown, and someone had given away their location."

"Uncle Frank is Dad's best friend. Was, I mean," Jack said.

"Yes."

"Remember he told you he'd been picked up by the Gestapo that day and they'd worked him over, then let him go when they found out he was German and said he'd spy for them? Do you think he gave Dad away?"

"He wasn't German," Helen said. "Those were his grandparents. He is as American as we are. Uncle Frank is a war hero. So was your father. We can't know what happened that night."

They were quiet, sitting with their thoughts.

Jack stood up and looked down at his mother. "Now that you're really a widow, are you going to marry Uncle Frank? Or Peter?"

Helen smiled wistfully. "I like Uncle Frank, but I doubt I'm going to marry him."

"I thought you and Peter would get together."

"Why would you think that?"

"I saw you together the night of the dance. On the beach."

He shouldn't have seen that, Helen thought, looking away.

"I thought you were at Mrs. Stamford's."

"I know. I came home. Something didn't seem right."

"That was just after Uncle Frank told me your father was dead, and Peter and I were beginning to realize how we felt about each other. I don't know what will happen, but if I were going to be with anyone, it would be more likely to be Peter."

"Will you?" Jack asked, looking as though a weight had been taken off his shoulders.

"We'll see. Peter has a say in this, too. But first I want to find out if Pauline knows more than she told us about what happened that week in 1944."

CHAPTER TWENTY-FOUR

A MAID knocked on Helen's door and handed her a sealed yellow envelope. It was only two days before she was to leave for Paris and she was afraid the cable was from Frank. But when she slit the envelope open, she saw that it was from Peter. It read:

BOOKING CALL FOR TEN AYEM YOUR TIME. STOP.
HAVE NEWS. STOP. LOVE. STOP. PETER.

It was close to ten, and Helen hurried downstairs to let Pauline know she was expecting an overseas call, and asked her to keep the line open.

"I hope it's not bad news," Pauline said.

"It's from a good friend. I promised to cable to let him know how our trip was going, and I've put it off. Perhaps he's just checking to see if we're okay."

"Quite a good friend?"

"Rather good, actually," Helen said, and blushed.

"Come into Louis-Arnaud's office, and wait for the call to come through. You'll have more privacy in there."

"Thank you," Helen said distractedly. She didn't have a good feeling about the cable. She was afraid that "news" meant something had happened to the Judge. If he has died, she thought, Peter will want to talk to me.

She sat at the count's desk and waited, taking his pen out of the inkwell and doodling on a piece of ivory paper engraved with the name of the château on the top. She bore down lightly so as not to affect the angle of the nib. When the phone rang, even though she had been waiting for it, the harsh double *brrrng-brrrng* startled her. To her dismay, the call was for the count, tying up the line. He was out for the morning, and she asked the caller to ring back at lunchtime. She sat up straight, and as she stared at the heavy black instrument it began to take on a threatening aspect. She hadn't noticed how menacing a phone could seem, when at any minute it could ring and convey something she could put off knowing a little longer.

Shortly after ten, the phone rang again, and she held the receiver to her ear, while the operator told her in French that there was a call for "Madame Vadsvort" and how many minutes had been booked. It was still difficult to get an open line for long in provincial France, where, between the Germans and the Resistance, so many lines of communication had been cut and were still not restored.

"Helen?" Peter shouted. She heard an echo, like the sighing of the sea, but his voice was coming through clearly.

"I'm here. You don't have to yell. Is everything all right?"

"First, are you okay? And Jack? Did you find what you were looking for?"

"Yes," Helen said bleakly.

"How are you feeling?"

"Hollowed out. Why did you call? Is the Judge okay? Nothing's happened to Kathleen?"

"We're all fine. But we're not at Wauregan."

"Why not?"

"Did you read about the hurricane we had a couple of days ago that swept up the East Coast and did a lot of damage?"

"We only get the French newspapers here. What happened?"

"Wauregan took the brunt of the storm. The entire place was evacuated. I took Gramps and Kathleen to Gramps's house on the mainland. While the colony was empty, the volunteer firemen were off-island. There was a fire, and two houses burned to the ground."

"My God! Whose houses?"

"Hang on, and I'll tell you. What I can gather from the people who are back there, the storm caused a power failure and when the power went back on, a surge started a blaze in the Williamses' house. Fortunately, the wind shifted, and the fire didn't spread too far, or the whole front row could have gone up."

"But the Williamses live right next to me!"

"That's why I'm calling."

"Are you telling me my house is gone?"

"I'm sorry. From what I hear, there's nothing left except smoking rubble."

Helen swallowed. And then, on the verge of the hysteria she

had been holding back, she said, "At least we won't be blocking your view of the ocean anymore."

"Don't say that."

"I didn't mean it. I can't take it in," she said. She wanted to put the receiver back on the hook and cry, but she kept talking.

"I can't imagine not spending my summers at Wauregan. I always said it was my safe place. Now I don't even have a house."

"But I do."

"What do you mean?"

"Gramps turned his house over to me a year ago, after I got out of the hospital. All legal; a deed and everything. He's even asked me to try out some of my new architectural ideas. He says he's sick of the gloom. The only problem is the Wauregan Rules: no single person without a family can own a house, unless he's a widow or a widower with grown children, like Gramps. But I have a solution to that.

"Come home, Helen."

"I will," she said. "But first I have some unfinished business here."

CHAPTER TWENTY-FIVE

AFTER she got off the phone, Helen bleakly told Pauline about what had happened at Wauregan.

"How awful," Pauline said. "Can you build a new house where the old one was?"

"I may not have to. But before I think about that, I need to know more about August 1944."

"Yes," Pauline said. "I think you do. There wasn't a wisp of fog. There's something wrong with what this Frank has told you. No one could forget that time. I was in close touch with my contact in the Resistance, hoping she could help me find out what had happened to Louis-Arnaud. The rumor was that a traitor had given away the location of the OSS radio operator and the airdrop."

"Is there any reason to think it could have been Frank?" Helen asked. Her tongue felt heavy, and she could hardly speak.

"You said he told you that the Gestapo had worked him over that day and only let him go because he said he'd spy for them. They wouldn't have released him if he hadn't given them something."

"How can we find out? Frank is Jack's godfather. I don't want to go through the rest of my life unfairly suspecting that he had something to do with Arthur's death."

"You don't have to," Pauline said. "I have an idea."

Then, as Jack and Louis-Arnaud strolled toward them, she smiled brightly, and said, "Just who we were about to look for. I'm borrowing Helen this afternoon.

"Thursday is my day to visit an old countess who lives nearby," she explained to Jack. "She's a little gaga, but she's lonely. Your mother will be a nice distraction for her."

Louis-Arnaud tried to catch her eye to see what she was up to, but she avoided looking at him.

"Maybe she can tell you stories about the war," Jack said.

"Perhaps," Pauline said. "But for the most part she lives in the distant past. Your mother will have the pleasure of hearing about the 1920s in the south of France. She was quite a character. Went water-skiing at night in her evening clothes and diamonds. Knew everyone. She's a piece of living history. I've heard the stories often, but the first time is fascinating. Unfortunately, she's rather deaf. She can't entertain more than two people at once, because she gets confused and can't hear, so you men will have to find another way to amuse yourselves."

Helen gave Pauline a sideways look, but her face showed no indication of what they had been talking about. It didn't sound as though the old lady would remember much, if anything, about the night Arthur disappeared.

After lunch, Pauline and Helen set off in the de Voubrays' Citröen.

"What's this about the countess?" Helen asked, as they drove down the allée that led out of the château.

"I invented her. That's why Louis-Arnaud gave me that funny look. There's someone I want you to meet. The woman I took messages to during the war. Maybe she'll be able to shed some light on what happened. She was much more involved than I was."

They drove into the village and drew up to the baker's shop across the street from the house Helen and Jack had gone to see. A buxom woman with gray hair pulled tightly in a bun and wearing a starched white apron stood behind a counter filled with baked goods. Her eyebrows were black over small bright brown eyes that peeked out from a skein of wrinkles. The buttery smell in the bakery was overwhelming, and Helen's mouth began to water. A thin girl of about thirteen, her hair in braids, hovered near the older woman. Granddaughter, Helen thought. Learning the trade.

After a few *ma chère comtesses* and *ma chère Madame Flauberts* had been exchanged, the bakery proprietress asked Pauline if she and her friend would like to come into the back room and have some freshly baked *tuiles* and a *café*, while her assistant watched the shop. Giving rapid-fire instructions to the young girl, she piled a plate with the delicate curled cookies, and led the way behind a curtain to a cheerful wallpapered sitting room, where armchairs were arranged around a table covered with a patterned cloth. This was the painting Helen had imagined when she first heard about the house where Arthur had been caught.

Tilting her head toward Helen, Madame Flaubert looked questioningly at Pauline.

Pauline introduced Helen and assured her that she could say anything in front of her, explaining that she was the wife of the American radio operator taken from across the street. Madame Flaubert raised her eyebrows. As the conversation continued in French, Helen followed most of it. When she lost track, she asked Pauline to translate.

"The countess tells me that you are meeting your husband's partner in Paris," Madame Flaubert said. "Does he look like a German officer, good looking and blond, a man who was with the American spy service during the war? Who escaped, but whose partner was captured?"

Helen nodded.

Madame Flaubert became agitated. Her hands trembled and her eyes flashed. "And you are sure that his partner was the radio operator who worked with the Resistance?"

"Yes," Helen said.

"In that case, I will tell you what I remember of that night. The moon was bright and my husband was the lookout, working with the Resistance, of course. He saw the Gestapo's cars, those poisonous black beetles, coming from many blocks away. In case the OSS men had not spotted the cars, he went to warn them. There is an escape tunnel the Resistance dug under our bakery. It leads to the houses across the street, and from there, to an alley. My husband raced into the tunnel and found the blond one running away. When my husband asked where the other man was, he said he hadn't spotted the Gestapo in time to warn his partner, and they had each been instructed to save himself at any cost.

"My husband was a fool. He said, 'Weren't you the lookout? If I could see them in time, why not you?'

"The man took his pistol, shot my husband in the stomach, and kept running. When my husband did not return, I went into the tunnel and found him. He was in a very bad way. He lived for three more days in agony before he died. He told me who shot him, but by then it was too late to catch the betrayer. We later heard he made it over the Pyrenees the same night he shot my husband, before anyone knew what he had done."

"What about the children he was helping escape?" Helen exclaimed.

"There were no children," Madame Flaubert said. "He was alone."

The color had drained out of Helen's face. "He invented the children?" She looked as though she might faint.

"So it would appear," Pauline said. "There's something else. A piece of the puzzle just dropped into place. Remember, *madame,* the Gestapo took over our house?"

"Who could forget? You brought us messages every week when you came to buy bread for them."

"The day after Monsieur Flaubert was shot, I heard the Germans talking at dinner about an American double agent they'd caught, and released on the understanding that he'd feed them information. But he'd disappeared the same night. Some of the men at the dinner table thought the partisans had heard of his treachery and executed him. Others suspected that he didn't want to continue to spy for them, so he escaped. I couldn't hear the whole conversation because I was in and out of the kitchen, serving the *salaud* Boches, and of course I had no idea that this had any connection to Arthur, or that he was even working in our area," Pauline said.

Madame Flaubert picked up the story. "Most of us believed that he had given away his partner and the operation. If we could have gotten our hands on him, he would have been—" She ran a finger sharply across her throat. "Did you talk to two taxi drivers yesterday near the house across the street? Were you with a young boy?"

"Yes," Helen said. "That was my son."

"By nightfall the news was all over town that the traitor might be in Paris. Is this the man?" she asked Helen.

"It must be," she said. "How many men died because of him?" She was shaking so hard she put her coffee cup down.

"Many. Women, too." To Pauline, she said, "You know Madame Grimaud, with one leg. She was in the party waiting for the airdrop. The Germans caught her. She has never told anyone how she lost her leg."

Pauline looked at Helen. She seemed to have grown smaller, and her pupils had shrunk, as she processed Frank's betrayal. Confused, and feeling helpless, she was emotionally winded.

"What do they do to traitors in America these days?" Pauline asked.

"Treason is a capital crime. I think it's still punishable by death," Helen said. "But who would testify against him?"

"No one," Madame Flaubert said.

"What am I going to do?" Helen asked.

Madame Flaubert's eyes narrowed. "This is a dangerous man. If he thinks that you found out what he did while you were here, who knows what could happen to you and your son."

"He didn't want me to come," Helen said. "I couldn't understand why he wouldn't join us. I thought he didn't want to relive that night."

"No. He didn't want to be recognized," Pauline said.

"Where are you staying in Paris?" Madame Flaubert asked briskly.

"I don't know," Helen said. "It's supposed to be a surprise. Frank is meeting us at the Gare de Lyon and taking us to the hotel. He says it is very authentic and French. Not like the big hotels that cater to rich foreigners."

"And when does your train arrive?"

"Hard to tell, with the railroad tracks in such bad shape. But we're supposed to arrive two days from now, around four in the afternoon."

"Where would you stay if you were on your own?"

"We've always stayed at the Ritz."

"Then I suggest you cable the hotel and reserve rooms for yourself and your son."

"That should be easy," Pauline said. "No one is in Paris in August."

"But Frank will be at the station," Helen said miserably.

"I'm afraid so," Pauline said. "This is quite frightening."

Helen suddenly felt ill.

"Is there a WC here?" she asked.

"Not exactly," Pauline said. "There's an outhouse in the garden."

When Helen stood up, her legs were trembling so violently she wasn't sure she could walk.

"Do you want me to come with you?" Pauline asked.

Helen put her hand over her mouth and shook her head. She walked unsteadily to the little wooden building, knelt on the hard-packed dirt floor, and held her head over the stinking hole. She vomited until nothing came up except foam. She was sweating and her mouth tasted foul. Despite what she had told Jack, she knew that she might have made a life with Frank, and never known the kind of man he was. When she looked for toilet paper to clean her face, she saw a neat stack of newspaper cut into squares. Thinking the newsprint might come off on her face, she wiped her mouth and forehead on her arm. She tried to breathe but the smell was too strong. Outside, she leaned against the frail wooden structure and looked up at the sky. It was still blue, and she was still standing. She and Jack would have to see Frank at the station, and when he heard of their change of plans, he, too, might decide to stay at the Ritz. Finally, her fear was overtaken by rage. She stood up and strode back into the little sitting room. "Tell me what to do," she asked.

"Rien. Nothing." Madame Flaubert's friendly plump face had turned hard. "Just take care of yourself and your son. For some of us, the war is not finished."

On an early September afternoon, a battered train arrived in Paris after a long, circuitous overnight trip. The platform was jammed with people, but as the train clattered into the station, Helen thought she glimpsed Frank through the dirty, scratched window. She was glad that he couldn't see her and read her expression. Then she lost sight of him, and assumed he was working his way through the crowd to find them. Her heart was thudding, her throat closed, and she was mortally afraid. She had practiced what she would say to Frank about why she and

Jack would be staying at the Ritz, rather than at his hotel, but nothing she came up with sounded sincere. To reassure herself that she would be safe, she focused on Madame Flaubert's sinister remark, which implied that somehow any danger Frank might or might not pose would be taken care of.

The train screeched to a stop and she waited as long as she could to dismount. Jack had sprung out ahead of her, and so she wouldn't lose him in the crowd, she reluctantly approached the top of the stairs. The conductor held out a hand to help her down, and she looked for Frank again. She didn't see him, but she noticed that in the place where he had been standing, the crowd was denser than elsewhere on the platform, and some kind of commotion was erupting.

With a growing sense of unease, she gestured for a porter in his distinctive black-visored cap with its red trim and his neat uniform jacket. She asked him to load their bags onto his cart and explained that she was looking for a friend who was to meet them. "Stay here," she instructed Jack, "and watch our bags." She still wasn't sure what she would say to Frank when she found him, but she didn't want Jack to witness their meeting.

Above the din of the station, she heard people calling loudly for help. She pushed her way through the throng until she saw what they were staring at.

Frank was lying on the platform, with a long knife sticking out of his back and his head turned to one side. She could not tell if he was alive.

They've murdered him! she thought. This was something out of Arthur's war, which she had imagined, but never fully taken in.

A gendarme had knelt down by the body, and Helen knelt

with him on the rough concrete. Tears began to drip from behind her glasses when she realized he was dead, although later, when she thought about the scene, she would never know whether she had been crying out of relief or sorrow. Frank's eyes were open, and it seemed that his bright blue gaze was fixed on her. But those eyes no longer had the power to charm or to deceive. Helen's fear disappeared as though it had been part of a bad dream. She could only feel pity for the innocent scholarship boy who had come to Yale, and been tempted to pretend he was someone else, until he no longer knew who he was—only what he wanted.

She leaned her face so close to his that a watcher might have taken them for lovers. He had no final words for her, but whatever he might have said did not matter now. At last, she was free.

WAR HERO KILLED

United Press, **Paris, September 14, 1948.** *Around 4:00 p.m. on September 13, Frank Hartman, an American, was knifed and killed by an unknown assailant in the Gare de Lyon in Paris. Mr. Hartman was a graduate of Yale University and its law school and one of the early recruits to the OSS. He served with distinction in France, receiving the Croix de Guerre and the Silver Star for bravery. Paris police report that there are no leads as to the killer. An unnamed source suggested that Mr. Hartman might have been mistaken for one of the German officers who occupied this city during the war. The only clue at the scene of the crime* *was a knife, which had a distinctive coffin-shaped button on the handle. Known as "Le Salaire de la Peur Coffin," such knives, often used by gangsters, became trademarks of Resistance assassinations. The fact that the killer left it in the victim indicates that this was a revenge murder.*

AUTHOR'S NOTE

The fictitious Wauregan colony has much in common with an idyllic small summer place where I spent several summers in the 1970s when my children were young, and which has changed very little in the intervening years. However, no character or names used in the story are based on any person, living or dead. The only events I have set at "Wauregan" that are not entirely invented are the "Sermons for the Children" in the colony's church, and the World War II stories I have adapted from the memories of Joan Berston, published as "World War II at POW" in *Point O'Woods 1898-1998: Celebrating the Centennial of the Point O'Woods Association*, presented by the Point O'Woods Historical Society, compiled and edited by Beverly S. Freeman.

The story about the Japanese who buried the American soldiers alive, and the dog that saved them, is adapted from one of the many books about the OSS that I read for background.

Although this story takes place nearly three-quarters of a century ago, certain themes resonate in the early twenty-first century.

In regard to war dogs, in the aftermath of the 2001 terrorist attack on the World Trade Center, trained German shepherds have become more familiar sights, even in civilian situations. The most famous shepherd was the dog parachuted into Pakistan with the team that killed Osama bin Laden. Many dogs that served in the conflicts in Iraq and Afghanistan are now retrained as therapy dogs, and used to help veterans suffering from post-traumatic stress. According to the American Kennel Club, German shepherds are now the second most popular dogs in America, with Labradors consistently first. A recent YouTube clip of a German shepherd waiting to be fed had received 94 million hits in February 2012.

As for those who saw action in the Second World War, it was considered unmanly to acknowledge the emotional effects of their experiences. The men and women who suffered usually tried to carry on with the lives they had led before the war, as though nothing had changed. However, as with some of the men at Wauregan, their disturbance was apt to seep out—examples are Dan's irrational jealousy; Sarge's brutality; Steve's impotence; the man who can't eat anything with bones; the veteran who dives under a table during the Independence Day fireworks; Peter's insomnia, and his sudden violent reaction to Sarge when he and his grandfather are guarding Sally Carter's house. Despite these problems, it was crucial to keep up appearances, and parents warned their children, "What happens at home, stays at home." Today, post-traumatic stress is frequently in the news, and is acknowledged as a common and severe condition, requiring treatment and rehabilitation.

Frank Hartman's fate was not unique. In the years following the war, there were many acts of vengeance against collaborators, spies, and traitors, particularly in France. It was rare, however, and possibly unheard of for an American member of the OSS to save him- or herself by giving away a compatriot or an operation, except under extreme torture. Frank's treachery should not cast aspersions on the loyalty or effectiveness of the dedicated members of the OSS, who risked and sometimes lost their lives in the European and Pacific theaters.

And finally, I have taken certain liberties with factual information. I put the *Ile de France* in the water a year before she was back in service. With apologies to astronomers, I moved the timing of the full moon in the summer of 1948 to suit the development of Helen and Peter's relationship. Their trip to the drive-in movie was on Monday, August 2, 1948, when, inconveniently for the story, the moon was almost entirely dark. The moon was full on July 20, August 19, and September 18 that year.

The term "devil dog" to describe Marines originated in World War I, when a German dispatch described the American troops as fighting like *"Teufel Hunden"* (or, more correctly—*Teufelshunde*), "Hounds from Hell," at the battle of Belleau Wood. According to Michael G. Lemish in his book *War Dogs: A History of Loyalty and Heroism,* members of the K-9 Corps that served with the Marines in World War II were also called "Devildogs." Lemish reports that some three thousand war dogs were returned to civilian life after World War II, and only four of them could not readapt. By contrast, dogs used in Vietnam were all euthanized or abandoned after the war, a tragic betrayal of "man's best friend."

The knife used at the end of the book is usually associated with gangsters (or, as my source said, "gangstairs") and was also favored by the Resistance for its long blade and ability to kill quietly and instantaneously.

ACKNOWLEDGMENTS

This book and its author owe the deepest gratitude to Lisa Gallagher, a superb agent, editor, and good and steadfast friend; Kathy Sagan, who was brave enough to publish and edit a first novel by a nonfiction author; Natasha Simons, who kept the ball rolling; and my husband, David Braga, whose patience, knowledge, and editorial skills I constantly tapped and tested. Beth Gutcheon encouraged me from the beginning and gave me invaluable advice about her own writing process. Art director Lisa Litwack gave *A Certain Summer* a beautiful cover, which conveys the spirit and period of the book. Nicholas Brown, who was fourteen years old at the time, explained the intricacies of catboat sailing, and he and his father, Jack, along with David Braga, kept me on track in regard to the sailing accident. Sailors should know that Beetle Cats are generally extremely reliable; the circumstances that caused *Red Wing* to capsize were exceptional. The "Sermon for the Children" is adapted from one given many years ago by the late Rev. Charles L. Copenhaver; he used an aerosol can of shaving cream to make his point, but in 1948, most men would have used shaving soap. Stories about war dogs are culled from many sources, most significantly *War Dogs of the Pacific,* a film by Harris Done (www.wardogsmovie.com); *War Dogs: A History of Loyalty and Heroism,* by Michael G. Lemish (Brassey's, 1996); *Hero Dogs: Secret Missions and Selfless Service,* preface by Ronald L. Aiello, text by Lance M. Bacon (White Star Publishers, 2012); and *Animal Heroes of the Great War,* by Ernest Harold Baynes (Macmillan Company, 1926). I also consulted many sources, including some dozen books, to learn about the OSS and its operations in France. Of particular help was *French Resistance Fighter: France's Secret Army,* by Terry Crowdy (Osprey Publishing, 2007), and *Vichy France: Old Guard and New Order, 1940-1944,* by Robert O. Paxton (Columbia University Press, 2001).

A CERTAIN SUMMER

PATRICIA BEARD

INTRODUCTION

It is the summer of 1948. Although World War II has been over for three years, for Helen Wadsworth, whose husband, Arthur, was declared mysteriously missing after an OSS operation in France in 1944, there can be no closure. Returning with her son to their beloved summer spot, the old-fashioned island community of Wauregan, she is haunted by memories of Arthur and the life they might have had, unable to move on because of the persistent hope that he might, somehow, still be alive.

But then Arthur's best friend, Frank—the man who was on the mission with him in France, and perhaps the only one who may know the truth about what happened—and Peter, a younger man who has been deeply scarred by his experiences in the war and who is trying to piece his life back together with the help of a German shepherd war dog named Max, both appear in her life, and she can't help but feel torn by her feelings for both men.

As Helen and the other inhabitants of the island struggle to come to terms with their pasts, and to figure out what they want for the future, Helen realizes that what happened to Arthur might be more complicated than it seems, and sets out to uncover the truth, so that, once and for all, she can be free.

QUESTIONS FOR DISCUSSION

1. Discuss the novel's title, *A Certain Summer*. Why do you think the author selected this title?

2. The novel is rich with detailed descriptions of the ocean, the sky, and the landscape of Wauregan. Is there a passage or scene involving nature that stood out for you? What role does the natural world, particularly in summer, play in the lives of the characters?

3. It could be argued that, in some ways, Wauregan is as much a character in the book as its inhabitants. Do you agree? What sort of setting does the island create for the novel? What emotions and impulses are being acted upon or repressed by its inhabitants because they are on Wauregan, away from the "outside" world?

4. What are the myths about the idyllic island summer the author refers to in the opening passage of the book? How about the "mystique" and the magic?

5. On page 16, the author writes: "When the men were mired in muddy trenches, on bombing runs, and in deadly battles, their dreams of the colony were as vivid as Technicolor movies with big-screen happy endings. It might be unrealistic to hope that a small insular summer place could restore what the war had stolen, but [war] was so surreal it was hard to recall even an ordinary peacetime day. The warriors' anticipation of the perfect families waiting for them in an ideal community were like the fantasies people at home shared

during rationing. . . [describing] the delicacies they would enjoy when they could buy anything they wanted, only to find, after a few postwar feasts, that for the most part, even good food was just food." Do you agree that, when we are deprived of something, whether it is food, the comforts of home life, or the love of another person, it takes on an almost fantastic magnitude in our minds, one that real life cannot match? Do you think this is true for memories, as well—for example, Helen's recollections of her relationship with Arthur? Discuss this idea as it relates to various characters in the novel.

6. Throughout the novel, memories of Arthur haunt Helen, and Wauregan is a tether to a part of the past that no longer exists for her. At the end, after finally learning the truth about what happened to Arthur, and with Frank dead and her house on Wauregan gone, she feels that she is finally free. Did you interpret that to mean free of the past, of her ambivalence about Frank and Peter, or of the limbo in which she has been living while she waited for definitive news about Arthur? Do you agree that she is "free," or do you think the novel suggests that the past can never be escaped?

7. After Frank has been killed, Helen reflects on page 312: "She could only feel pity for the innocent scholarship boy who had come to Yale, and been tempted to pretend he was someone else, until he no longer knew who he was—only what he wanted." Discuss the role of identity throughout the book. How does wartime change the way we define our identities, and the ways others define us?

8. There are various examples of marriage, romance, and sexual relationships in this novel. Based on your reading, what do you make of the attitudes about marriage during this time? What about attitudes toward fidelity, sex, or love? What role do you think the war had in the way relationships were formed and carried out in this novel? Provide examples.

9. Which characters won your sympathy and why? Did this

change over the course of the novel? Did your notion of what was best or right shift in the course of your reading?

10. On page 292, Pauline takes Helen to the room the German soldiers have defaced and tells her, "Louis-Arnaud said this place had seen many things in five hundred years, and this is part of its history. If we restored it, we would be pretending that these horrible things hadn't happened. We keep this room to remember the filth people can stoop to, and act before evil prevails." Do you agree with Louis-Arnaud that it is important to keep reminders of the lowest points in human history, as a warning for the future? Or do you think that preserving such markers are roadblocks to moving forward?

11. The book opens with the line "Nothing ever changed at Wauregan." Do you think, ultimately, this proves true? Do you think it's possible for a place not to change, at its core? Why do you think people find comfort in the idea of a place that "never changes"? In 1948, at Wauregan, what elements of the colony's traditions have been successfully maintained? What has been disrupted? Are the disruptions permanent, or are they particular to the postwar period?

12. On page 221, the minister, Dr. Waters says: "'Don't pass along stories that can hurt others. As my mother used to warn me, 'If you don't have something nice to say, don't say anything.' Let's attempt to find something good to say about each other, or hold our tongues.'" And Pauline notes on page 292: "In even the most beautiful garden, a poisonous snake can crawl out from under a rock and bite you . . . . You may recover, but the next time, you will be careful where you step." How do you think each of these statements applies to the events in the novel?

13. World War II was a catalyst for enormous social and cultural change, and although the Wauregan colonists try to shield themselves, no character in *A Certain Summer* is left untouched. Discuss some examples. How does Helen's life exemplify these changes? Whose life do you think was most altered by the war?

14. What did you think of the conclusion of the novel? Did it turn out as you expected? Would you have ended it differently? If so, how?

15. On page 4, one Wauregan resident tells Arthur: "In certain summer places, we try to leave all that behind and just be good neighbors." When do the inhabitants of Wauregan succeed in being good neighbors to each other, when do they fail, and why?

ENHANCE YOUR BOOK CLUB

In the novel, Helen mentions two books that were very popular at the time: *The Egg and I* and *Forever Amber*. Pick a book published in 1948 to read for your next meeting. Among those that hold up well are *Dinner at Antoine's* by Frances Parkinson Keyes, a murder mystery in which, as in *A Certain Summer*, "place" (in this case, New Orleans) is a major element of the book—in addition, one of the characters is a World War II soldier, mistakenly declared dead. Another choice is Norman Mailer's first novel, *The Naked and the Dead*, which chronicles his experiences during the Philippines Campaign in World War II.

Or, have a retro film night: rent the movie versions of *The Egg and I*, *Forever Amber*, or the classic 1948 film *Key Largo*, starring Humphrey Bogart and Lauren Bacall, in which a storm—also as in *A Certain Summer*—plays a significant part in the story. The romantic comedy *A Foreign Affair*, starring Greta Garbo, and set in occupied Berlin just after the war, was also released in 1948, and deals with aftershocks from the war.

Helen's mother-in-law's special iced tea, steeped with fresh mint, sugar, and mixed with orange juice; the judge's favorite coconut cake with lemon curd filling; tomato aspic with cucumbers; and coleslaw with bacon are among the delectable summer treats mentioned in the book. Make and bring your favorite summer foods to your book club meeting and have a Wauregan-style feast, whatever the season.

The loveable Max is an important character in the novel. Do some research on war dogs and present your findings to the group. Consider checking out some of the sources the author used in her research, including *War Dogs of the Pacific*, a film by Harris Done (www.wardogsmovie.com), the book *War Dogs: A History of Loyalty and Heroism* by Michael G. Lemish, published by Brassey's, Washington, D.C., 1996; and *Hero Dogs: Secret Missions and Selfless Service* by Lance M. Bacon, published by White Star Publishers (www.whitestar.it).

AUTHOR'S Q&A—PATRICIA BEARD

Q: What inspired you to write *A Certain Summer*?

A: I have wanted to write about the American tradition of the family summer community for a long time. It has a special resonance for me, as when I was a little girl, my family spent summers in a small summer place in Maine; and when my children were young, we summered in a community similar to Wauregan. For many people, the memories of childhood are most vivid when they take place in summer. I wanted to explore that, and celebrate it.

Q: You are known as an author of nonfiction books. What made you decide to write a novel?

A: In nonfiction, I am restricted to what I can know, and that often limits the use of dialogue; fiction freed me to use more of my creative energy. A crossover is that while *A Certain Summer* is not autobiographical, as so many first novels are, it is set in a world I know well.

Q: How has your experience writing nonfiction influenced *A Certain Summer*?

A: Throughout the book, I had opportunities to research subjects that interested me: among them were the emotional and social influences in the aftermath of a "good war"; the historic role of war dogs; and the way the OSS and French Resistance operated.

Q: Are your characters based on real people?
A: No, with one exception: Kathleen is based on a woman who helped me bring up my children and who was such an important part of our lives that my daughter named her first child after her. But "Kathleen's" stories from Ireland come from research and my imagination.

Q: Why did you set your novel in 1948?
A: Partly nostalgia. There were many similarities to the 1950s, when I grew up. And partly because I'm interested in transition. In 1948 society was on the cusp of change, yet at Wauregan, the members of the community tried to keep the past alive. I think the traditional structure of Wauregan provided a needed balance.

Q: In what ways is Helen a modern character? Are you like Helen?
A: Helen is more independent than many of the women in the story, because she has been on her own since her husband left to serve in the OSS. Am I like her? Since I invented her, she does have some of my qualities. And like Helen, I am tall and thin, wear glasses, and am a graduate of Bryn Mawr College. However, I grew up in Manhattan, not in the Midwest, and my grandfather was not a railroad baron—although I've taken the liberty of borrowing the nickname of James J. Hill of the Great Northern Railway, who is the great-grandfather of my children on their father's side.

Q: What are some of the myths you refer to at the beginning of the book?
A: The most important is the idea of the "family summer place." Until women entered the workforce in large numbers, summer colonies were nearly entirely inhabited by mothers and children during the week. Fathers came on weekends, and for short vacations. On Sunday nights, when the men returned to their jobs in the cities, life returned to the world of women and children.

Q: Is Wauregan exceptional, or is it similar to other summer places?

A: Except for the geography, it could be transposed to most regions of the United States, and many different social and economic groups.

Q: In those colonies is it true that "nothing has changed" in the past two generations?

A: In the ones I have known, the basic values remain the same, although the tradition of multigenerational families is somewhat diluted, as it's much less common for young men and women to marry their childhood friends, "newcomers" enter, who might not have been as welcome a couple of generations ago, but who often refresh a place that can become ingrown. It works well as long as they share the community's essential values. Working mothers, the higher incidence of divorce, and increased informality have also shifted the dynamics of traditional summer places, often for the better, but in those like Wauregan, the essence remains.

Q: There are a number of instances of trust and betrayal in the story. Why?

A: Those are among the universal questions: Who can I trust? Who can't I trust? How can I know?

Q: Why did you include a German shepherd?

A: I love just about any kind of dog. I've never lived with a German shepherd, but I have known some, and they have a special quality of loyalty, gentleness, and the potential to be fiercely protective. Those are qualities I like in men, too.

Q: Some of the men at Wauregan suffer from what we now recognize as post-traumatic stress disorder. The war dog, Max, was "deprogrammed" before he was returned to civilian life. Do you

think it would have helped men returning from the war if there had been a required readjustment period, even if it was brief, before they were flung back into civilian life?

A: It would have been hard to establish, as the men who had been in combat and their families were eager to be reunited. But, with knowledgeable counseling, it might have helped, and would be helpful now for returning veterans.

Q: Were you rooting for Helen to end up with Peter, Frank, or for her husband, Arthur, who was missing in action, to return?

A: See what you think when you read the book! Then tell me who you were rooting for, and whether it changed as you read along.

Q: How did you come up with some of the episodes in the story?

A: I made up most of them, but some came bubbling to the surface from stories I'd heard. For example, my mother told me about a woman who went off with her lover in a seaplane during the week, while her husband was away. Mother said the other women in the community knew about it, but didn't tell their husbands because they were afraid the men would become suspicious about what was going on when they weren't there. I admit that it's also true that my son was kicked out of sports group one summer. I can't remember why, he was only about eight years old, and he was readmitted after he apologized for whatever transgression started the problem.

Q: What are the elements of summer in a small colony that most appeal to you?

A: I love knowing the parents of my friends, my children's friends, and the next generation—the grandchildren. And I love the peacefulness of island life. I write during the summer, but it feels different to be working on an island than in my office at home.

Q: Do you still spend summers at the community on which Wauregan is based?

A: No. I haven't been there since the late 1970s.

Q: When you write nonfiction, you haven't had to describe sex scenes. There is quite a bit of romance in *A Certain Summer*. How did you deal with sex?

A: Delicately. Some things should remain private, even in fiction. And there's always the reader's imagination to fill in the gaps.

Q: You have a significant sailing scene in *A Certain Summer*. Are you a sailor?

A: I enjoy sailing—as a passenger. I counted on my husband and some friends, including a fourteen-year-old boy, to advise me.

Q: For a summer place, you don't place much emphasis on sports, except sailing. Why not?

A: Helen and Peter are both avid swimmers, of course, as was Arthur, but except for tennis and sailing, the emphasis at Wauregan is not on competitive sports. For example, there is no golf course. As for me, my favorite "sport" is reading under an umbrella on the beach.

Q: Do you plan to write more novels?

A: Absolutely. I have an idea for the next one, which will also be set in the World War II period, but before the war, rather than after it. The story will include a complicated romance, espionage and danger, and authentic historical detail. I'm thinking about how to include a dog and I expect I'll find a way.